# BETA

JASINDA WILDER

# 1

## WAKING UP

WAKING UP HAS TURNED INTO ONE OF MY FAVORITE games. The first question is always who's awake first, Roth or me? If it's me, it's my job—self-appointed— to make sure he wakes up in the best possible way. In other words, with my hands and mouth around his morning wood. And if he's awake first, he pretends to be asleep, so I can wake him up that way.

The second question I ask myself every morning is where in the world are we? Because it's different every week or two. Two weeks ago, I woke up in Vancouver. I still had one of Roth's neckties knotted around one wrist, the remnant of a long and scream-filled night spent tied spread-eagle to the bed. Roth didn't untie me until I'd come...god, like six times? Seven? And when he did finally untie me, well, let's just say I don't think he'll play the "torture Kyrie with multiple orgasms without letting her touch him back" game again any time soon. I literally attacked him. The claw marks raking down his back are still healing. I fucked him so hard I actually think I nearly broke his cock. I *think* that's possible. Pretty sure it is, and I'm pretty sure I nearly accomplished it.

This morning I woke up and took stock. A little sore between the thighs, but nothaing too bad. Roth was snoring, so I knew I was awake first. I breathed in, sighed, stretched. I blinked my eyes open, catching a whiff of salt sea air and the sound of waves crashing. The bed rocked gently from side to side. We were in a small, wood-paneled room with low ceilings and an open window. There was just room enough for the bed and a small chest of drawers. But the room was moving. Why was the room moving?

Where were we? It took a few minutes for memories of the preceding weeks to bubble up. A week in Vancouver…a long, *long* flight to Tokyo. A week in Japan. God, what a week. So many tours, so much hiking, so much sushi and sake. I'm not sure I'll ever drink sake again, that's for sure.

Tokyo, Nagoya, Osaka, Kyoto…. I remembered the flight out of Kyoto, the flight attendants all dressed identically, down to their hairdos and the little scarf-tie thing knotted just so.

Then where did we go?

A seagull cawed, and I heard voices off in the distance, chattering rapidly. But they were not speaking Japanese.

"*Nhât nó lên!*" The angry voice echoed across the water, faint and distant.

Vietnam. That's where we were. Hanoi.

Roth had bought us a houseboat, paid for it in cash, and then piloted it himself up the Red River all the way to Hanoi from a little village on the Gulf of Tonkin. We took it slow, stopping often to take on supplies and admire the scenery. We ate, drank, slept, and fucked. We checked out temples, hiked out into the farmlands and up into the hills, hiring an interpreter/guide to show us the best places off the beaten path. That's the thing about Roth: He never behaves like a tourist. He always seems to belong wherever we are, and he always makes sure we're safe.

We arrived in Hanoi last night, and Roth found some little old lady to cook us a huge dinner on the houseboat. He paid her enough U.S. dollars that she left looking slightly faint from shock.

After dinner, he uncorked a bottle of some local wine or liquor—I wasn't sure which—that was insanely strong. After a couple of small glasses, I was hammered. Roth took full advantage, laying me on my belly and drilling me from behind until we both came. That was it, because I passed out after that.

Once in a night isn't anywhere near enough to sate my Valentine, so I owed him this morning.

Roth was lying on his side, facing away from me. The sheet was low around his hips, showing me his broad, rippling back. His blond hair had grown out over the last few months, enough that it brushed his collar when he had a shirt on, and it hung down past his cheekbones. He'd grown a bit of a beard, too. Being fair as he was, he didn't grow a thick beard, just a fine coating of blond hair on his cheeks and jaw. Sexy. Oh, so sexy.

I hadn't realized it was possible to feel this strongly about anyone. I'd realized pretty quickly that what I felt for Valentine was love, and that had been scary enough by itself. I wasn't prepared to fall in love. Especially not with a man like Valentine. But as the weeks turned into months and I saw the world at his side, I realized what I'd felt for him back in Manhattan had really only been the beginning. The tip of the iceberg. The tiniest scraping sample off the top. The longer I spent with him, the more I realized how deep and intense my feelings for him were. I wanted to be with him every second of every day. I lived for the moments when I could make him smile, when I could see the soft, tender side of him that existed only for me.

Valentine was the best thing that had ever happened to me.

I cuddled up against him, pressed my lips to the back of his shoulder, and kissed, running my hand down his thick bicep. I found his hip and pushed the sheet away. I peered over his shoulder to watch as I cupped his balls in my hand. That, I'd found, was the best way to get him hard if he was still asleep. Massage slowly, gently, maybe a little pressure to his taint, and the sleeping giant would respond. Sure enough, within a minute or so, his cock was engorged and his breathing was changing. He groaned, his abdominal muscles tensing, arms raised over his head. He rolled to his back, stretched, and flexed his hips to drive his dick into my fist.

I glanced up at him, finding his eyes on me. "Morning."

He grinned at me, a slow, sleepy smile. "Good morning, my lovely."

"I passed out last night, huh?"

"Yes. Snake wine does you in rather quickly, it seems." He watched as I stroked him slowly, one hand sliding from root to tip and back down in a smooth glide.

"Guess so."

"You passed out before we got to do the one thing I'd been wanting to do to you on this boat," he said between yawns.

"Which is?"

"Mmmmm." He closed his eyes and lifted his hips. "Would you like to find out?"

I just gave him my small, secret smile, the one that meant I wasn't going to argue either way. The *do as you wis*h grin.

Roth growled low in his throat and sat up, pushing me off him. He grabbed the blanket, a large, thin piece of dark green fleece, and draped it from his shoulders, wrapping the ends around both of us as I stood in front of him. He gestured at the door leading from the cabin up to the deck, and I ascended, squeaking as Roth's fingers traced a line up my ass crack. He just chuckled and kept fondling and fingering me, making the trip up the ladder a little difficult, but fun. On the deck, Roth kept the blanket around both of us and guided me to the bow, which curved up elegantly to about waist height. Hanoi was spread out before us, dim in the early morning haze. There was another houseboat some two hundred feet away, and a third the same distance away on the other side, but there was no motion from either. A fishing scow plied the water about a thousand feet up-current and drifted toward us with fishing nets being hauled in, voices echoing now and again.

"Grab the bow," Roth whispered in my ear. I took hold of the bow with both hands, then turned my head to watch him, but he made a negative sound. "Act like you're just staring out at the city. And try to keep your voice down."

I took the edges of the blanket and held on to it for him, keeping it pulled around us as Roth's hands slid around my belly and descended between my thighs.

Oh, shit. Staying quiet was not one of my strong suits.

He had me writhing and moaning within seconds, pressing into his touch and biting my lip to keep from screaming. It didn't take long before I was coming for the first time, and then he was bending at the knees, fingers of one hand on my pussy, the other around his cock, feeding it into me. I bent forward over the bow, spread my legs wide, and took him.

The fishing scow was getting closer, floating downstream, angled slightly so they'd slide right by us.

"Oh god, Roth. Hurry. I'm so close."

"Don't come yet. Not yet."

"I can't help it. I'm about to—"

He slowed his pace immediately. "Not yet, Kyrie. Not yet."

The scow neared. Faces turned to regard us, eyes narrowed, suspicious. Roth just waved, and I heard the fishermen exchange comments, laughing. At that exact moment, Roth flexed his hips and drove into me. I wasn't expecting it, and I let out a loud whimper, and all the fishermen guffawed. But at a glare from Roth, the helmsman gunned the engine, and they were soon past. Then Roth was moving again, and I was coming apart despite his exhortations to wait…wait.

"Come with me, Valentine!"

He came. Oh, dear god, did he come. So, so hard. He filled me with his come, and then kept driving, coming and coming, and I could only clench around him and bend over farther and keep taking him, gasping in the morning air.

Two weeks later, we were in a chateau in the hills of southern France. I was waking up, playing my game. Taking stock and guessing at our location.

But this time, something was wrong.

I sat up suddenly, totally awake. Roth wasn't in bed. He never, ever left me alone in the mornings. He never got out of bed before me. I glanced at the bathroom, but it was dark and silent.

My heart was pounding, sweat beading on my forehead.

"Roth?" My voice was tentative, quiet, echoing in the expansive bedroom.

Silence.

The bed beside me was rumpled, still warm from his body heat. The pillow was indented where his head had been. There was a note. A white scrap of torn paper was pinned to the pillow with a long, thin silver knife. The message was written in red ink in neat, feminine, looping handwriting:

*He belongs to me.*

# 2

## PANIC

"No. Nonono." I reached out for the knife and the paper, but stopped short of touching either.

*He belongs to me.* The ink was crimson, the color of fresh blood. Was it blood? Roth's blood? No, it couldn't be. It was too neat, too clean, each pen stroke precise. Blood would smear, right? Oh god. Oh god. Who would do this? Who *could* do this? We went to bed drunk last night…I knew that much. But not *that* drunk. Not so drunk that someone could have kidnapped a man like Valentine Roth right out of the bed beside me while I slept.

But he was gone.

I scrambled out of bed; the six hundred year-old oak floors were cool under my bare feet. The four-poster bed was even older than that, Roth had told me. This chateau was one of two he owned in France. This one, in the Languedoc-Rousillon region, sat nestled between an old cathedral and a sprawling vineyard. There wasn't much land attached to this chateau, just enough for the house and a small yard, but it was quaint, ancient, and beautiful. Peaceful. His other chateau was part of a winery in the Alsace-Lorraine area, and that was to be our next stop.

Maybe Roth was in the kitchen? Maybe this was something new. Some ridiculous game. I hurried downstairs to the galley kitchen, which was dark and quiet, three empty bottles of merlot clustered together on the counter, a corkscrew beside them with a cork still in it. The den was empty as well, the fireplace dark now except for a few embers glowing a dull orange. A cashmere throw blanket lay rumpled on the floor in front of the fireplace, and I remembered lying on my back right there last night, the blanket on Roth's shoulders as he moved above me, his arms thick pillars beside my face, firelight glinting off his skin, shimmering in his arresting blue eyes. He'd finished inside me, leaving me shaking and breathless from the force of my orgasm, and then he'd lifted me in his arms and carried me, still trembling from the aftershocks, to our bed. He'd nestled behind me, his hand a warm, reassuring presence on my stomach, his chest at my back, his lips kissing my shoulder as he murmured, "I love you, I love you, I love you," in my ear. I fell asleep like that, cradled by him, his warmth cocooning me, his strength sheltering me.

I was worried and frightened now, and I choked back a sob and tried the wine cellar, cool and dry and temperature-controlled to preserve the hundreds of bottles of wine, each worth hundreds and thousands of dollars. All worthless to me if Roth was gone. He wasn't there. Of course he wasn't. I knew he wouldn't be, but I had to look anyway.

Still naked, I threw open the door to the garage and flicked on a light. The Range Rover, black and gleaming and silent. The Aston Martin, red and sleek, also empty. The keys to each were on hooks just inside the house.

I stumbled back to the bedroom, shaking all over now, hands trembling, panting in short, panicked breaths.

*What do I do? What do I do?* The answer came immediately: *Harris. Call Harris.*

My cell phone was on the nightstand, plugged in to charge. There were only four contacts in my phonebook: Valentine, Harris, Layla, and Cal. Valentine's phone was on his nightstand, still connected to the charger. His clothes were on the floor, where we'd shed them the previous evening before taking a shower. God, the shower. It was small, a typical European shower. But somehow Roth had still managed to pin me up against the wall and ravish me until I couldn't breathe.

Everywhere I looked, there were memories of Roth. The bed, the shower, the kitchen—my bare ass on the counter, cabinet handle in my back, Roth lifting up on his toes to drive into me—the den, even the garage. I'd sucked him off in the garage, and he'd returned the favor, lifting me onto the hood of the Rover and performing his uniquely talented brand of cunnilingus on me until I begged him to let me stop coming.

And everywhere I looked, there he was. Telling me he loved me. Him, Valentine Roth, gorgeous, ripped, talented, gazillionaire businessman. He *loved* me. And he never got tired of telling me, showing me, making sure I knew I belonged to him.

I tripped and fell onto the bed. Sobbing. And when I managed to open my eyes, all I could see was the knife, black handle, silver blade curving and serpentine and razor-sharp, evil. The note, a torn scrap of paper and the blood-red ink.

I grabbed my phone, ripped the charger cord free, and pressed the "home" button. I swiped it to unlock it, then tapped Harris's name.

"Miss St. Claire." His voice, cool and calm, was there before it rang a second time. "How may I help you, ma'am?"

"He's gone—he's—they…someone took him! He's gone, Harris. Help me. Help me!" I wasn't making sense and I knew it, but I couldn't breathe, couldn't think.

"*Kyrie.*" His voice cut through my panic. "Breathe. Take a moment and breathe."

I took three deep breaths, in through my mouth, out through my nose. I tried again. "I woke up just now. Maybe ten minutes ago. We're in—in France. Valentine is gone, Harris."

"Where did he go? To the shops, perhaps? Out for coffees?"

"No, Harris! You *don't understand!*" I was shrieking, shouting. "There's a note, a fucking note with a goddamn knife!"

"I'm trying to understand, Miss St. Claire. Are you saying someone kidnapped Mr. Roth?"

"YES!" I screamed it, so loud and shrill it hurt my throat. I had to swallow and breathe and start over. "The note — someone stabbed a big knife through the note into the pillow. It's a woman's handwriting. It says—god, god. It says, 'he belongs to me.'"

"This is serious? For real? You aren't joking?"

"DO I *SOUND* LIKE I'M FUCKING JOKING?"
I fell forward onto the bed, phone pressed to my ear,
sobbing. "Who would do this…who? Why? What do
I do, Harris?"

"Is there anything else apart from the knife and
the note?"

"No."

"Just those words? No demands or anything?"

I shook my head even though I knew, rationally,
that Harris couldn't see me. "No. No. Just the note,
just those words. His phone, the cars, his clothes…
everything. It's all here. I've looked everywhere, but
he's gone. Who took him, Harris?"

"I have a couple of ideas. It's going to be okay,
Miss St. Claire. We'll find him. Just stay there and
don't touch anything. Get dressed, but don't go anywhere. Don't call anyone. *No one,* do you understand
me? Not Layla, not the police, no one."

"Okay."

"Say it. Repeat it for me."

"I won't go anywhere. I won't call anyone. I'll
stay here and wait for you."

"Yes. I'm in London, so I'll be there in a matter
of hours." His voice was calm and collected, and that
reassured me somehow.

"Okay." I swallowed hard and tried to sound
calm. "Harris? Who could have done this?"

"We'll speak when I arrive, Miss St. Claire. Until then, try to remain calm. Get something to eat. Pack a bag of your clothes. Sensible clothes, sensible shoes. Necessary personal items. Do not touch anything of Mr. Roth's, especially not the note or the knife."

"Okay. I understand." My voice was quiet, barely audible.

"We'll find him, Miss St. Claire. I promise you. You have my word." Something cold in Harris's voice scared me. But that was good. I needed the scary bodyguard Harris right now, not the polite driver and friend.

I hung up the phone, unplugged the charger cord, and wrapped it into a tiny bundle, tucking it into my purse. I showered quickly, harshly suppressing the images of the last time I was in this shower. I lathered, rinsed, and got out, dried off. Brushed my hair, tied it up still wet into a messy chignon. Jeans and a T-shirt, my hiking boots. Roth had insisted on buying me a bunch of outdoor gear before we set out on our big trip. He'd bought me a set of luggage and pretty much a whole new wardrobe. Jeans, T-shirts, sweatshirts and sweaters, khaki shorts and tank tops, a rain slicker, expensive hiking boots, hats, sunglasses, pretty much every kind of outfit for every kind of climate. And somehow he'd gotten it all into two big Louis Vuitton suitcases and a backpack. He always packed for us, saying he had a foolproof system.

So right now I tried to replicate his method, rolling the clothes rather than folding them, packing them down deep into the bottom of my backpack. A couple pair of jeans, shirts, my favorite hoodie, some shorts and socks and underwear and a spare bra, toiletries. I put my purse in the backpack as well, and laced up my hiking boots, tied a sweater around my waist.

Why was I packing? I'd followed Harris's instructions, but I didn't quite understand why I needed to pack and why I was now ready to leave at a moment's notice.

Once I was packed, I went into the kitchen and made what I thought of as a "French breakfast," a baguette purchased the evening before, some Brie, fresh sliced fruit, and a cup of coffee. With Roth, everything tasted better. Plain cheese tasted like heaven, coffee was thick and rich and always perfectly doctored, bread was crusty on the outside and soft and warm on the inside. But now, alone, everything was tasteless, and I couldn't stop thinking, couldn't stop wondering.

How? Who? Why? If there had been a demand or something, I could have understood a little. An old enemy out for revenge, someone whose business

Roth had taken over and chopped up. Someone simply wanting a ransom. But the feminine handwriting had me stumped. How could a woman kidnap
a huge, muscular, powerful man like Roth? It didn't
make sense. It shouldn't be possible.

I fidgeted. Paced. Repacked. I stared at the note,
trying not to hyperventilate. After an eternity, I
checked the time on my phone; barely an hour had
passed. Even breaking every speed limit between
here and London, Harris couldn't be here in anything less than four hours. What the hell was I supposed to do until then? I'd be insane in four hours.

I needed to get out of the chateau. I *had* to. I
couldn't stay here for another minute, not with that
note and the ominous presence of the knife. But
Harris had specifically told me not to leave, not for
anything.

I tried to distract myself with the TV, but most
of it was in French, with a couple of UK channels
coming in rather poorly. I clicked it off. The man I
loved was missing, and I was supposed to just cool
my heels watching TV?

Hell, no.

So I paced some more, refusing to check the
time. I sat, knees bouncing, chewing my nails, thinking my girlfriend back in Detroit, Layla, would be
furious if she saw my fingernails all chewed up.

I managed to pass another hour, and then a third.

Then I heard tires on the gravel drive, the low rumble of an engine, the quiet *thunk* of a car door closing. I leapt to my feet, scrambled to the window, and peeked out. A low, sleek, black two-door Audi with darkly tinted windows sat in the driveway. A man stood leaning with his back against the hood, holding a cell phone to his ear. Tall and thin, dark hair slicked back, swarthy features, clean-shaven and wearing a slim black suit with a narrow black tie, white shirt. He nodded every once in a while, then thumbed the phone to end the call and shoved it in his pocket.

Two things worried me: one, he wasn't Harris, and two, he had a handgun held casually in his right hand. As I watched, he ejected the clip out of the bottom of the pistol, glanced at it, replaced it in the chamber, and then pulled back the slide. He did this with a practiced ease that made my gut churn. This wasn't right. Not right at all.

I didn't stop to think. Slinging my backpack over my shoulders, I dashed through the house to the garage. I snatched the Rover's key fob off the hook, stuffed it into my pocket, and went to hit the button that would open the garage door. But then I paused and listened. The front door was locked; I knew that for a fact. I'd locked it myself while waiting for Harris.

Silence, long and thick.

And then the smashing of glass. I imagined a pistol butt going through the small squares of painted glass in the front door, a hand sliding through to unlock and open the door. I waited until I heard the door creak open and close again before sliding into the driver's seat of the Rover. I waited another few moments, hoping that the man, whoever he was, would check the upstairs bedrooms first.

I put my foot to the brake and touched the ignition button, opening the garage at the same time. The engine purred to life, and the garage door rolled up on oiled tracks. Thank god Roth kept everything he owned in pristine condition. As soon as the door was open high enough, I threw the Rover in reverse and gunned the engine, cutting around the Audi parked directly behind me. The truck bumped onto the grass, tearing up the sod, but then I was on the gravel of the drive, jerking the gear shift into drive and flooring the pedal. Dirt and gravel sprayed out, and the Rover leaped forward.

*Crack. Crack. Crackcrack.*

Was that gunfire?

I looked in the rearview mirror just in time to see the rear window splinter into a spider web as a bullet hit it. Then it collapsed altogether as a second round hit the glass. I screamed as a third round ricocheted off the side mirror, mere inches from my face. I spun the wheel, hit the brake, and then gunned the engine to bring the Rover around in a tight ninety-degree turn onto another side road. I heard an engine roar, and I knew the Audi was not far behind me.

I didn't have time to even be afraid. The wind whistling through the shattered back window was evidence enough that this was no joke and that each choice I made from this moment on would determine whether I lived or died. I jerked the Rover around a left turn and then a right, driving too fast down the quiet early morning streets of a sleepy little French village. I didn't even know the name of the town—I just knew it was somewhere in the far south of France. Near Marseilles, maybe? My knowledge of French geography was pretty much nonexistent. I was used to sitting in the passenger seat as Roth drove, letting him take me where he wanted to go.

A street sign ahead of me snapped backward, the metal dented with the impact of a bullet.

What was going on? Who was shooting at me, and why? Where was Harris?

I yanked the SUV into another left turn, and then a right, and I was out of the village and onto a straight two-lane highway leading out and away, vineyards on either side. I floored the gas pedal, feeling the powerful Range Rover engine bolt the vehicle forward. The needle quickly passed the forty miles per hour mark, then fifty. I risked a glance in the rearview mirror and saw the Audi behind me, about a quarter mile away and closing fast.

I'd watched Roth make a few phone calls in this car, so I knew what to do. I hit the command button, and told the system to call Harris.

The trill of a ringer filled the car, once, twice, and then Harris's voice. "Miss St. Claire. Is everything all right?"

"No. It's not all fucking right, Harris." I gripped the wheel in both hands, the gas pedal floored, and the speedometer needle passing seventy. "A guy showed up. A black Audi. He had a gun. It wasn't you, and it didn't feel right, so I took the Rover and left, but now he's chasing me. He's shooting at me. I'm scared." I tried to stay calm, but only managed to sound robotic.

"Shit." I heard a rustling on the other side of the line, and then the roar of an engine and tires squealing. "Are you hurt?"

"No. But he shot out the back window, and one of the side mirrors. He's right behind me, and he's gaining on me. I don't know what to do. He'll kill me if he catches me. I know he will."

"Drive as fast as you safely can and don't stop for anything. I'm coming for you. I'm not far away."

"I don't know where I'm going, Harris!" The Rover was doing over a hundred now, and my ability to control the vehicle at this speed was shaky at best.

"There's only one highway where you are. Which way did you turn out of the village?"

"Right."

"Then you're heading toward me. You're in the Rover?"

"Yes."

A pause, tires squealing again, a horn in the distance. Sirens. "Good. Just keep going. Plow through anything that tries to stop you. Just go."

"I am."

At that moment, the right side mirror shattered and I shrieked, my hands jerking on the wheel. The Rover wobbled, and I fought to correct it, tapping the brake and wrestling the wheel to keep the vehicle from flipping. I was fishtailing all over the road, the tires screaming. As soon as I felt the Rover stabilize again, I hit the gas and was pushed back into the seat as the engine roared forward. The Audi was right behind me now, and I heard the reports of the pistol barking behind me.

There was a slow-moving truck ahead of me, a semi groaning up the steep grade. I slid out into the oncoming traffic lane and flew past it, then had to swallow a scream as I jerked the wheel to the right once more, cutting in front of the semi and narrowly avoiding a tan sedan of some kind. The semi blared its horn and flashed its lights, as did the sedan. I risked another backward glance and saw that the Audi had passed the semi as well.

Another pistol shot echoed, and I heard the impact as the bullet hit somewhere in the rear, one of the brake lights maybe, or the trunk hatch.

I'd never disconnected the call, and apparently neither had Harris, because I heard him cursing. "What was that? Are you okay?"

"Yeah, yeah. He's still right behind me, and he's shooting at me." I checked the rearview mirror. "He's catching up, Harris."

"Keep going. Don't let him catch you. Ram him off the road if you have to."

I had the gas pedal floored, and I was inching back up to over a hundred miles per hour, the countryside and other traffic flying by in a blur. Several drivers were honking and gesticulating wildly at me. I approached another car from behind, this one a little Peugeot or something, puttering along without a care in the world. The road began to curve, the grade falling away to one side, vineyards arching into the distance in endless rows. I eased off the gas, letting the needle sink back down, but the Peugeot was still ahead of me, and I knew I'd have to pass him. I waited until the last second, trying to peer as far around the curve as I could, which wasn't far. I slid out into the opposing lane, gunned the engine, and began to accelerate past the tiny vehicle. My heart was in my throat, my stomach revolting in terror as I saw a line of heavily laden flatbed semis approaching, lights flashing, horns blaring. The driver of the Peugeot was pissed that I was trying to pass him, and he attempted to accelerate and block me.

"Let me the fuck over, asshole!" I screamed.

Harris's voice filled the car. "Do what you have to do, Kyrie. Don't think. Just do it."

I was nearly past the Peugeot, the tail end of my Rover just barely overlapping his front quarter panel. I shoved down my emotions, gripped the steering wheel in two shaking hands, twisting the leather and taking deep breaths. Milliseconds were passing like hours. The semis were less than a hundred yards away and closing quickly. The Peugeot was still trying to outpace me. I wanted to close my eyes, but I couldn't. I didn't have the luxury of another breath, or of even thinking about it. There was no time for hesitation. I pulled the wheel to the right and felt the crunch of metal on metal. I heard the squeal of tires and the frantic blare of the horn.

*Crackcrackcrack.* Gunshots echoed, three of them, and the passenger seat of the Rover exploded in a burst of cloth and stuffing, the windshield spider-webbing low near the dashboard, and then I heard another squeal of tires, glanced in my rear view mirror to see the Peugeot spinning, fishtailing, and then the front right tire caught and it went flying, launched toward me. The semis were beside me now, horns going as if honking would stop the unfolding horror. The Peugeot somersaulted through the air and slammed into a passing semi with a deafening crash and a fiery explosion.

"Ohshitohshitohshit…." I was hyperventilating, screaming. "I killed him, I killedhimikilledhim—ohmygod what did I do?"

"Enough!" Harris's voice cut through, loud and sharp, silencing me. "You're staying alive. That is your only concern. Keep driving. Don't stop."

"I—I—Harris, people are—are dead because of me!"

"Better them than you," he said, his voice cold and emotionless. "Besides, you'd be surprised at what people can survive."

"But the Peugeot exploded!"

"Is the Audi still behind you?"

I glanced in the rearview mirror, seeing only billowing black smoke and yellow-orange flames.

"I don't—I don't think—" I never got to finish. A low black shape emerged from the smoke and the wreckage, weaving onto the shoulder and back onto the main road, and then gunning the engine. "Shit! He's still back there."

I risked another backward glance, saw a hand extend out of the driver-side window, a silver pistol clutched in the fist. I watched the pistol jerk, a brief bark of flame, and then heard the *thunk* of a bullet hitting the body of the Rover.

"I see the smoke ahead. I'm almost there," I heard Harris say. "Honk your horn and flash your brights."

I laid on the horn and tugged the brights lever, keeping the pedal floored, trying to stay ahead of the Audi. The gun cracked again, and I heard another *thunk*. Looking ahead, I saw a silver BMW approaching, lights flashing.

"That's me," Harris said. "Silver Beamer. Now, here's what's gonna happen. When I count to three, you're gonna hit your brakes. Ease off the gas right now. Keep the wheel straight. When I say 'three,' you *stand* on those brakes. Let him rear-end you. As soon as he does, you hit the gas and take off. Got it?"

"Got it." It was all I could say.

"Ready?"

"No!"

"Too bad. One. Two…THREE!" He shouted the last word.

I'd eased off the gas when he told me to, bringing my speed down to below seventy…sixty…fifty, and the Audi was right behind me, black grille and silver rings growing larger in my rear view mirror. On "THREE!" I put both feet on the brakes and leaned all my weight on the pedal. The wheel jerked and shuddered, the back tires fishtailed, and I fought to keep the Rover straight. I felt a sickening crunch, and the Rover was thrown forward. I glanced in the rearview mirror, and I could see the driver, the man from the chateau, hooked nose, deep-set black eyes, lip curling in a sneer, showing white teeth. It was a fractional image, seen in a split-second glance in the mirror, but it was burned indelibly on my brain.

And then I heard a secondary squeal of tires from somewhere ahead and to the left. I threw my weight onto the gas pedal and felt the Rover bolt forward, throwing me back in my seat. I caught a glimpse of Harris in the window of the BMW, arcing in a sliding curve as he slammed on his brakes and threw the wheel over. Another momentary tableau, a panic-burned Polaroid image flashing into my skull: Harris, spinning his steering wheel hand over hand, face calm and emotionless. And then… *crunchCRASH*.

BMW met Audi, and the black vehicle went tumbling sideways, roof-tires-roof-tires, metal crumpling, and glass flying. Harris's car stuttered and rocked to a stop, and I was stopped too some-how, fifty feet away, and watched as smoke, thick and black, curled and coiled up from the overturned Audi. Harris stepped calmly from the driver's side of the BMW, leaving the door open. I watched, my hand over my mouth, as he reached into his suit coat with a gloved hand and withdrew a huge black pis-tol, then moved to kneel by the smashed-open win-dow of the Audi. I shook my head, whether in denial or horror, I wasn't sure. Harris twisted low, peering into the front passenger side of the Audi. He shoved the pistol through, and I saw a flash, heard the bark, and saw a red mist spatter through the shattered windshield.

As if nothing had happened, Harris stood up, replaced his weapon in the holster at his shoulder. He wiped his face with a handkerchief, wiped his hands, then placed the cloth in his back pocket. He pointed at me, held up one finger, which I took to mean *wait*. So I waited, watching. He leaned into the open door of the BMW and pushed a button, free-ing the trunk hatch. He crossed around, lifted two black duffel bags from the trunk. He left the trunk open, left the door open, and strode calmly to where I waited in the Rover. He opened the passenger-side rear door and tossed the bags inside.

"I'll drive," he said, then shut the door. Gratefully, I shoved open my door and moved around the hood. Halfway around, my knees gave out, my stomach heaving. I fell to the asphalt, bile on my tongue. I felt Harris lifting me to my feet. "We don't have time for you to break down just yet, Miss St. Claire. Where there's one of that sort of man, there's more. We need to move."

He helped me into the passenger seat and buckled me in. I was out of it, adrenaline receding, leaving me shaken and shaking, dizzy, nauseous. I blinked, and the Rover was moving, air rushing past from my face from the shattered window, and then I blinked again and we were weaving through the wreckage we'd just left behind—twisted and jackknifed semis, a crumpled Peugeot. Once we were out of the wreckage, Harris gunned the engine, and then I blinked again and we were bouncing over a dirt road and approaching the chateau. Then we were in the garage and Harris was helping me out, putting me in the passenger seat of the Aston Martin, buckling me in.

"Wait here. Let me check out the scene upstairs." He tossed the two duffel bags and my backpack in the trunk, and then vanished into the house.

I concentrated on breathing in, breathing out. I tried to block out the horrific images: the twisting, spinning Peugeot. The jackknifing semi. The rolling Audi. The spitting spray of blood.

What the hell was going on? Where was Roth? Why were people shooting at me and chasing me?

Harris slid into the driver's seat, threw the car into gear, and backed out. He said nothing, only brought the sleek red sports car onto the road, pointing us in the opposite direction from where we'd come. Sirens howled in the distance.

Fifteen minutes passed, and we were rolling between rows of grapevines, the sun shining, and the land peaceful and silent. As if nothing had happened. As if Harris and I were merely two friends out for a drive.

I couldn't take it anymore. "Harris? What the *fuck* is going on?"

He let out a sigh, the only sign of emotion a slight twitch in the muscles of his jaw. "It's complicated."

"This is Roth we're talking about. Everything is complicated."

"Well, obviously he was kidnapped."

"By whom? How? Why? Who could take him out of our bed in the middle of the night without waking me up?"

"Do you know much about the world Mr. Roth came out of?"

"A little. He was an arms dealer, wasn't he?"

"Correct. But that's not a world one simply walks away from." Harris paused for a long moment, considering. "I think we have a case of jealousy going on."

"Jealousy?"

"Miss St. Claire, you know how private Mr. Roth is. I'm somewhat stuck in that I'm not sure how much I'm allowed to tell you. What has he or hasn't he told you, what does he want you to know?"

"*Harris.* That's bullshit. I was almost killed several times just now. I was *shot* at. Roth is *gone.* He was taken from me, taken out of our fucking bed while I slept! I think I have a right to know what's going on, don't you?"

"I understand that. However, the problem is, I myself do not know very much." He pinched his lower lip between thumb and forefinger. "Here's what I know. Roth dealt in crates of assault rifles, rocket launchers, grenades. Small things like that. Nothing huge. In the circles Roth operated in, he was a small but important fish surrounded by some big, man-eating sharks. Back then, he was a young man with a big attitude. He'd made some good decisions, some good investments early on, built up a good client base and a decent stash of capital."

Harris paused to slow the Aston Martin and make a right turn onto a wider highway, and then resumed speaking. "But then he got involved with a girl. Gina Karahalios. He met her in a discotheque in Athens, had no idea who she was. Just thought she was another pretty Greek girl he could have a fling with for a night and move on. Well, turns out Gina was the daughter of one the most dangerous men in the world, Vitaly Karahalios, a drug dealer, smuggler, and major arms dealer. When Gina brought her new boy toy home with her, Vitaly recognized his promising talent. That meeting? It was Roth's downfall. He ended up working for Vitaly, running errands and doing dirty work. It was never part of Roth's plan, to hear him tell it, but he didn't have much choice. You don't say no to a man like Vitaly Karahalios.

"And his daughter? She's her father's daughter in every way, cut from the same cloth: cunning, violent, dangerous, manipulative. And she had her hooks in Roth, had them in deep. He wanted out, though. From the start, he wanted out. He never wanted to get involved in that kind of business. He never wanted to be a criminal. He was just trying to make ends meet. That's how he explained it to me, at least. He started out doing a favor for a friend in return for investment capital. Deliver some boxes, get paid, and don't ask questions. So he did it. And then again. Then, sort of by accident, he discovered he was running boxes of small arms. Well, by then, the money he was making doing that started eclipsing his legitimate business income. For a kid in his early twenties, pulling in twenty or thirty grand for a single afternoon's work? Easy choice. But then he met Gina, and everything spiraled out of control."

"Sounds like Roth glossed over a few facts when he told me all of this."

"One thing I have learned, working for Valentine Roth: He will never tell you an outright lie. But he will often leave out facts, keep the whole of the truth from you. I've seen this in his business dealings many times. It is part of his way. He doesn't consider it lying, or even an omission. The flow of information is vital in any business. He learned early on in life to never reveal too much, and now it's just…how he is." Harris shrugged.

"I'm still not understanding how we got from that whole story about Vitaly and Gina to people shooting at *me*."

"This is where my knowledge of events is somewhat sparse. Something went wrong. He tried to get out, I think. Tried to go legitimate. The Karahalios family wasn't thrilled with that decision, I think. And now, for some reason, I think Gina is out for revenge, or to get him back, or something. I don't know what she wants. I'm not even sure I've made the right guess, quite honestly, but it's the only thing that makes sense to me, based on my limited knowledge."

"So what do we do? How do we find him and get him back?"

Harris didn't answer for so long I wasn't sure if he'd heard me. "I'm not sure. Number-one priority right now is to get you somewhere safe while I figure out a plan. The problem is, that chateau was supposed to be a safe house. It was purchased through a ridiculously complicated series of fronts and subsidiary companies. If Gina or her father or whoever it was could find you two there? I'm not convinced that any of our preexisting properties are going to be safe. The Karahalios reach is enormous. That man I just disposed of is only one of many. Probably the first one sent after you. There will be more. When he doesn't report back, more will come. And soon."

I let a few minutes pass, watching the landscape slide by the window. Eventually I had to ask. "So where are we going now?"

"Marseilles."

"And then?"

"And then I make some phone calls."

# 3

## MARSEILLES

Harris drove us to Marseilles, and we arrived late in the afternoon. He seemed to have a particular destination in mind, because he wove through the narrow streets without hesitation. He stopped on a street that sloped steeply down toward the sea, parked the Aston Martin and set the handbrake, then popped the trunk and slid out. Harris closed the trunk, my backpack over one shoulder, and jerked his chin at me, indicating that I should follow.

In other circumstances, I would have loved to have taken a few moments to appreciate the beauty of Marseilles. It was the Old World at its finest, ancient buildings rolling low over the hills in their march down to the Mediterranean, bathed in golden sunlight. The sea sparkled cobalt in the distance, white sails dotting the bay. As it was, I spared only a moment, and then I followed Harris through a low, narrow doorway into a dark cafe. There was a short length of bar on one wall, an aged slab of scratched, scarred, pitted, and polished wood with a brass foot-rail underneath running at ankle height. A few small round tables were scattered in a random pattern, each one empty. An old man stood behind the bar, a pipe held to his mouth, billowing sweet-smelling smoke. He had white hair, a neatly trimmed white beard, dark, deep-set eyes, and tanned, weathered skin, the wrinkles on his face etched so deeply that they looked like scars in his skin. His gaze raked over me, assessing me, and then he said something in low, rapid French.

"Just long enough to make some arrangements," Harris responded in English. "Couple hours, if that. Thanks, Henri." He pronounced the name the French way, *Anhrrrree*. The old man nodded, and Harris handed me my backpack, pointed at a stool. "Have a seat, Miss St. Claire." I sat, and he leaned against the bar beside me. "I've got to make some arrangements. See a few people. You'll stay here with Henri. I won't be more than an hour or two, hope-fully, and then we'll be on our way."

"Wait, you're leaving me here? Alone, with him?" I hated how panicked I sounded. "What if—what if they followed us? Or they find me?"

"God help them, in that case," Harris said, the ghost of a smirk on his lips.

Henri clamped the pipe between his teeth, puffed a plume of smoke toward the ceiling as he reached under the bar and came up with a massive shotgun. I didn't know much about guns, but I knew this one wasn't a typical hunting shotgun. It was long and black, with a single wide-mouthed barrel and a shortened stock, making it resemble a machine gun or assault rifle. Another reach under the counter produced a box of shells, and Henri began calmly inserting them into the shotgun, and then into a series of loops on the side of the weapon. Then he lined up a dozen more shells on the bar top.

"Oh. Oh. Okay." I swallowed and stared at the wicked-looking weapon.

Henri twitched the corner of his mouth in a flash of a smile. "Safe. No worries." His accent was so thick the words twisted and curled in on themselves.

"I'll be back. Just sit tight, okay? Don't leave Henri's sight." Harris moved toward the door, then stopped and turned back to me. "You got a cell phone with you?"

"Yeah, of course." I lifted my shoulder to indicate the backpack. "In my purse."

"Turn it off and give it to Henri." He stood, waiting, and I realized he meant right away.

I slung my bag around to my lap, unzipped it, and dug in my purse for my iPhone. I held the power button and swiped the phone off, then handed it to Henri, who turned and tossed it into the sink, which was full of soapy water.

"Um. All right." I sighed wistfully.

"Tracking a cellphone is the easiest thing in the world. Most people know this as a kind of abstract fact, having seen it on movies and TV or whatever, and for most people, under most circumstances, it doesn't matter. You have nothing to hide, no reason to care. But you, in these circumstances? It matters. Karahalios has the resources to track you that way, trust me. Hopefully, he hasn't already."

"Oh. Yeah, I guess that makes sense."

Harris left, and I watched him go with a twinge of trepidation. I sat on the bar stool in silence as Henri smoked his pipe, seemingly content to merely wait.

After what felt like half an hour of dead silence, no TV above the bar, no music playing, no conversation, Henri glanced at me. "Drink?"

I shrugged and nodded. "Sure. Thanks."

Henri twisted in place, grabbed a dusty brown bottle from a shelf and two wine glasses. He uncorked the bottle, and poured a generous measure of deep ruby liquid into each, then slid one glass toward me with a finger. He lifted his glass toward me in a silent toast and took a sip. I matched his toast and drank my own, and felt the rich, slow burn of a dry, expensive merlot.

We drank in silence.

I tried not to think or worry or conjecture. But it was useless. My brain whirled and spun, and the wine, even with as little as I drank, left me heady and loose. I pictured Valentine tied to a chair, being beaten, or tortured. The more I tried to block the image, the more it kept coming back, until it was all I could think about. All I could see, every time I blinked.

Valentine was missing and presumed kidnapped, if Harris was right, by a violent crime lord. And I was sitting in a bar in Marseilles, drinking wine?

An hour passed somehow. Another. So much waiting. I hated waiting. I'd always hated waiting.

Tires squealed outside in the street, brakes protesting, an engine roared. Instantly, Henri was in motion, grabbing me by the sleeve and pulling me around behind the bar, shoving me down into a crouch. His hand on my shoulder, holding me down, was huge and hard, rough as concrete. I could see the shelf underneath the bar, and it was stocked with all kinds of things. A green rotary phone. Several boxes of shotgun shells. A huge silver pistol. A machete. A smaller black pistol, several other boxes full of rounds for the handguns, I assumed, as well as a stack of spare clips, some glinting with rounds, others empty. Bottles of alcohol, a pack of cigarettes, books of matches and ashtrays and a packet of pipe tobacco.

I glanced up at Henri, who had the shotgun to his shoulder, pipe still in his teeth, aiming the weapon at the door. Car doors slammed, and I peeked up to watch Henri as he stepped out from behind the bar, moving in the slow crouching shuffle of someone who has had tactical training of some kind. He moved to stand beside the door so that when it swung inward, he would be able to blast whoever stepped through. I ducked back down behind the bar.

My heart hammered in my chest, my stomach lodged in my throat.

Hinges creaked slowly. A foot shuffled on the wood floor.

*BOOM!—BOOM!—BOOM!* Three bellowing, deafening blasts of the shotgun, followed by the sound of wet splatter. Bodies hitting the floor.

"Stay down," Henri called out. "Do not move."

I stayed down. My lungs wouldn't work. I was close to hyperventilating, sucking in short, shallow breaths and letting them out with a whine in my throat.

"They are done. Is okay. You safe now." I heard the sound of something sliding across the wood planks of the floor. "But still, stay down. Not good for you to see."

No arguments from me there. I hugged my knees and waited, listening as Henri dragged three heavy bodies I didn't want to see across the floor and down some stairs. I continued to sit on the floor behind the bar for another half hour as Henri mopped and scrubbed.

Finally, he appeared behind the bar. "All done. Go sit, now." He washed his hands in the sink, dried them, then grabbed a book of matches and relit his pipe, sipped at his wine.

And just like that, everything was back to normal. Sitting at the bar with a glass of half-finished wine. As if three men hadn't just died.

I opened my mouth to ask a question, but Henri shook his head. "Do not ask. You do not want to know."

"The police?" I asked anyway. "Won't they—"

"*Non.* Not here. They will not come here."

That was a mystifying answer, one that I wasn't sure I wanted to know more about.

My heart leapt into my throat again when the door opened suddenly and Henri jerked the shotgun to his shoulder. Harris stepped through. He'd changed out of the suit into a pair of blue jeans and thick black V-neck sweater, the sleeves pushed up to his elbows. "Just me. Just me." He sniffed the air, his eyes darting from the floor at his feet to the door, and then to Henri and the shotgun. "Something happen?"

Henri set the shotgun on the bar, speaking in rapid French, gesturing at a door in the back of the bar.

"Persistent fuckers," Harris muttered.

Henri barked a laugh. "Vitaly Karahalios? He does not give up."

"You know anything about his daughter, Gina?"

Henri spat on the floor, a spiteful, angry gesture. "*Evil.* Worse than her father." He glanced at me, speculation in his gaze. "Ahhh. Now I see. This is about the girl, *non?*"

"That's what I think." Harris gestured at the door in the back of the bar, ostensibly meaning the bodies beyond it. "They're Vitaly's men, yes?"

Henri nodded. "*Oui.* I am as sure of this as one can be without knowing for certain. Who else could find her here, and risk my wrath?"

"Good point." Harris gestured at me with his fingers, indicating that I should go with him. "Thanks, Henri. I'll be in touch." Harris reached into the back pocket of his jeans, and it didn't escape my notice that Henri tensed at the motion, his hand resting on the shotgun. Harris held up a thick white envelope, which clearly contained a thick sheaf of Euros, setting it on the bar near Henri.

"I do not need this," Henri said, shaking his head.

"For your trouble."

Henri winked at me. "Protecting a beautiful woman is never trouble." He pushed the envelope away, a gesture that contained a strong note of finality. "I owe Roth my life. This was my honor."

Harris nodded and stuffed the envelope back in his jeans pocket. "All right. You know how to reach me. You hear anything, see anything, find anything out, let me know, okay?"

"*Oui*. Of course." Henri held up a finger. "Wait. A moment, wait." He twisted to reach under the bar, set the small black pistol on the bar, then two clips and the box of rounds. "For her. Teach her. You and I will not always be around, *non?*"

I shook my head. "I can't. I wouldn't—"

Henri held up his hand, glaring at me, and I fell silent. "You can. You *will*. Those men? Mercy is a thing they do not know. Better to die than let them get their filthy hands on you, yes? Better yet, you kill them first. Learn. For Roth, learn."

I picked up the handgun. It was heavier than I'd thought it would be, and cold to the touch. "Is it safe? To put it in my bag, I mean."

Henri snorted. "What good does it do in your purse? Can you reach it there so swiftly? *Non.* Look. Your first lesson." He clamped his pipe in his teeth and puffed, then grabbed the gun from me, pushed a button on the side, and the clip ejected. He held it sideway, pulled back the slide. A round clattered onto the bar. "*Now* it is safe." He knocked the clip back in, pulled and released the slide, and then held the pistol so I could watch as he thumbed a switch near the trigger. "Safety on. *Now* it is safe. Push the button to shoot. And if you shoot? You shoot once, one time only, and you kill. Only shoot to kill."

I swallowed hard and backed away. This was absurd. What was happening to me? How could this be my life now? A few short months ago, I was a broke and starving girl, alone in the world. And then I was collected by Roth, and everything changed. I became his, willingly his. He took me away from everything. He was showing me the world. We'd visited a dozen or so countries so far, and I'd discovered exactly how big the world was, and just how many places there were to see, and I realized I wanted to see *all* of them.

But only with Roth.

And he was gone. My idyllic little world—traveling with my Valentine, eating and drinking and fucking and sailing and hiking and *living*—had been shattered.

I'd been shot at. Chased. I'd hidden behind a bar like something from a Hollywood movie as shotguns went off around me.

And now I was supposed to take a gun and shoot people with it? I'd never touched a gun in my life. Not even so much as a BB gun.

"Take the gun, Miss St. Claire. We don't have time for you to have qualms about it right now. Take it and put it at the small of your back, just like in the movies." Harris was at my side, talking quietly to me.

He took the pistol from Henri and placed it in my hand. The heft of it was the cold, hard weight of reality. This was not a toy. It was a weapon, meant to kill. I reached around behind me, put it between my underwear and the waist of my jeans. It felt alien and heavy resting there, cold against my skin. I tugged my shirt down over it. Surely everyone who looked at me would know I had it? I kept pulling at my shirt, pushing the handle this way and that. It was far more uncomfortable than I'd thought it would be.

My jeans were tight-fitting, so adding the barrel of a handgun stretched them so tight they pulled against my belly. And how was I supposed to sit down? Wouldn't it fall out, or become even more obvious?

"Put the sweater on," Harris instructed. I did so, and he grabbed the spare clips, handed one to me, and then stuffed the rest and the box of shells into my backpack, rearranging things inside so they weren't on top. "Put that in your pocket, and stop fidgeting with the gun. With the sweater on, no one can tell."

"*I* can tell."

"Good. That's the point. I'll give you some lessons once we're in transit."

"I feel stupid. I've never even shot a BB gun, Harris."

"Then don't touch it unless I say so. The most important thing to know is point it away from you and me. Keep that in mind, and you'll be fine." He lifted a hand in a wave to Henri, and then pulled me out the door. "Now, we need to move."

Out on the street, evening was giving way to dusk. Couples strolled down the steep incline, hand in hand. A businessman in a three-piece suit power-walked up the hill, a cell phone to his ear. Cars passed going down the hill, brakes squealing, engines idling high and gears downshifting. Harris

pulled me into a walk down the hill, keeping hold of
my arm. He said nothing, and neither did I. Down,
down, down to the sea. The sound of waves lapping
and seagulls cawing met my ears, and then I smelled
the brine on a stiff wind. Lines clinked against masts,
flags snapped. Harris guided us through throngs
of people, past cafes and seaside bars, eventually
leading us out onto the docks among hundreds of
boats, some with sails and some without. Tiny fishing vessels and mammoth yachts and everything in
between.

One hand on my elbow, the other shoved into
his hip pocket, Harris seemed deceptively at ease,
relaxed. I could feel him scanning, however, and
every once in a while he'd twist around to scan
behind us, doing so casually, as if he was nothing
more than a tourist taking in the sights. Pier after
pier stretched out and away, each one with a dozen
boats on each side. Marseilles stood above us, a massive, looming, and ancient presence in the lowering
dusk. Harris led me past half a dozen piers before
cutting over onto one, and then he took us to the
very end of the dock and halted in front of a medi-
um-sized boat.

Ships or boats or whatever were something I
knew nothing about. This one wasn't a sailboat,
but rather a smaller version of the massive yachts

visible elsewhere in the bay. It didn't look particularly impressive, or new. Usually, if something belonged to Roth, it was the best available. Not necessarily the biggest or most ostentatious, but just the highest quality. This boat looked…understated, and that was putting it nicely. It was the kind of thing that wouldn't stand out in any way, no matter where we were. Which, it occurred to me, may have been the intention.

As if reading my mind, Harris sent me an apologetic grin. "Not what you're used to with Mr. Roth, I imagine, but this was the best I could do on short notice. It'll do the job, though."

"How'd you get it?"

"Traded the Aston for it, plus some cash." He stepped aboard and held his hand out, helping me across and onto the yacht. "It's on the older side, but it's got a few things most boats like it don't have."

"Like what?"

Harris didn't answer immediately. Instead, he untied the lines keeping the boat moored to the dock, and then led the way to the wheelhouse. He took a seat, and I sat nearby, waiting. Harris put the boat in reverse and expertly backed out of the slip, angling the bow toward open water, then pushed the throttle forward.

"Well, anonymity, for one thing. The slip itself was…borrowed, and the boat's papers are untraceable. It just means anyone looking for us—Vitaly's men, for example—will have a harder time finding us. I didn't think about your cell phone soon enough, which is the only reason they were able to track us to Marseilles. Stupid of me, honestly. Good thing Henri is the 'shoot first and don't ask any questions' type."

"Who *is* Henri?"

Harris shrugged. "That's a tricky question to answer." He glanced at me. "Mr. Roth used to run in some shady circles. I think you know that. And even now he still retains contact with some old…friends and acquaintances. Henri is one of those. Honestly, I don't know much about him myself, just that he's tough as nails, cold as ice, and loyal as hell. As long as he's on your side. And he's *very* much on Mr. Roth's side."

"He said something about owing Valentine his life," I said.

Harris checked behind us, and then returned his attention to navigating past the breakwater and out into the trackless azure expanse of the Mediterranean. "Yeah, that's a story I don't know. Henri was a smuggler, I think. My guess is that he and Mr. Roth got into a tight spot, and Roth got them out."

I shifted uncomfortably. "When Roth told me about his old life, he made it sound like he was just a businessman. Like he just…handed over some boxes and took some cash, and that was it. Like it wasn't… dangerous."

Harris chuckled. "He *would* say that. And that's how it was, mostly. Not even that, really. Arms dealing is just another business, in some ways. The deals happen in a hotel bar, or in some corner of a nightclub. Prices and goods are discussed over some drinks, the parties shake on it, and that's about it. Lackeys do the rest. But Valentine didn't have employees back then. He did it all himself. Acquired goods, negotiated the deals, did the delivery. That's where it got dangerous. The types of people who deal in weapons aren't always the nicest sorts, obviously. And sometimes they're notably lacking in what you might call…scruples. Meaning, they'll try to take what they want and find a way to not pay for it. Especially when dealing with some twenty-year-old kid doing business on his own, with no firepower backup, no one standing behind him as a presence, you know? Tells you how good he was that he never got killed doing what he did, the way he did it. I think he came close a few times—more than

he'd ever admit to, though. Like with Henri. He's a
wily old cat, Henri is. Not the kind of guy who is
easily backed into a corner. And not the type of guy
who would lightly, or easily, admit to owing someone his life. What he did today, taking out those
guys? That was a big deal for him. He's in semi-
retirement, you could say. Doesn't really do business
anymore. Tries to keep a low profile." Harris pushed
the throttle open, and the bow skimmed over the
water, barely touching down. Harris set our destination in the GPS unit and then returned his attention to our conversation. "So, offing three of Vitaly's
goons? That could open him up to retaliation."

"Oh."

"Yeah. Oh."

I swallowed hard, hoping Henri wouldn't get in
any trouble because of me. "Where are we going?" I
asked.

"Greece."

# 4

## CAPTIVE

*VALENTINE*

MY HEAD THROBBED. THAT WAS MY FIRST REALIZATION. IT pounded and ached like fuck. It felt like a thousand hammers were pounding on my skull. Why did my head hurt so badly?

I tried to touch my fingers to my forehead, but couldn't. My hand wouldn't move. I jerked it, but it was…restrained. My eyes slid open, warily, painfully. Even my eyelids hurt. Blinding light assaulted my eyes. I had to blink and squint and twist my head to the side. I shut my eyes again and peered through slitted lids.

The sunlight was blinding, and it bounced off the waves like so many knives. A seagull cawed. An

osprey keened. I could hear the waves crashing outside the window. Oh god, my head…it was sluggish,
thick. I was having trouble getting my bearings.

Gradually my eyes adjusted to the light, and
I craned my neck, looking for a hint as to where I
was, or why my hands were restrained. Was this a
new game of Kyrie's? I tugged hard, but my wrist
was bound firmly to the bedpost. Bedpost? The bed
in the Languedoc chateau didn't have posts. It was
a platform bed, the headboard mounted directly
to the wall. And the chateau wasn't on the sea. This
incredible brightness reminded me of something.
Something familiar, an old, haunting memory.

I twisted my head and strained to see out the
window, where I saw flat-topped white roofs, white-
washed buildings with blue doors and shutters, and
more than a few roofs and cupolas painted that same
distinctive bright blue. I could see that the buildings
descended down the hillside in serried ranks, bare
rock peeking through in places, the sea rippling in
the distance, far below.

In an instant, I knew exactly where I was.

Oia, Greece.

Shit. No, no. Shit, no. How did I get *here?* The
blue of the sea was a perfect azure rippling with the
occasional whitecap, sails dotting the blue; there's
nowhere on earth quite like the Aegean. Oia is a city

carved out of the rock on an island a hundred and fifty miles southeast of Athens, a quaint, quintessentially Aegean village.

Vitaly Karahalios kept an estate on Oia.

I tugged each of my limbs. I was bound spread-eagled to the bed. Brass rails two inches in diameter spanned between the stout upright posts at each corner, handcuffs shackling me in place. The headboard was set against a wall with windows running in almost a complete circle around the circumference of the room, which was clearly a rotunda, offering a spectacular view of the entire island, with the tiny fishing village of Ormos Armeni visible to the south.

I heard a lock twist and turned my attention to the doorway directly opposite the bed. The door was thick, dark wood reinforced with black straps of metal, locked from the outside. The door swung open, revealing the one woman on the entire earth I would have given my entire fortune to never see again.

Gina Karahalios.

Time had favored her. Fifteen years ago, Gina had been a fresh, nubile girl of nineteen, slim and delicate and almost too angularly beautiful. Now...? Now she was all woman, a bit of weight giving her curves and making her even more beautiful. Her thick, straight black hair hung to her waist in loose locks glinting in the sun, dark as a raven's wing. Her skin was the flawless golden tan of a Greek woman raised in the Aegean sun. She wore a white dress, sleeveless, cut in a deep V between her plump breasts, the hem flirting just above her ankles. The dress was long and fluttering, molded so tightly to her curves as to be immodestly revealing.

Her eyes, though. Those hadn't changed. Black as her hair, gleaming with wicked intelligence, cold, cruel, calculating. Predatory. Seductive. Those eyes could fix on you and make you squirm, no matter who you were. Even her father was a little afraid of Gina, I think, and that was saying something. I'd once watched Vitaly slit a man's throat with a steak knife and then go back to eating.

She stood at the foot of the bed, one arm wrapped around her waist, the other hand at her mouth, touching two fingers to her lips in a thoughtful posture. Her hip was popped out, knee drawn up. Gina never merely sat or stood or lay; she posed. She was always, *always* aware of how she looked, how she was seen.

"Val. My god, Val. Age looks good on you." Her voice was a little deeper, a little smoother, and she spoke in very lightly accented English.

"You too, Gina."

"It's good to see you, I must say."

"I can't say I agree there, actually." I tugged my hand against the bond. "Let me go. Let me go now, and we can forget this happened. This doesn't have to be a big deal."

She grinned, the curve of her lips reminding me somehow of a viper eying a hapless mouse. "Oh, no. Oh, no, no, no. I don't think you understand, dear Val. You don't understand at all."

"What, Gina? What do I not understand?"

"This." She waved at me, the bonds, and the bed. "This situation."

I had to dispel my trepidation. Gina had been capable of damn near anything fifteen years ago. Something told me she was even more dangerous and unpredictable now.

"So, help me understand. Why am I here? Why am I handcuffed to the bed?"

"You used to like playing these games with me, Val. Don't you remember that night? You *must* remember. Cyprus? Yes, it was Cyprus. The Four Seasons. You were meeting…who was it? Uri? Uri Domashev. You got such a good deal that night. I think you must remember this—in fact, I know you do. You never forget things. You made the deal with Uri. You fleeced him, scalped him dry, and he knew it, and he couldn't do a fucking thing about it. I was very proud of you that night. And I showed you. I let you tie my hands to the balcony, and you fucked me from behind until I screamed so loud people complained, but of course everyone knows you don't tell me what to do, so they couldn't make us be quiet. You let me tie you up that night, too. Remember? I used your shoelaces. That was a good night." She bit her lower lip and wiggled her eyebrows. "Tell me you remember, Val."

I remembered. Oh, Jesus, I remembered. You didn't forget someone like Gina. "Of course I remember. But Gina, that was fifteen years ago. Things have changed." I tried to keep my voice low, tried to stay calm. "A *lot* has changed. You tried to have me killed, if you'll remember. And now you kidnap me? Come on. Untie me and let me go."

"Oh, no. I don't think so. You're not remembering right." She moved around the bed to stand beside me. "I didn't try to have you killed, silly. That was Papa. He felt you'd outlived your usefulness, plus there was the fact that you were *abandoning* me….he wasn't happy. And I even tried to talk him out of it."

"Gina…Micha *told* me you'd sent him. Before I put a bullet in his brain, he told me you'd paid him a hundred grand to take me out. He told me you'd instructed him to make me *suffer*." I paused to let that sink in. "If he'd just shot me, it would've worked. I never even saw him coming. But he tried to hurt me first. And that was his mistake. That was *your* mistake. I let it go, Gina. I didn't hold it against you. I didn't try to get even. I went my own way and left you alone."

"You *left me,* Val." Her voice went thin and low and growling. "You *left* me."

"Your father wanted me to be a hit man. He wanted me to do things I wasn't comfortable with. He wouldn't take no for an answer, so I cashed out."

"You don't just *cash out* on us, Val. It's not that simple."

"It should've been."

"But it's not. It's *not.* You're *mine.*" She leaned over me, touched a long, blood-red fingernail to my chest, over the sheet still covering me. "I let you have some time to think, okay? I let you have your fun. I wanted you to…age a bit. You were too young to appreciate me then, I think. I don't like boys, and you were just a boy back then. You needed some seasoning, so when you got away, I decided to let you go. But you're mine. You've always been mine. You were my favorite, Val. There've been others, of course, but none of them was *you.* They couldn't satisfy me the way you did, even back then. I've kept an eye on you, you know. You've had *lots* of practice. You should be able to satisfy me now. It's been a long time since I've been truly satisfied with a man."

I barely suppressed a shudder. "Gina, this is crazy. You have to let me go. I don't belong to you. I'm in love with someone else, all right?"

She narrowed her eyes, and I saw something else in her gaze: a hint of something dark and manic and insane. Jealousy. "That bitch doesn't own you. I do." She abruptly straightened and turned away, examining her fingernails. "But no matter. Alec should have taken care of her by now."

My blood ran cold. "Gina…what did you do?" She didn't answer, just twisted her head on her neck to grin at me slyly. "*WHAT DID YOU DO?*" I shouted the last part so loud my voice went hoarse.

"Disposed of unneeded distractions, my dear Valentine. That's all." She bit her thumbnail coyly, a choreographed gesture of icy insouciance.

"If you hurt her, so help me…you'd better pray I don't get free. I'll kill you. I don't hurt women, but if you harm a hair on Kyrie's head, you'll pay for it. You'll regret it."

"You won't do a damned thing, Val." She pivoted on her heel, grabbed the sheet draped over my chest, and flung it back. I was stark naked beneath it, a fact I'd tried not to think about till then. "You've gone soft. You always had your friend Harris do your dirty work. Don't pretend, all right? I know you better than that."

"If you think for one second that I've gone soft, then you don't know a single thing about me, Gina."

She quirked an eyebrow. "Ah. There's a bit of that steel spine you used to have." She perched her hip on the edge of the bed, partially facing me. I glared at her, stared her down, refusing to flinch as her fingers rested on my chest and tickled downward. "Other parts of you used to be like steel, too."

I tried to arch away, twisting to avoid her touch. "Don't fucking touch me, you viper."

There was nowhere to go, and she ignored my efforts to get away from her questing hand, just like she ignored my protest and my insult. Her attention was focused on my body, her eyes roaming and devouring, her lips curled in a cruel smile.

"You used to respond so beautifully, Valentine. I barely had to touch you, and you'd be ready to come all over me. Are you still that responsive? Hmmm?" She wrapped her fingers around my flaccid cock.

I closed my eyes and thought about that day fifteen years ago when she'd sent Micha to torture and kill me. I thought about the pain of his knife in my back, inches from piercing my heart. I thought about the fight, every move agony, wrestling the gun from his fingers. I thought about shooting him in the kneecap and pressing the gun to his forehead until he told me Gina had sent him. How she'd caught wind of my plan to disappear, and had obviously not been willing to let me go that easily. For the first time in fifteen years, I thought about the moment I'd pulled the trigger. Micha had been going for a hideout pistol, so I'd had to shoot him. Blood had spattered everywhere. I'd vomited all over Micha's twitching corpse. With the knife still in my back, I'd run. Stumbled onto my sailboat stocked in preparation for my departure. I sailed toward Athens, but only made it as far as Milos before I had to stop and find a doctor. I'd paid him ten thousand dollars to fix me and keep quiet about it.

The self-distraction program was working, because Gina hissed in frustration and leaped off the bed. She paced the length of the room, enraged by my lack of response to her ministrations. "You aren't cooperating, Valentine. That's not how this goes."

I barked in laughter. "What did you think—that I'd wake up, kidnapped and cuffed to a bed, and be happy to see you?"

She whirled on me, eyes blazing in fury. "You... will...be...*mine*. You *are* mine. I will make sure of it."

"I belong with Kyrie, not you." I knew as soon as the words left my mouth that I shouldn't have said it.

"She was already going to die, but now? I think maybe she will suffer first. I think maybe I will have her brought in. Maybe I will make her watch me fuck you. Maybe I will take what I want from you and then kill you, and then kill her." She leaned over me again, caressing my chest, my thighs, my cock, and my testicles, her touch gentle in contrast to her words. "I'll do it myself, too. I've had plenty of practice at that, you know. I've got a few rather lovely techniques." She licked her lips, shifting tactics abruptly. "But first? I've got to get you hard. I'd rather not drug you, but I will if I have to. Let's try this first. You used to love this."

She lowered her mouth to me, started working me gently and insistently, skillfully. I kept my mind occupied, thought of all the worst moments of my life, all the painful, embarrassing, horrible memories. Anything to keep from responding. I focused on the horror of my position, on the anger. On the shame.

It didn't work. She got the response from me she wanted, and seemed to take immense and vocal satisfaction in that fact.

She stopped when she felt me start to harden, spat me out with a wet *pop*. "There we are. God, Val. You are more beautiful than I had remembered. I'm going to enjoy this very, *very* much." There was a small table next to the bed, with two drawers. She opened one, pulled out a small rubber ring and a bottle of lubricant. I wasn't fully hard yet. She squirted some of the lube onto her palm and smeared it onto the ring, then onto me. I closed my eyes and tried to force myself down, thought of Micha's spasming body and the blood and gore flooding the street. It started to work, but by then Gina had the cock ring on me and was stroking me into hardness with quick, vigorous pumps of her hands. I hated that I had so little control over myself. That I couldn't stop the response to physical stimulation. I wasn't aroused, but my traitorous body responded out of my control.

Jesus, it hurt. The ring was meant for a much smaller man, and the blood flow was restricted, so I couldn't subside even if I wanted to.

*I'm sorry, Kyrie.*

"Why are you fighting this, you silly man? Don't you remember all the good times we had together?" She was sitting beside me again, acting calm and cool as if she wasn't forcing this on me.

"I remember never being able to satisfy you, that's what I remember. I remember nothing I did was ever good enough. I remember you screaming at me when I came too soon. I remember you convincing me to let you tie me up, and then you didn't let me go. Just like this. You had me tied up for hours that night in Cyprus. *That's* what I remember." I spoke through gritted teeth, tasting the revulsion on my tongue, at the back of my throat like bitter bile. "You've always been a goddamn psychopath. I realized that the first time we fucked. You always wanted more. Something else. Something even more fucked up."

I was slipping. Regressing. My speech was reverting to the way I'd spoken back then, vulgar language with the English accent. I'd worked hard to distance myself from who I'd been, worked hard to clean up my speech. I'd stopped cursing, straightened my accent as much as possible, spoke properly, formally. I forced myself to speak, look, and act like the man I wanted to be: a respectable, legitimate businessman. Fifteen minutes with Gina, and I was regressing.

She just grinned. "Oh, Valentine. You have *no* idea." She was stroking my length, almost idly. Petting. "I've been practicing for this. I know you, Val. I knew you'd fight me. But you can't. You can't fight me. You're trying right now. You're trying to think of something else so you won't react. Aren't you? But just—just stop fighting for a moment and *feel*. It feels good, doesn't it? It hurts, just a little. I'm just getting started, Valentine. Fight all you want, but you'll give in to me. You'll give me what I want."

I fought it. Fought hard. Kept my eyes closed and denied her, denied myself sensation. "Never."

"Maybe you need some…inspiration." She let me go and slid off the bed. "Watch."

I kept my eyes shut. I knew what her game was. I wanted to think of Kyrie, but refused. I wouldn't think of her in this situation. I wouldn't betray her. Not willingly.

"*WATCH*." She spat the word out, furious. Something cold and sharp touched my Adam's apple. "Don't toy with me, Valentine."

I opened my eyes. Gina was standing near my head, a short, wicked-looking black folding knife held to my throat. Her face was expressionless, a blank mask. She kept the razor-sharp point to my throat for a few beats, then pulled it away and folded the blade into the handle. As soon as the knife was closed, the mask fell away. I recognized the look on her face as what she thought of as "seductive." Pouting, slightly smirking lips, puppy-dog eyes. She wouldn't kill me yet, I knew that much, but if I didn't cooperate to some degree, she'd find some awful and inventive way to punish me. So I watched.

I watched, and for the first time in my life, watching as a beautiful woman stripped down to nothing in front of me failed to incite any kind of reaction in me. She wasn't Kyrie. Until Kyrie, I'd never loved a woman. Girls were girls, and they'd never meant anything to me beyond a few hours of fun and pleasure. They were all largely interchangeable. A naked woman was something to be appreciated and, if circumstances permitted, thoroughly enjoyed. And then Kyrie happened, and love happened, and everything changed.

Gina was a beautiful woman. A work of art, really. But she was just that: art, sculpture. Her makeup was perfect. Her hair was perfect. And even as she reached behind her back and unzipped the dress and let it fall to pool around her ankles, she was careful to make sure nothing was out of order. She paused after the dress was off, making sure I appreciated the hours spent in the gym, the diets, the expensive lingerie.

On any other woman, those would be positive qualities. But with Gina, that's all there was. It was window dressing, disguising the cruel, empty soul beneath. Her eyes never left mine as she reached behind her back and unclasped her bra, then held an arm barred across her chest, keeping the bra in place as she withdrew first one arm and then the other. When the straps were off her shoulders, she let the undergarment drop with a flourish, setting her massive tits bouncing. Ugh. She'd had implants. An additional twenty pounds, even on her svelte frame, couldn't explain the jump from small C-cup to large DD-cup. She'd also pierced her nipples; a thick silver bar was positioned horizontally between each nipple.

Piercings and implants were fine. If that's what a woman was into, if that made her feel good about herself, great, fine. It simply wasn't to my taste. My personal preference was for natural bodies, no implants, and no piercings. I liked a woman as she was. That, at least partially, was why I'd been so attracted to Kyrie. She was the epitome of feminine beauty to me. She needed no makeup, no expensive clothing or lingerie or implants to be lush and gorgeous. Her breasts were naturally big, firm, high, and taut, with large areolae and thick pink nipples, unadorned and begging to be tasted. The curves of her body were…perfect. Wide, swaying hips, strong, thick thighs, long legs. She wasn't stick-thin. That look had never appealed to me. I'd dallied with a few model-thin women before Kyrie came along, and they were beautiful women in their own way, and certainly other men found them desirable. But to me, Kyrie was what I wanted. She was perfection to me. Curves. Flesh to hold and feel and clutch and kiss.

A slap across my face brought me back to the present. "*Look* at me, Val."

"My name isn't Val, Gina. My name is Valentine."

"But I've always called you Val."

"You don't get to do that anymore." I lifted my chin and let her see the depth of my revulsion and derision. "You can keep me tied up here as long as you want. You can drug me and cut me and threaten me all you wish. You can take whatever you want from me. None of that will change a thing. Not a thing. I won't love you. I won't be attracted to you. I won't want you. I won't even *like* you."

She wasn't wearing any underwear. Whether she'd shed them while I was spaced out thinking of Kyrie or whether she'd never been wearing them, I couldn't remember. She was shaved bare—there was not a single hair anywhere on her body below her neck.

"You're lying. You want this. You're trying not to want it, but you do."

I didn't bother arguing with her. I just kept my eyes focused on hers, refusing to give her the satisfaction of my gaze on her body. She sashayed closer to me, putting a sway in her hips, a bounce to her cleavage. Her black eyes watched mine, and I saw them narrow at my lack of reaction. She didn't falter in her runway walk, though it was obvious she was aware of the sun shining through the window behind her, outlining her, the wind skirling through the room, tossing her hair.

Finally, she was at the bed. Leaning over me, staring down at me. Climbing onto the bed. Straddling me. She put her hands on my chest, curled her long red fingernails into my skin and muscle, gouging deep. That had always been her thing, digging in with her nails. Establishing dominance, maybe? Or maybe it was supposed to be erotic? I never liked it, and had told her so on more than one occasion. If she got lost in the heat and throes of ecstasy, Kyrie would occasionally scratch me or grab my shoulders hard enough to leave indents. With Gina…it was intentional. It was meant to cause pain and to remind me that she could draw blood if she wanted.

There was nothing I could do to stop her. Try to buck her off, maybe. That'd work once maybe, if that. Eventually she'd just tie me down and do what she wanted anyway. And, aside from that, the struggle was half the fun for her, I think. Seeing me fight it, seeing me reduced to this, tied up and at her mercy? That was the fun for her. Or at least part of it.

She slid her body along mine, writhing her core against my pained, imprisoned member. Shudders of revulsion shook through me.

"Don't do this, Gina." I couldn't help it—I had to try. "Please. This isn't how you want this."

"Oh, no?" She ground herself against me, teasing. I slid through the creases of her flesh. She was wet with desire. "Feel that? That says otherwise. This is *exactly* how I want it. You are *mine*, my dearest Valentine. I want you at my mercy. I want you squirming and begging. So *beg*, Valentine. Beg me to stop. It'll only make my cunt that much wetter for you."

Such a vulgar woman. Putrid. "This is rape, you know." I sounded cool and calm, as if rage and horror weren't rifling through me.

She smiled, a wicked curve of her lips, her tongue dragging along her upper lip, slowly, deliberately, cloyingly. "Exactly. That's exactly what this is."

She arched her spine out, fingernails gouging into my skin, drawing blood. She tilted her head back on her shoulders, hair hanging and waving and tickling and draping over one shoulder in a blue-black cascade, sliding her core against me, pressing the tip of me to her entrance. I gripped the cool brass of the headboard, shook it, strained against it, felt my stomach revolting, my mind whirling and my soul protesting. I thrashed until my wrists bled, and Gina held on and let me buck as if she was riding a wild bronco. Shame seared me. I was helpless. For all my money, all my power, all my physical strength, I was totally helpless. Emotional agony blazed within me. I was betraying Kyrie by allowing this to happen. Helpless or not, there had to be some way for me to stop what Gina was doing to me.

"Last time I'll say this, Gina. Stop now. Let me go. I'll forget this happened, and we can go our separate ways."

"Or?"

"You'll have to kill me when you're finished with me. If I get free, I will stop at nothing to destroy you, your father, and everything you hold dear."

"Here's an interesting fact, Valentine." She braced herself with one hand on my chest, reached down between us, and gripped me in her fist. "I don't hold anything dear. Do what you wish to my father. I'd thank you for doing it, and I'd even help you do it. You know nothing of me. Nothing of what I've endured since you escaped me the last time."

*I'm sorry, Kyrie. I love you.* The thoughts blew through me, attached to my mind, and hung there like burrs, repeating and repeating and repeating as Gina lowered her hips with agonizing slowness, penetrating herself with me. I focused on the ceiling, and then tried closing my eyes. I focused on anything, everything, except her. Except what was happening to me. Stroke after stroke, her body arching and writhing and rising and falling above me, Gina brought herself to climax, screaming like a banshee in my ear. I felt nothing. The burn of the need to release was nothing but pain, nothing but a raw physical reaction to stimulus, as natural and unstoppable as breathing or eating or excreting.

She came—or pretended to—twice more, and then slid off me, leaving me aching and painfully hardened. "Mmmmm. That was good. Thank you, Val."

"Fuck you."

"No, fuck *you*. Fuck you very much. I just did, and I'm going to again." She licked her lips and caressed my length, arranging herself on a chair in the corner. "I just needed a quick break before we continue."

I closed my eyes and focused on each breath in, each breath out. I counted my breaths....one, two, three...forty-six, forty-seven, forty-eight...one hundred and two, one hundred and three, one hundred and four....

I'd reached three hundred and nineteen when I felt the bed dip and her cool hands on my thighs, then the wet warmth of her mouth on my cock. "Mmmm. Yum. You taste like me."

I remained motionless, ignoring the pain, the feel of her mouth, and the weight of her body as she straddled me once more. I ignored the burn, the agonizing pressure welling up inside me. Ignored the hate, the shame, the fury. Ignored it all. Pushed it all down.

*Feel nothing. Feel nothing. Feel nothing.*

Gina brought herself to thrashing, ululating orgasm three times, and there was nothing I could do, no way to stop it, no way to do anything but endure it.

I felt, vaguely, distantly, the throbbing aching pulse of my own release nearing. Never in my life had I wanted anything less than to give her the satisfaction of my body, of my release. It was inevitable, however.

I clenched my teeth together so hard my molars creaked and my jaw ached. I held back. Held back.

"GIVE IT TO ME!" Gina shrieked, writhing on me, slamming down and up and down and up and down.

Flesh on flesh. Her nails dragging down my chest. Heat, pressure. Pain.

I tightened every muscle in my body, curled my toes in, and pulled on the handcuffs binding me to the bed and rendering me helpless, drawing on the pain of my bloody wrists and turning it to rage and strength. My biceps and triceps tightened, pulsed, my thighs turned to rock and my calves to stone, my lungs ceased to draw breath and my heart pounded like tympanic thunder in my chest, and still Gina attempted to elicit my release from me, and still I refused her.

Strength ebbed, ebbed. Gina was panting and sweating above me, at last showing the strain of exertion, her hair wisping and pasted to her forehead. She flung herself off me with a feral groan of frustration.

"You'll regret this, Valentine," she hissed, her face inches from mine. I kept my eyes shut and my body tensed, shaking, my energy and the ability to hold back waning. She licked my cheek, the corner of my mouth. "Oh, yes. You'll regret this."

She sucked my lower lip into her mouth and tugged, nibbled, and I could feel her grin, feeling the delight in my pain.

She bit, hard enough to draw a grunt from me, breaking skin and drawing blood once more.

Abruptly, she was gone. I was left aching, the cock ring still on. I let my muscles relax, let my breath go, dizziness washing through me.

I remained painfully engorged for an hour before it began to subside.

And that was when she returned, showered and in a blue dress this time, hair coiffured perfectly once more. She had a small pill bottle, which she set on the table beside the bed, then perched a buttock on the bed beside me.

"If you won't cooperate willingly...." She blinked slowly, a small smile on her lips, then twisted the top off the bottle and shook a small white pill into her hand. "This is an experimental drug I procured from a lab in Prague. It's not licensed anywhere in the world, and is banned in several countries throughout the EU. I couldn't even begin to pronounce the name of it. Something scientific and complicated and stupid. But those I've...spoken to...who have used it claim it works wonders. Magical, some said. Hours and hours and *hours* of uncontrollable arousal. What was the phrase the one man used? Oh, yes. He claimed it turned him into a rutting beast. This should be fun."

I pressed my lips together, clenched my jaw, and stared her down.

She only laughed. "You think you can resist? You can't. You can't stop me."

She reached down between my legs and slipped the cock ring off, then covered me up to the waist with the flat sheet. After a glance and a grin at me, she put two fingers to her lips and gave a short, sharp whistle. The door opened, and two short, squat, powerfully built men dressed in black business suits with white shirts and slim black ties came into the room. Bulges at their chests indicated that they were armed. The two men were nearly identical, possibly twins, brothers at the very least, each of them having slicked-back black hair, similar dark eyes, the same swarthy complexion and cruel, cold gazes.

Gina said something in Greek, and the two men moved to stand on either side of the bed. One of them took my jaw in his hand, squeezing and pinching, shoving his index finger and thumb into my cheek, between my teeth, forcibly separating my jaw. I twisted and bucked, wrenched my head from side to side, but I couldn't dislodge his grip on my jaw.

"You'd better quit struggling, Val," Gina said. "I really don't mind a bit of blood on my lovers, you know. I'm perfectly willing to let Stefanos and Tobias soften you up a bit. So really, dear, it's best to just go along."

I couldn't speak to tell her to fuck off, or I would have. My mouth was pried open, and Gina placed the pill on my tongue with absurd delicacy. Immediately, my saliva began to dissolve the chemical compound, bitterness leaking onto my tongue, into my mouth. The cruel, painful grip on my jaw, the thick finger and thumb between my teeth, kept me from spitting it out. Working my tongue only moved it farther back in my mouth so the quickly dissolving mixture sluiced down my throat, choking me. Acidic gall burned my taste buds, scorched down my esophagus. I choked, coughed, my own spit gagging me, but the pincers between my mandibles remained in place, keeping my head tipped back, my jaw pried apart.

I fought, jerking on the cuffs, each tug of my wrists sending pain shooting through me. I felt blood trickling down my forearms.

Reflex took over, and I swallowed, the need to breathe dominating my will to resist.

"Good." Gina patted my chest. "Good boy. That should take effect within a few hours. I'll be back. Until then…don't go anywhere!" She laughed at her own joke, leading the two thugs out of the room.

I could still taste the bitter grit of the pill on my tongue. Summoning as much saliva as I could, I spat to the side, watching the gobbet land on the floor. It was too late, though. The chemical was already inside me; the question was whether it would work, and how, and if I could find a way to resist the effects.

An unknowable amount of time later, hours, perhaps, or even longer, I felt the stirrings deep within me of the experimental drug taking hold. It felt like need. Not just need, no, nothing that easy or simple. Oh, no. This was frantic, primal, manic, blood- and bone- and soul-deep animalistic desperation. It began in my gut, a roiling, a tightening. My fists curled around the chain of the handcuffs, the pain of my raw wrists fading. Thoughts were impossible. Logic was erased. Memory was nothing.

I was need. I was the embodiment of insatiable, rapacious sexual hunger.

Need curled inside me, pounded through me, wrenched my muscles into spasming throbbing pulsation, my hips grinding at the air. I *needed*. This was about release, this was about…about quenching the fire inside me, and in that moment, with the drug coursing through me, I would take anything at all, anything that would slake my thirst, anything that would fill the raging void within me.

Someone was growling, a feral snarl. Me? Was that me? Yes, it was. Sweat coated my skin. My cock was a white-hot iron rod.

The door opened, and Gina entered, hips sashaying in a sultry sway, a satisfied smile on her painted ruby-red lips.

Within the space of a breath, I was a starving lion chained in the corner of a cage, a bloody hunk of fresh meat just out of reach.

My entire body writhed on the bed, seeking flesh, seeking heat, seeking release. Gina halted just out of reach, her tongue sliding along her lips, eyeing me. My thrashing had dislodged the sheet long ago, leaving me bared to her gaze. Her hand drifted out, clasped around my cock, and slid down.

I growled, thrashed, pushed my hips up into her touch.

"Ah, yes. Much better," she murmured.

Despite the hold of the drug on my body and my mind, there was a seed, a tiny speck of myself, somewhere deep within the recesses of my soul, untouched, untainted. And that minuscule, fading spark knew this was wrong, this was not what I wanted. It knew this primal need that had been artificially catalyzed within me was a sexual assault of the worst kind. My will, my desire, the truth and fidelity of my soul and my being, had been stripped from me. I'd been reduced to an animal, all higher functions ripped away, leaving me chained to a bed for the use of a soulless demon-bitch of a woman.

And there was not a fucking thing I could do about it. I wasn't even left with the will to resist the need inside me. All I had was the spark of knowing how wrong, how shameful, how evil this was.

Gina slid astride me, nails digging into my chest, and slid me inside her body.

The spark of my soul screamed in protest, unheard beyond the walls of my prison.

# 5

## ACROSS THE MEDITERRANEAN

"Good. Now push the slide into place. Right, just like that. Perfect. Now pull it back. Good job, Kyrie." Harris took the pistol from me and set it on the table between us. "Now do it again, and this time I'm not going to coach you."

I picked up the heavy black gun and began the process of stripping it down, removing each piece and laying it on the table in the order Harris had shown me. When the weapon was down to components, I put it back together again, faster than the last time. I'd been doing this for the past two hours, disassembling and reassembling the pistol Henri had given me. The first time, it had seemed foreign and impossible, like putting together a puzzle without any guidelines or edge pieces or a picture for reference. But with Harris's patient instruction, it got easier. Now I could do it on my own, without him showing me which piece went where.

It was bizarre, me, a middle-class white girl from Metro Detroit, erstwhile college student and starving bachelorette, learning to strip a Glock.

Harris stood up and went below deck, returning with three empty soda cans. Jerking his head to indicate that I should follow him, Harris went to the stern of the boat and tossed a can into the water. "Shoot it." He pointed at the can.

"But…the boat is moving, and the water is moving. How can I possibly—"

"I don't expect you to hit it from here. It's a tough shot even for a skilled marksman. The point is just to give you something to shoot at. Just try."

The red can was bobbing in the wake, now a good thirty feet astern. I held the pistol in both hands, arms extended out in front of me. Harris moved my left hand so my fingers were overlapping my right hand, nudged my feet shoulder-width apart, putting me in the stance he'd shown me before we started disassembling.

I took a deep breath, let it out slowly, and squeezed the trigger. Except the safety was still on. I thumbed the button, and then took aim once more at the can, which was now a tiny red dot fifty feet away and bobbing on the waves.

*BANG!* The gun jerked upward, the noise and the violence startling me. I knew I hadn't hit the can, obviously, but I was curious to know how close I'd gotten. I glanced at Harris, who nodded.

"Good." He tossed another can in. "Try again."

I aimed at the second can, let out my breath, and squeezed. This time, I saw the water spray up where the bullet struck, a good two feet to the left of and well below the can at which I was aiming. I watched the motion of the soda can, waited until it was at the bottom of a wave trough, and squeezed off a round. This time, the can *plinked* and disappeared under the water. It was only fifteen feet away, but still, I'd hit it, and that was something.

"Excellent, Kyrie. Excellent." He tossed the third can in. "Once more."

I tracked the bobbing of the can, waited, then fired. Missed. I let out a breath, fired, missed again. The can was now barely visible in the blue of the Aegean.

I lowered the pistol and flicked the safety on. "It's too far away."

Harris just grinned, reached behind his back for his gun, lifted it, and assumed what I thought of as the military stance, his body sideways, both arms crooked, right hand holding the butt of the pistol, left hand cupped under his right. He paused for a split second, and then squeezed off three rounds in such fast succession that it sounded like a single loud roar. I had my eye on the can and watched it rupture, water geysering as the rounds plowed into the waves.

"I've spent hundreds of hours at the range," he explained, placing his pistol in the back of his jeans. "But you did really good for your first time. I mainly just wanted you to have a feel for how loud it is, for the kick. And again, it's just for last-resort emergencies. If you aim it at someone, you'd better be prepared to shoot them."

"I don't know if I'm capable of that," I admitted, following Harris into the pilot's cabin.

Harris settled into the pilot's seat, disengaged the autopilot, and nudged the throttle lever forward. "Of course you're not. You can't be sure what you're capable of until you're forced to find out."

"Is it hard? Shooting someone?"

Harris let out long breath. "Yes. It is. The first time, it's...awful. Not sure what else I can say. I threw up the first time I killed a man. And you know, if it ever becomes *easy,* it's time to find another line of work. It's hard every time."

Hours passed, and I watched the horizon in silence, the evening sky deepening to darkness as the waves churned beneath the hull.

"Will we reach Greece tonight?" I asked.

Harris shook his head, seeming amused at my question. "Oh, no. It's over a thousand nautical miles from Marseilles to Athens. It'll take us a few days to make the trip. I'm heading for Palermo first, to restock and refuel, and then will make for Athens."

"Oh." Apparently my understanding of Mediterranean geography was somewhat lacking.

"We'll find him."

"When? And how?" My voice was soft and quiet and hesitant, betraying my doubt.

Harris didn't answer right away. "I'm working on the how. As for when? As soon as we can, I suppose. If Gina Karahalios has him, getting him back could be tricky. The other question is whether Vitaly is involved. There are a lot of variables to deal with, and…it's just me. I can't risk bringing anyone else in. I shouldn't have involved Henri, but I did."

"I'm here."

"I know. But…how do I say this without sounding insulting? I was an Army Ranger."

"And I'm just…what? What am I?" Now that the question was aired, I realized it had been percolating inside me for a long time.

Harris glanced at me. "I didn't mean to incite an existential crisis, Miss St. Claire."

"You didn't. It's been happening all along, I'm finally just talking about it, I guess."

"I understand." He sighed. "You know, I joined the Army as an eighteen year-old kid. I was bored. I came from a totally normal family. Had a mom and a dad and two sisters. No drama, nothing interesting. But I had no idea what I wanted to do with myself. I graduated, and spent six months just... literally fucking around. That was all I did. Went to parties and hooked up. But even that got boring. So, one day, I happened to walk by a recruiter's office. He was standing outside, smoking a cigarette. I bummed one off him, and we started talking. Damned good salesman that he was, he had me signing up by the time I was done with my smoke." Harris laughed. "I *hated* the Army for the first two years. But then I got into an off-base brawl with a couple of Rangers and got my ass handed to me. The same guys who beat the shit out of me ended up buying me beer and convinced me to try out for Ranger school. After months of work I got in, and that was the beginning of things for me. I had something I *wanted,* suddenly. It provided the motivation to *try.*"

It was odd to think about Harris as anything other than the buttoned-up and endlessly capable man I'd come to know.

I looked at him again. He was over six feet tall, but just barely, and was slender in a whipcord, razor-blade sort of way. He had short, dark brown hair and vivid, intelligent green eyes that could be either friendly and warm as summer grass, or as cold and frightening as chips of ancient jade. He wasn't classically handsome; his features were too rugged for that. He was striking, but not so much that he'd stand out in a crowd. He was intense, exuding competence and power. He moved with an easy grace, the kind of predatory prowl of someone capable of extreme violence, someone who is intensely fit, athletic, his body honed to a razor edge. Looking at him, it was impossible to determine how old he was. Over thirty, for sure, and certainly less than fifty.

Silence descended, and stayed for a long time. I sat in the chair beside Harris and watched the stars prick and poke the blackness with points of silver, multiplying from thousands to millions to quintillions to an innumerable multitude. The boat ascended gentle rolling waves and slid down into the troughs, tilted and rolled, bucked and bobbled, churning through the waves and the darkness, and only the unpredictable motion of the sea kept the journey from hypnotizing sameness. There was nothing to see but the ever-moving sea and the sky, black with shaken-salt stars.

I nodded off and was woken by the low rumble of the boat's engine cutting out and the lapping of bay waves. I rubbed my eyes and stretched as Harris docked the boat, tied the moor line, and returned to the cabin.

"We'll sleep on the boat," he said. "There are two cabins. Lock yours, and sleep with the gun close by. I don't expect trouble here, but it pays to be ready."

I nodded and followed him below, then entered one of the bedrooms, locked the door, crawled onto the bed fully clothed, and tried not to think about how much I missed Valentine.

I woke up to the shrill caw of seagulls and the gentle lap of waves against the hull, the gentle hum of the engine revving up, voices in the distance. I rose and ascended to the wheelhouse, took my seat beside Harris, squinting at the blinding sunlight scintillating off diamond-and-blue waves.

"Good morning, Miss St. Claire," Harris said.

He twisted the wheel, bringing the bow of the boat about, pushed the throttle lever, and the craft moved forward. He handed me a green Thermos. I twisted the silver top off and poured a measure of thick black coffee, sipped it gratefully.

"You could've slept longer, you know."

I shrugged, sipped. "It's fine. We're restocked and everything?"

Harris nodded. "Refueled, some food, and a few other things."

Something in his voice alerted me. "A few other things, huh?"

Harris shrugged. "I'm developing a plan. I'm hoping I'll be able to work things out without involving you, but I'm afraid I may not have much choice. There are just…too many variables. I don't know. We'll see."

"I'm not sure I like the sound of that."

"I only know the Karahalios family by reputation and from what little Mr. Roth has told me. They're brutal, thorough, and have essentially endless resources." He guided the boat out of the bay and into open water, then fiddled with the GPS and autopilot, setting our next destination. "What I've heard is that Vitaly is the kind of kingpin the Greek government is wary to tangle with because, in the current economic and political situation, he has too much influence."

"And he has Valentine?"

"I'm not sure Vitaly himself actually has him. I think it's his daughter, Roth's former girlfriend. That doesn't make her any safer to mess with, since, as far as I know, she has her father's resources at her disposal, as well as her own."

I swallowed hard. "And we, you and me, are going to—what? Just walk up, knock on the door, and ask for him back? Walk in and shoot her?"

Harris did a shrug-and-nod thing. "Basically, yeah. Although I'm going to try to divert some attention elsewhere first, and hope it buys us enough time to get Mr. Roth and get out."

"And then? If these people are as scary as you're saying, what chance do we have of actually getting away?"

Harris let out a breath. "I don't know. I really don't. I wish I had something comforting to say to you, but I just don't. Would you rather turn around and go home? Just leave him?"

I shot him a glare. "Of course not."

"Okay, then. We'll just have to wing it and hope. It's not like I can just muster some army of henchmen or something."

I watched the waves dance and gyrate, trying desperately not to think about what Valentine was going through. "I'll tell you this much, Harris: I'm not going to be sitting in some hotel room or in the cabin of this boat waiting with my thumb up my ass, okay? Whatever happens, I'm going with you. I know I don't have your training, but...Valentine is the man I love, and I can't just sit around, hoping and waiting."

"I know. But what good is rescuing him if you're dead?" Harris gave me a long, penetrating look. "You've changed him, Kyrie. You have. And for the better."

"He's changed me, too."

Forty-eight hours later, we were docking in Athens—the Marina Zea, Harris informed me. We shouldered our bags, ensured our pistols were safely secured but within reach, and set off on foot down the marina dock. The marina was set in a wide, circular bay with docks jutting out into the center, boats of all sizes moored and waiting for their owners. Beyond, multi-story apartment buildings rose in a ring, balconies and flat roofs ascending in serried ranks. From a distance they all looked uniformly white, but as we made our way from the docks closer to the city proper, I realized each building was different, some pink, some white, some yellow, but most of them adhered to the same basic design, block-shaped, balconies facing the street, with shops and stores and restaurants below at ground level.

There was a sense of age to the city that was immediately palpable, even from a distance, even without having spent more than five minutes here.

We wove through the marina, passing trucks carrying loads of various kinds, families, groups of businessmen, gaggles of laughing children, pairs of women, couples, locals and tourists and old men with white hair and wizened, wrinkled faces.

We came to a place where the buildings closed in tight on our left, a portion of the marina on our right fenced-off for construction, the pavement narrowing to a space barely wide enough for us to walk side by side. Harris stopped, eyeing the cityscape around us. We were in front of a graffiti-scarred, old, low white building, boarded off and empty, a ten-foot-high chain link fence to one side. Located at the water's edge were partially constructed piers and bare concrete pillars standing sentry in the dark waters. The city noise was dampened, muffled, and distant. There was no one in sight, the only cars passing back and forth half a mile away.

"I don't like this," Harris said, reaching behind his back to draw his pistol. "Something's not right."

As if his words were a cue, a battered blue metal door swung open, the door heavily marked with white spray paint graffiti every bit as illegible as the graffiti on the abandoned buildings and freeway overpasses back in Detroit. The door squeaked ominously and a man stepped out, followed by three more. Each man was dressed alike, in a sleek dark suit and a black T-shirt. Each man held a machine gun, the tiny kind I thought might be an Uzi.

"Took you long enough to get here," one of them said. "We expected you yesterday."

Harris stepped sideways so his body blocked mine. He said nothing, only stood silent with his pistol at his thigh.

"Nothing to say?" The speaker was a short, ugly young man wearing a sparse black goatee, his face marred by severe acne. His eyes were cruel and cold and dull. "Come on, then. She is expecting you two."

"Fuck off." Harris tilted his head to the side.

"I think no." He glanced to either side in an exaggerated gesture, looking at his three companions. "We are four. You are two. We have these." He waggled his machine gun. "You come now. Drop the gun."

Harris looked sidelong at me. He seemed to be contemplating something. "How about you first?" He returned his attention to the men in front of us.

I didn't see a way out of this.

I slid farther behind Harris, letting his body completely block mine. Hoping I was being discreet, I reached behind my back and withdrew my pistol, gingerly, quietly thumbing the safety off. What was I doing? I couldn't do this. They had machine guns. I couldn't do this.

Apparently I wasn't being discreet enough, because one of the men shouted something in Greek, stepping toward me, lifting his gun. Three short, angry steps, and he was beside Harris and I was twisting away from him, loath to let him get his hands on me. Time distorted then, milliseconds drawing out even as everything sped up. Harris pivoted, his arm flashing out and wrapping around my attacker's throat, jerking him in front of him. The Uzi waved, spat fire and noise, and then Harris's pistol barked once and blood sprayed. I shrieked, but my hands were clutching my pistol in front of me, feet shoulder width apart, pistol cupped and supported as Harris had shown me, and my finger was tightening on the trigger, the black barrel leveled at one of the men. Harris shoved the dead body forward and stepped swiftly to one side, his pistol barking, once—twice—three times. Uzis chattered and the dead body jerked and burst red, but then the guns were silenced and bodies were crumpling, and I was still standing with my pistol held out in front of me, finger on the trigger, barrel shaking, pointing at empty space.

"Kyrie. Put it away. It's over." Harris spoke from beside me, his voice too calm. "Put it down. Put the safety on. Now, Kyrie. *Now.*"

I flinched at the whip-sharp note in his voice and lowered the weapon, pushing the button in to secure the pistol, returned it to the small of my back.

"I couldn't—I couldn't—" My voice cracked.

Harris's hand touched my shoulder. "I hope you get through all this without ever needing to. I really do." He bent and grabbed two handfuls of pant leg. "Come on. Help me pull these assholes out of the way." Harris dragged the body backward a few feet, and then realized blood was leaving a wide trail. "Fuck it. Leave 'em. We need to move."

He set off in a trot, stepping over bodies without a second glance. I followed less surely, unable to look away from the blood and the staring eyes and the gaping holes. Harris returned, grabbed my arm, and pulled me into a run, slowing only once we hit a main road and were able to get lost in the bustling crowd. I wasn't following Harris at that point so much as being pulled by him without resisting. Seeing men shot and killed…I couldn't move past it. Knowing someone had died was one thing, knowing someone had likely died when I rammed the Peugeot was one thing…what had just happened, that was something totally else.

Harris had us weaving in an erratic pattern, left here, right at this corner, down this alley and backtracking, and then we were on a bus and smashed between a crushing crowd of sweating locals. I was still nauseous and seeing holes in torsos and staring, unseeing eyes.

Harris's voice filled my ear in a barely audible whisper. "I know you're in shock, Kyrie, but you need to pull it together. It was us or them."

I answered in a harsh rasp. "I *know*. I just— god...I keep seeing them."

"I understand, believe me." The bus turned, and we swayed to one side. He used the commotion to pull my shirt down lower to cover my gun. "Next time you pull that out, you *shoot*, okay? Don't think—don't even really try to aim. Just point at center mass and pull the trigger. If you draw it, you shoot it. Got me?"

I nodded. "Got it. I'm sorry. I just...froze."

"And that's how you get killed in those situations. You *can't* freeze." His voice was totally calm, as if we were discussing sports or the weather.

"I was *scared,* Harris. They had fucking *machine guns.* I was about to *die.*"

He let out a breath. "I know. I know." He touched my shoulder in a gesture that was part friendly affection and part apology. "I'm sorry we're in this. I'm sorry *you're* in this."

"I just—I just want Valentine back."

"Me, too." He patted my shoulder again. "And we'll get him back."

"Promise?"

Harris was a long time responding. "No. I can't promise that."

# 6

## DROWNING

*VALENTINE*

Curtains of distortion swept across my brain, the ceiling and floor wavering and twisting. Heat billowed through me. I was on fire. I was burning alive, skin crackling. I was so hot my skin must surely be blistering, but I didn't dare look. Nausea rocketed through me in a sudden burst.

I felt vomit in my throat, at the back of my teeth. I could only crane my neck and hope I didn't choke as I spewed all over the bed and the floor and myself.

Once my stomach was empty, I felt a sweat break out over my skin, cooling me to shivers.

My penis ached. My skin crawled. Eyes closed, eyes open, I saw over and over the repulsive vision of Gina writhing on top of me, clawing me, leaving bloody gashes gouged down my chest. I heard her voice, calling out as if in the grip of ecstasy. I felt her on me, and I wished I could vomit again.

When the door swung silently open, I saw her in triplicate. She wore a green miniskirt, tight as a second skin, molded to her thighs and ass, barely long enough to cover the bottom of her buttocks. Long tanned legs, four-inch ivory heels, sleeveless ivory blouse cut low between her breasts. I clenched my eyes, opened them, saw a single image, which blurred and multiplied.

"Val. My, my, my. Such a mess. The medication has side effects, it seems." She rounded the foot of the bed and sat at my side—the side I hadn't vomited all over. The back of her hand touched my forehead. "You're burning up."

I twisted away from her touch, and her eyes narrowed. "Get away from me."

She stood up, tugged at her blouse. "I thought we were past this, Valentine." I didn't bother responding, and she snapped her fingers. The same two thugs as before appeared in the doorway. "He needs to be cleaned up." She wrinkled her nose and gestured at me.

This was my chance. I knew it, felt it coming. One of the men produced a key from his pants pocket and unlocked the end of the handcuffs on my right hand. My wrist was still shackled, but free from the bed. Then he freed my foot on the same side. The thug passed the key to his brother, who unlocked my left hand and foot .

One of the thugs backed away and drew a huge silver pistol from a shoulder holster. "Up. Stand up," he growled. "Nothing funny."

I slowly slid my legs to one side of the bed and attempted to sit up. My entire body protested, dizziness sweeping through me as I levered myself to a sitting position. My stomach roiled, heaved, but I shoved it down, gritting my teeth and forcing myself to my feet. I had to brace myself with a hand on the headboard as the world spun and dipped beneath me. Gina was watching from beside the doorway, her purse over her shoulder. She dug in her purse, rifling through it for god knows what.

A meaty, clammy hand clapped around my forearm, jerked me forward, off balance. I stumbled, wobbled, dizziness and riotous nausea rollercoastering through me. I could see four of everything, then three, one, and two, and then it was all a myriad of shapes and colors and bodies and blue sky, blue water, white roofs and walls and blue doors and a black-suited thug in front of me, catching me, something cold and silver and hard between us.

My stomach heaved, bile streaming between my teeth and down my chin as I tried to contain it, and then an idea hit me and I let it go, let it pour out of me and all over Tobias or Stefanos or whoever this fuckhole in front of me was. Vomit hit his suit coat, shirt front, face, and he cursed in Greek, but I was already grabbing his hand, fumbling half-blindly, taking his sudden distraction as an opportunity to twist his hand so the barrel of his gun pointed at himself, and my finger found the trigger and jerked it.

*BANG!* The pistol went off with a deafening crash. It kicked back and into my chest, the recoil of the absurdly massive handgun knocking me backward. I snatched the gun, still dizzy, seeing too many of everything, still heaving, stumbling. I fell backward three, four, five steps, hit the wall, pointing the pistol with one hand at the other black-suited thug, who advanced slowly, his own gun drawn.

"You kill my brother." He was inches from me, his silver gun with a wide black mouth pointed in front of one of my eyes.

"Tobias." Gina's voice was a low, threatening razor. "Take the gun from him and get him cleaned up."

"But Stefanos—"

"Is dead." She pulled a tube of lipstick from her purse, applied it slowly, pursed her lips, and put the tube away. "Do I look like I give a fuck?"

Tobias muttered something in Greek under his breath, but he holstered his pistol. I had no chance of resisting as his fist flashed out and connected with my cheekbone. I fell sideways, and the pistol was stripped from my hand. I was dragged by my wrists out of the room and into a bathroom, huge and echoing, all marble and glass.

He let me go, and my head smacked painfully against the marble floor. I heard water running, and then I was dragged across the bathroom, the grooves between the tiles plucking at my hair and scraping my scalp, and then icy water sluiced down onto my face and chest, and I was trying to roll away, but the stream came from a handheld wand and I was sprayed down head to toe, and no matter which way I turned or rolled or how I curled up, the frigid water beat against my skin like knives of ice.

I heard a footstep on the tile somewhere near my feet, and I felt a presence over me, the stream of water battering against my chest, so cold now I was numb. A fist clenched my hair, jerked my head backward, and the spray was moved to slice into my eyes and my nose and my mouth, and I was drowning, drowning, unable to breathe or even keep from inhaling the water. Coughing, I couldn't turn away, could only pull brutally against the hand gripping my hair, ripping hunks out by the roots in an attempt to get away.

And then the water was off and rancid breath huffed against my face, and a voice grumbled in my ear, "I'll fucking kill you. I do not care what the crazy bitch says, I will kill you. Slowly. You will suffer. Suffer much. Anyone you love, I will kill."

I slammed forward with my head, felt my forehead connect with flesh and bone, felt a tooth cut open my forehead. Tobias stumbled backward, and then lashed out with his foot into my gut. I curled inward, gasping for breath, gagging as the world went white.

"Enough, Tobias. Your silly revenge can wait. Bring him back to the room."

I was dragged back across the bathroom, down a short hallway, and into the too-bright bedroom, which now smelled of antiseptic. I still couldn't breathe, coughing up water and seeing stars. I felt myself lifted under the armpits, and—at the end of my strength—willingly crawled onto the bed, curling into myself and fighting for breath past the weight of water in my throat and lungs and the ache of the blow to my stomach.

The door closed, and I felt the bed dip near my bent knees. "Well. I hope that was worth it, Val. You got yourself hurt on top of being sick, *and* you made an enemy. Tobias is a psychopath, you know. And coming from *me*, that's saying something."

Her hand touched my shoulder and stroked my arm, brushed my wet hair out of my eye. I was soaking wet, shivering, head pounding furiously, skin tight and tingling with the ache of a fever.

I jerked away from her. "Don't—" I devolved into hacking, spat up a mouthful of phlegm and water. "Don't touch me!" My voice was a hoarse rasp. "Don't you fucking touch me."

"A little late for that," she said, sounding amused. "You should rest now. I've got plans for you for later."

"You might as well kill me," I grated through my teeth.

"Ha. No. I don't think so. Not yet at least. I haven't had my fill of you." She reached for my wrist, clicked the handcuff to the bed, did the same for my other wrist, securing both wrists before I knew what she was doing.

I fought her with my feet as she reached for my ankles, kicked at her, connecting with her hip and then her stomach, knocking her backward. She stumbled, righted herself, smoothed her skirt and blouse, combed her fingers through her hair, and stood panting just out of reach.

"You know, I suppose I should mention that your little slut has eluded me so far. And the more you fight me, the more trouble you cause, the worse things will be for her when I finally catch her." Gina examined her fingernails, and then grinned at me evilly. "I'm sure Tobias would have a fun time with her. I might bring another bed in here and cuff her to it, too. And then you can watch as my men and Daddy's run a train on her. How about that? Dozens of men fucking her, right in front of you? You'd have to watch. And then she'd watch while I fuck you. I could get some of my girlfriends in here, and *they'll* fuck you too. And then, when we're all sick of you two, I'll kill you. Her, then you? Hmmm. Maybe. Or you, then her? I don't know. I'll have to think about it some more."

She rummaged in her purse and came up with a compact pistol. A Walther PPK, by the look of it. She rounded the end of the bed, staying out of reach of my feet, touched the barrel to my temple. "Now. I'm going to cuff your feet. And if you fight me, I'll shoot you. But I won't kill, not yet. I'll bring your little whore in here and let everyone I know fuck her in front of you. Or you can cooperate. If you do, I'll spare her. Meaning I'll just put a bullet in her skull. Easy choice, no?"

I went still, let her cuff my ankles to the bed once more.

"Good. You're learning." Gina patted my thigh, then turned and sauntered out of the room. "I'll be back after you've had a chance to rest."

Kyrie sat astride me, blonde hair loose around her shoulders, naked and gleaming and perfect. We moved together, her ass gliding across my thighs, her breasts swaying, her cerulean eyes locked on mine, tender and wavering with emotion. I reached for her, needing to touch her, feel her, caress her, but something stopped me. She grinned. "Not yet," she whispered, her words out of synch with the motion of her lips.

Her palms on my chest, Kyrie leaned over me, hair draping like a curtain around my face so the sun glinted through her blonde locks. She slid forward, and I felt her core drag along my cock, wet and hot and slick, and I only knew that I needed her. She smiled, a gentle curve of her lips, and the taut pink tip of her nipple touched my forehead, soft and warm. I reveled in the feel of her skin, the touch of her flesh. The peak of her perfect breast drifting softly down my face, over my nose and lips, and I took the nipple between my teeth—

"Oh…Val…yes—" she whimpered.

And then everything distorted. I looked up, blinking, and blonde hair became black and blue eyes became dark, and I screamed, a guttural roar in my throat, my body arching and bucking, throwing a startled Gina off me.

I clenched my teeth and screamed again until my throat went hoarse and gave out, eyes squeezed shut, the agony of being ripped from the dream too much to take, the horror of knowing I'd touched *her*, had *her* repulsive skin against mine, and I'd mistaken it for Kyrie's, thought it was Kyrie loving me when, in reality, it had been Gina assaulting me.

Gina stood up, naked. "Why do you keep fighting me?" She swayed over to the side of the bed, leaned over me, cupped her breast in one hand and traced idle patterns on my face with her nipple. She moved it to touch my cheek, my chin. Dragged her breast across my lips, quickly. I thought about biting her, but didn't. I showed no emotion, no reaction. She pressed the inside of her opposite breast to my face, suffocating me between her tits. I held my breath and closed my eyes and waited. She slid astride me, bottom lip between her teeth in what was meant to be a seductive, erotic pose. She crushed her core against my cock, with no response. Now I was totally repulsed, furious, disgusted, and no force on earth could bring me to arousal.

"Come on, Val. Play with me." She lifted my limp member in her hand, toying with me.

"I'd rather die."

"Oh, that'll happen soon enough." She let go of me, leaned forward, and pulled open the drawer of the nightstand. The bottle of pills rattled, and she opened the top, shook one out into her palm. I pressed my lips together, clenched my teeth. "You can make this easy, or you can make this hard."

I just glared at her, lips compressed into a thin line.

"The hard way, then." She shook her head and tisked as if scolding me.

She moved off me and put on a purple silk dressing robe that was hanging over the back of a chair. For the first time, I noticed two large black plastic buckets, a silver pitcher, and a stack of white towels on the floor near the door. Gina placed the pill on the nightstand, glancing at me meaningfully. She then unfolded a towel and placed it beneath my head. Next, she carefully dragged both buckets across the floor, the effort needed to do so making it clear they were both full to the brim with water. Finally, she took the pitcher and scooped it full of water, then set it on the nightstand beside the pill.

"I will ask you again, Valentine Roth. Will you take the pill, or no?" I lifted my chin, wrapped my fists around the chains of the handcuffs. "Very well, then. The hard way it is." She laughed, a merry little giggle. "Hard for you, I should say. Fun for me. I've always rather enjoyed this particular little game."

She lifted the pitcher in one hand, slid her other palm over my forehead, and buried it in my hair, a brief caress, and then she took a fistful of hair and jerked viciously. Holding my head tipped backward, she tilted the pitcher so a few drops of water pattered on my nose, mouth, and eyes. I tried to turn my head to the side, but her grip on my hair was immoveable. She was *strong*. I felt roots give way, and then she was pouring a little more water onto my face. This time, some went up my nose, and I gasped, snorted. While I was coughing, she poured more water onto me, this time directly into my mouth. And she kept pouring. Panic surged through me. I shook my head, not even feeling the hair being ripped out of my scalp, and she kept pouring, hitting my eyes and nose, jerking my face back into place so the slow and steady gush of water hit the back of my throat. I was drowning, drowning. Just when I thought I would surely succumb and die, she righted the pitcher and ended the stream of water.

I coughed, gasped, arched my back, and tried

to breathe. My mouth was open wide as I choked, fighting for breath. And that was when she placed the pill on my tongue, poured a tiny measure of water into my mouth, and then pinched my nose shut. I had no choice but to swallow or die, and my body wouldn't allow me to die. I tried, seeing Kyrie's face, tried to keep my esophagus closed as darkness weighed down, panic a raw and bone-deep horror inside me, the need to breathe, to live, to keep fighting winning out.

I swallowed, and gagged as the pill went down, and resumed coughing the water from my lungs.

For the next hour, Gina tortured me with the pitcher of water. She would refill, sit beside me, and pour water onto my face. A little, just enough to make me sputter, and then she'd wait, let me catch my breath, and when I had, she would slowly empty the pitcher into my eyes and throat and nose, always stopping when I was moments from drowning.

I'd already swallowed her pill, so this was just for fun.

I felt the chemicals begin to burn inside me, a slow, distant warming of banked coals deep in my blood and bones.

A fist pounded on the door, and Gina barked a question in Greek. A young man burst through the door, spitting out rapid-fire Greek, clearly panicked.

Gina, still holding a full pitcher of water, swore softly in English: "Shit." She sighed, hesitated, and then upended the pitcher onto my face. "It appears as if your little whore is coming for you. She's caused me no end of trouble, you know. I'm going to have fun peeling the skin from her bones once I've caught her."

I shook the water from my face, spat, coughed, and watched as Gina waved the young man away. When he was gone, she tossed the now-wet purple robe aside and dressed in a pair of white linen slacks and matching shirt, then slid her feet into a pair of red sandals.

"I'm going to kill her slowly, Valentine. I'm going to have her raped, and I'm going to kill her." She pulled her pistol out of her purse, checked the load of the clip, and then glanced at me. "She killed Alec. Or someone did. Shot him in the head. I had a lot of fun with him. It will be hard to replace someone as eager to please as him. He liked to give me cunnilingus, and he was rather skilled at it. Now I'll have to train someone else." Despite the icy calm with which she said these words, there was a gleam of maddened rage in her glittering black eyes.

She left the room, the lock clicking behind her. A silence descended then, which stretched out for a time I couldn't measure, and then hell broke loose.

# 7

## ASSAULT

I RAN BEHIND HARRIS, MY LUNGS BURNING AND MY LEGS aching.

Harris had, in the end, decided the only real possibility was to just go for it. After some investigation and asking questions I wanted to know nothing about, he came up with a location for Gina Karahalios. She was living on an island about hundred and fifty miles southeast, in a place called Oia. We took the yacht from Athens across the Aegean and through a cluster of islands of various sizes, docking on the far side of the island from where Gina's house, according to Harris's information, was located.

We started out slowly, simply strolling through the countryside as if we were tourists like any others.

We caught an ancient, rumbling bus and took it on a clattering, scary journey over hills and around cliff faces, eventually getting off at the outskirts of Oia. It was a picturesque place, square white houses with blue doors and shutters marching down to the sea, which glittered in the distance, far below. The sun shone bright, a few wisps of cloud drifting slowly here and there. Buses rumbled, a few cars passed here and there. An old man held on to the halter of a gray donkey pulling a cart full of fruit.

Harris pointed to a huge house high up on a hill, a sprawling estate with turrets and cupolas all painted the same blue as everything else. "There. That's it."

The road leading up to the house in question was winding and narrow and steep, and there was a wall surrounding the house, seven feet high and made of white-washed bricks with bits of broken glass twinkling and gleaming on the top edge.

Harris eyed the way up. "This is going to be rough. Stay right behind me." He twisted a long cylinder onto the barrel of his pistol, dug three clips out of his backpack, and stuffed them into his pocket. "Come on. Let's get this over with."

And he took off running up the hill, hugging the side of the road. There was no one on the streets this far up, this close to the estate. Curtains twitched and faces peered out, watching us, seemingly unsurprised to see a drawn gun. I followed him up the hill, ignoring the jelly-weakness in my thighs and the ache of oxygen-deprived lungs. We reached the last row of houses before the road curved toward the gated entrance, and then Harris stopped and ducked against the corner of a house. Even he was breathing hard and sweating. I was gasping and dripping sweat, and barely able to stand upright.

"Take a minute and catch your breath. I'll be right back." Harris dug several small packages from his backpack, things shaped like bricks with wires attached.

"Harris? What are those?"

"Distractions."

"Jesus. What is this, *Die Hard?*" This last was to myself, though, because Harris was already across the road and pressed flat to the wall beside the electronically controlled gates. He peeled something from the back of the bomb and pressed the package to the wall beside the gate, touched a button or switch—I couldn't make out which from this distance—and then moved in a crouch around the corner and out of sight. After a few minutes, he returned at a sprint and moved into the doorway beside me.

He was breathing deeply, a sheen of sweat on his forehead. "Kyrie, I don't know what we're going to find when we go in there. Maybe nothing. Maybe something awful. I don't know. Just…be prepared for anything. And above all, stay right behind me, no matter what."

I nodded, unable to speak.

The explosion was a deafening *CRUMP*, followed by a pattering rain of debris and shouts in Greek. Harris drew his pistol and nodded at me, and then we set out across the street, into the cloud of smoke around the gateway. I tugged my shirt up around my nose and mouth and held it there as we entered the pall of dust and debris, following close behind Harris, who seemed unaffected by the acrid smoke. A shape resolved in the sun-fractured shadows of the smoke. Harris's pistol made a quiet barking sound, not unlike a firecracker, but much louder than I expected a silenced pistol to be. The shape dropped. Another replaced it, and Harris shot that one, too. Then we were through, and I was stepping on something at once soft and hard, rolling out from under my foot. I felt my stomach lurch and refused to look down, simply adjusted my footing and stayed tight behind Harris. He swiveled from side to side, and his pistol cracked, again and again, and then there was the *crackcrackcrack* of a machine gun, dust spitting up from the shattered marble tiles near our feet, but the shooter was quickly brought down by Harris.

He was moving with the graceful, predatory economy of a professional warrior, partially crouched, feet silent, body angled, swiveling and pivoting as if his upper half was a gun turret. When he fired his gun, he didn't stop, didn't slow, just kept on gliding with serpentine swiftness, the pistol barking and jerking in his hands nonstop.

I felt nothing. All emotions, all senses were switched off, shoved down, and I tried to pretend I was in a movie, that this was all pretend, but I couldn't. Not totally. I had a gun, too, but I didn't dare draw it. Couldn't, wouldn't, not unless I was ready to shoot and kill, and I knew I wasn't. Then, before I knew it, we were standing outside the house itself.

Harris exchanged clips in a swift, practiced motion, stopped with his back to the wall, pivoted, and peered up a stairway. I couldn't have told you what the house we were in looked like, except for an impression of marble floors and white walls and dark beams on the ceiling. Harris kept his back to the far wall as he slithered up the stairwell, peering up and angling to see around corners. His pistol fired, twice, a third time, and I was right behind him, glancing behind me every so often.

As we rounded the corner of the stairs, I saw a shadow moving on the landing beneath us. I tapped Harris on the shoulder, pointed down without speaking. He nodded, in a crouch that spanned three stairs, aimed his pistol downward, and waited. A body wielding a wicked-looking black assault rifle appeared in the doorway, and Harris shot him twice. I looked away after the first shot, and then Harris was tapping me on the knee, and I had to follow him.

A woman's voice was shouting in Greek, pausing now and then, clearly engaged in an argument over the phone. This was followed by silence and then the sound of an engine roaring, and the whine of helicopter blades powering up. Harris was paused in the doorway of the stairwell, just out of sight, waiting until the helicopter took off. He then jerked his head for me to follow, heading for a door at the end of a short hallway. A man stood outside it, an M-16 held in his hands. He saw Harris, but a moment too late. Harris shoved me to one side and lunged, the M-16 ripping the air, but Harris's pistol was already cracking, rounds slamming into the guard's body within the blink of an eye. Harris pushed me out of the way.

I hit the wall hard enough to knock the breath out of me, and I stood gasping as Harris rifled through the dead man's pockets and came up with a small handcuff key. Harris jerked at it the locked door, cursed, searched the man's pockets again, and then cursed again before stepping back and kicking the door just to the left of the handle. The frame splintered but held, and he kicked it again. This time, it flung open, and Harris stepped through, pausing to grab the M-16.

I was right behind Harris as soon as the door burst open.

Harris let the assault rifle droop, shock clearly overtaking him. I couldn't see around him, could only see a bed, a brass footboard, and a foot handcuffed to the railing, a bit of bare leg. I knew that foot. I knew the curl of hair on the toes and the scar on his ankle where he said he'd cut it open rock climbing, and I knew the scrim of fine blond hair on his leg, the scar on his calf from the muffler of a dirt bike.

"Valentine!" I lunged around Harris, but stopped in shock.

He was totally nude, cuffed spread-eagle to the bed, his hair wet and matted to his scalp, blood trickling down his forehead. He was alive, though, eyes wide and crazed, teeth bared in a rictus of madness. He had a massive erection, so engorged his veins stood out throbbing and purple. A pill bottle sat on a side table, as well as a silver pitcher. He was sweating, writhing, spine arching and hips lunging. His wrists and ankles were bloody, rubbed raw from his thrashing against the cuffs.

"What the fuck is wrong with him, Harris?"

"Drugs is my guess. A drug to make him…do what she wanted, when he wouldn't cooperate."

"How are we going to get him out of here in this state?" I glanced at Harris, who only shook his head.

"I don't know. But we have to." He handed me the key he'd gotten from the dead man. "Uncuff him. Leave the cuffs on his wrists for now, though. I don't know how crazy the drug'll make him. I might have to subdue him till it wears off." He sounded too calm, and I darted a glance into Harris's eyes. It clearly disturbed him to see Valentine this way.

Roth, who was always in control, always calm and collected. Roth, seemingly the master of his universe, reduced to a naked, crazed beast.

I wanted to cry, but I didn't. I moved to Valentine's side, touched his face. Wiped the blood from his forehead, the wet hair from where it was pasted to his temple. "Valentine? Baby? It's me. It's Kyrie. I'm here. Harris is here. We're gonna get you out of here, okay?"

He growled in his throat, but his eyes latched onto me. His gaze darkened, shifted. "Not you. Get away from me, you bitch. Get away. Fucking kill me, you cunt. Stay away or kill me. I won't do it. Not again. I won't. Won't."

Tears started in my eyes, my throat closed. "Valentine? It's me. It's really me." I'd never heard Valentine talk that way, so coarse, so vulgar, and so full of rage and disgust. He didn't recognize me. That had to be it. He wouldn't talk to me that way. He loved me. Right? I forced myself to believe that, knelt beside him so my face was level with his. "Roth? Valentine? It's me. It's Kyrie. Listen to me. Listen to my voice. It's me."

"Kyrie?" He sounded hesitant. Skeptical.

"Miss St. Claire. We have to go." Harris stood in the doorway, rifle pointed down the hallway. "The second charge is about to go off, and we have to be there when it does."

"Give me a second. He thinks I'm—I'm her."

"We don't *have* a second. She'll be back with a goddamn truckload of men with guns, okay? They're coming here, and we have to be gone before they do." He bent, went through the dead man's pockets a third time, coming up with a spare magazine, which he used to replace the partially depleted one in the gun.

I squeezed my eyes shut and prayed a prayer to whatever might or might not be out there, and kissed Valentine. A slow, deep kiss. The kind that said *I love you—I love you—I love you.* "It's me. It's me."

He didn't respond to the kiss. I pulled away, and he blinked, looked at me. "Kyrie? You're real?"

"Yeah, I'm real. And we have to get out of here, okay? Can you walk?"

"I—god—I don't—don't know." He seemed barely able to form words, muscles tensing and flexing, each shift and jerk of his hands drawing fresh blood from his wrists and ankles. "I'll try."

I fitted the tiny key into the handcuff attached to the bed, released it, then unlocked his other hand and both feet as quickly as I could. Valentine lunged off the bed, tripped over the sheets, and stumbled to the floor, scrambled away on his backside into the corner. I snatched a towel from a stack on the floor—not daring to wonder what had gone on with the buckets and pitcher and towels—and approached him.

"Come on, baby. Stand up, okay? We have to get out of here." I held up the towel.

Valentine levered himself to his feet, and stood pressed even deeper into the corner. He seemed afraid of me, wary of me, as if I wasn't who I said I was. "Stay—stay back. Don't touch me. Don't fucking touch me." He flexed his hands into fists and released them, shook them, rubbed his face and sucked in deep breaths and let them out. Squeezed his eyes shut and opened them, staring at me with a bizarre mix of desperation, lust, and worry. "Tell me something only you'd know."

"It's really me, Valentine, I swear—"

"TELL ME!" he shouted, his voice raw and hoarse.

I wracked my brain. "You sent me three checks! The message on those three checks was '*you belong to me.*'" I took another step closer to him, the towel held out for him.

Crackcrackcrack. The M-16 rattled, deafeningly loud. "We have to fucking *go!*" Harris shouted.

Valentine snatched the towel and wrapped it around his waist, covering his still massive erection. "Don't touch me. Please. I can't—I'm not me right now, and I can't—I'm—*fuck*—" he cut off with a growl, shoving past me, without touching me. "Let's go."

He stopped, unbuckled the dead guard's belt and jerked the pants off him, stepped into them, and tied the belt in a knot. The pants were several inches too short, the waist too loose, and the belt too long, but he was covered to an extent.

Harris set off with Valentine on his heels, me in the rear. Down the stairs, around the corner away from the front gate, and through a courtyard. A boxy Mercedes SUV, a Jaguar, and a Rolls Royce sat in the courtyard, gleaming in the sunlight. Harris ducked to peer into the Mercedes, checked the driver's-side door handle. It was unlocked, and he bent in, came up with a keyless ignition fob.

"Get in." He gestured at both of us. "Kyrie in the front. Mr. Roth, you get in the back." He glanced at his watch. "*Now,* please."

I slid into the front seat while Roth got in the back, and as soon as we were in and the doors closed, Harris had the car bolting backward, spinning around. A blinding flash lit up the courtyard, accompanied by an explosion that flung chunks of rock and brick and mortar into the air. Windows smashed, car alarms set to blaring. The roof of the Jaguar was caved in by a hunk of brick, and the driver's-side window of the Rolls shattered. A huge piece of brick hit the hood of our Mercedes, denting it, and another hit the roof near my head.

Harris gunned the engine, and the powerful V-8 rocketed the car forward through the hole made by the bomb. The tires hit bits of brick, and the car jolted, bounced, and then we were hauling too fast down a hill, braking and squealing around a corner and then another, and then we were aiming for the coastline. A helicopter thumped in the distance.

I glanced back at Roth, who was hunched over in the seat, sweat coating his back and shoulders. He was shaking all over, handcuffs still dangling from his wrists and ankles. I risked reaching a hand out, touching his shoulder. He flinched away, glancing up at me with wild, bloodshot eyes.

"*Don't!*" he hissed. "I can't control it."

"What did she do to you?" I whispered, more to myself than to him. "You can't control what?"

"Myself. I need—I need—" He didn't finish, though, biting off mid-sentence and ducking his head, grabbing the chains of the handcuffs and pulling hard, drawing blood, as the pain offered lucidity.

"Leave him be for now," Harris said. "Take a look behind us. Anyone following? You see that helo?"

I peered back. "No, no. I don't see anyone behind us, and the helicopter…it's there, but it's out over the water, flying toward the island. I don't think it's following us."

We were racing around a curve on the hillside, the sea far, far below. A bus rushed past us, too close, our mirror almost scraping the side of the bus. In the back seat, Roth was rocking and growling, his hand going to his crotch and grinding himself as if the pain of his engorged penis was just too much. And then he jerked his hand away and grabbed the back of Harris's seat, and his fingers went white with the force of his grip.

He glanced up at me, saw me watching. "Don't look at me, Kyrie. Don't you fucking dare look at me. You see the state I'm in? I'm crazy right now, baby. Crazy." He grinned, a feral leer. "You wanna help me out, love?" He'd never sounded so English as then, the way his words twisted, the way his voice deepened and his lips curled.

*He's not himself.* I repeated that in my mind, hating the words coming from his mouth and the way he said them.

"You want my cock, don't you, Kyrie? You see it? I'm fucking crazy right now. I can't stand it. I need you." He reached for me, eyes hot and leering and ravenous. With a spear of pain in my heart as I did so, I backed out of his reach.

"Roth. It's not you. That's not you." I fought the tears. "It's not you."

His face twisted, and he hunched over. "Fuck. *Fuck.*" He rubbed his face with both hands, spoke through his fingers. "Don't come near me. Don't touch me. Don't look at me." The hate, the disgust, the raw vitriol in his voice made me flinch, shudder, and made the tears stream down my face.

Harris stopped the SUV on a side street, beckoning for me to follow him. I slid out of the car and shouldered my backpack, waiting until Roth was in front of me before following Harris. We made our way through the sleepy village by the sea, fishing boats plying the waters in the distance, guitar music playing somewhere, water lapping at boat hulls and chucking at dock pylons. Our yacht stood out among the old fishing boats and small skiffs. We boarded, and Harris had us untied and was backing out before Roth and I had even sat down. Roth headed for the stairs leading below, and I followed him, dropping the backpack to the deck.

He pushed through the doorway of the stateroom I'd slept in, perhaps by accident, or perhaps because he could smell me on the blankets. I followed, hesitant but determined. Locked the door behind us. This was Valentine. My Valentine. I couldn't leave him alone, not now, not like this.

He whirled, chest heaving, sweat gleaming on his skin, on his bulging muscles. His blond hair was long and damp, curling at his neck, his pale blue eyes crazed and wild. His hands shook. The handcuffs dangled, silver streaked with blood.

"Why are you here?" he demanded, his voice low and threatening.

"I—I can't leave you alone. I just got you back. I can't leave you. I won't." I stood straight and unflinching as he took a slow, prowling step toward me. "It's me, Valentine. It's Kyrie. I'm here. I love you. I love you."

His fingers twitched and curled. I trusted him. I knew him. Even in the hold of some drug, I knew he wouldn't hurt me. He loved me. I trusted in that.

His trembling fingers lifted and touched my cheek. I felt a tear there, though I hadn't realized I was crying. He smeared it away. His breathing was erratic and panting, his chest rising and falling, his jaw working, every muscle taut and tensed. His finger slid across my cheek, down my neck, stopping at my clavicle and dropping away. I stood still, letting him touch me, denying the fear I felt in my gut. He leaned in, put his nose to the side of my neck, inhaling deeply. For some reason, my gaze locked on the bed, a low frame bolted to the wall. The bars of the frame were narrow enough that I could cuff him to it, if I had to.

Why did I think that? Why? I'd just rescued him—why would I need to restrain him?

His inhalation turned to a kiss, lips sliding across my skin. I went stone still, hands at my sides, fear churning in my gut. Was this my Roth kissing me? Or was it the leering beast from the car that'd looked at me like he wanted to eat me? I wanted to kiss him, to remind him who I was, who we were. I touched his jaw, lifted his face.

"Roth?" I searched his eyes.

The next few seconds happened in a blur too fast to comprehend. Somehow, I was on the bed and Roth was ripping my shirt apart, baring my bra, which he tugged down, bending and kissing my breasts as his hands jerked at my pants, the button fly and the zipper.

"Roth, wait—"

He didn't wait. My pants were off, the pistol thumping to the floor beside the bed, and he was above me, handcuff bracelets cold against my forearms. His hands were on my wrists, pinning me. He'd shed the borrowed pants at some point, was naked now.

"Kyrie...god*damn,* Kyrie. It's you. I can smell you. I can taste you. You're you. You're really you. I dreamed you once, but it was her," he growled in my ear, and I whimpered at the mad hunger in his voice.

"Roth, baby, let me up, okay?"

I was lost in the terrifying juxtaposition of sensations. I loved being beneath Roth, I loved the feel of his body hot and hard and huge over mine, I loved the smell of his skin and the strength in his hands and the press of his cock against my core just before he pushed in. I loved all that, cherished it, and needed it.

But this?

This wasn't that. This was madness. Drug-induced insanity. A crazed need he couldn't control, and he wasn't listening to me as I whimpered, as I struggled against his crushing grip on my wrists, fighting panic as I struggled against him.

"Let go, Valentine," I whispered. I lifted up and put my mouth to his ear. "Let me go. Please."

He pulled back and looked down at me, his eyes wide and mad and dark and alien. "I need—I *need* this."

I shook my head, managed to get a wrist free. I touched his cheek, fighting tears. "Not like this, Valentine. Please." I pushed at his chest, gently, delicately, pleadingly.

He was shaking all over. Warring within himself. I felt him at my entrance, and in this moment, with this Roth, I wanted to press my thighs closed to him, and that made tears leak out. His hips flexed, his eyes narrowing, jaw clenching, and I felt him slide in a little, his broad head parting me just slightly.

My breath came in gasps. "Roth, no. No. Not like this. This isn't you. *Please,* Roth."

He growled, his lips curling into a rictus, his eyes squeezing shut. I felt him shaking all over, felt him tensed tighter than a guitar string, every sinew and muscle rock hard. With what seemed to be a physically painful effort, a supreme exertion of will over his body, he moved just enough that I could scramble out from beneath him. He flopped to the mattress and twisted onto his back.

And then, with a supreme effort of will, he took the end of the handcuffs and clicked them around the rails of the bed frame, one and then the other.

Knowing what he'd been subjected to, I couldn't escape the enormity of what he'd just done—for me, to protect me from himself—by voluntarily handcuffing himself to the bed.

"Kyrie. Kyrie." His voice broke. "Don't—please—don't leave me, Kyrie. Don't leave."

I was crying in earnest now, barely able to see through the tears. I stood beside the bed, watching blood stream down his wrists. "Valentine. I'm here." I collapsed to my knees, rested my head on the pillow beside his. Put my palm to his feverish cheek.

"Why?"

"Because I love you."

# 8

## TAMING THE MONSTER

*VALENTINE*

I fought the drug. Fought the madness. In the back of my head, I knew I'd almost done something unforgivable. But I couldn't think of that. Not yet. I couldn't think of anything but the pain, the pressure, and the wild need for touch, for flesh, for release, for sex. I needed sex. I needed release. It was a primal need.

I cracked open an eye and saw Kyrie sitting on the floor beside the bed, naked but for her bra, tugged down to bare her breasts. "Go. Leave me. You shouldn't see me like this."

She was watching me, tears in her eyes. "I'm not leaving, Valentine. I won't." She sniffled and wiped her eyes, then moved gingerly to sit near my feet. "Talk to me. I'm here. You can say anything. I love you. I know this isn't you, this is—whatever she gave you."

"A pill." I strained to touch her. "Something experimental. A libido enhancer. Not—not like Viagra. It doesn't just make me hard, it makes me… *need*. God, that's not—fuck, it hurts—'need' isn't even close to a strong enough word."

She stroked hair away from my eye with a tender finger. "Valentine…what can I do?"

"Nothing. Nothing." I squeezed my eyes shut and rode the wave of boiling frantic ravenous hunger.

I couldn't bear to look at her. It was too hard, too much. She was so lovely, so beautiful, so lush. Her long, muscular, tanned legs, crossed to put her core in shadow. Her stomach, flat and firm yet cushioned with a layer of silken flesh. Her ribs, rippling into view as she shifted slightly. Her tits, spilling over the edge of her bra, a plain white utilitarian underwire bra, in that moment somehow the sexiest thing I'd ever seen. The bra was out of alignment, and she was too upset to adjust it. A hint of areola at her left boob teased me, had me growling and desperate to get my hands free, to rip the stupid garment away so I could see all of her perfect tits.

"I can't just sit here and—and watch you go crazy, Valentine."

"Then don't. Just go. Get the fuck out of here." I turned my head away and kept my eyes shut, waiting for the click of the door closing behind her.

Instead, I felt the bed dip, felt her sit beside me. "Never." Her voice was low, hesitant. "I'm here, Valentine. I'm here. I love you. I still belong to you. I'm not leaving."

"You have to—have to get away from me. It's too much. You're too much. I can fucking *smell* you, Kyrie. I can smell your sweat, and I—god, *god*—I can smell your pussy. I can practically taste your skin. Jesus, Kyrie. I'm so hard it hurts." I was writhing, pulling at the handcuffs, and for a second I was back in the bed waiting for Gina to take what she wanted, and I had to look at Kyrie, tried to remind myself I wasn't there anymore.

She was crying, silent tears trickling down her cheeks. "Let me help you."

"How? How can you help me?" I didn't dare open my eyes. If I looked at her, the need would overwhelm me.

"Help…relieve the—the pressure."

My eyes flicked open, and my gaze focused on Kyrie like a laser. "You'd do that? Even after what I… what I almost did?"

Her face crumpled. "But you didn't, Valentine. You didn't."

"I *wanted* to, though."

"But you *didn't*."

A heated blast of desperate need billowed through me. I couldn't breathe for the pressure, for the need, for the ache in my bones and my blood. Kyrie was sitting beside me, and I could smell her. I hadn't exaggerated when I'd told her I could smell her pussy. My senses were attuned, honed by the drug, and as she shifted, I could smell her, perfume and musk and sweat and essence and all woman.

I arched my spine, thrusting my chest upward, digging my heels into the mattress, tugging at the cuffs. Wildness, feral hunger, a driving furious thirst, my eyes on Kyrie. If I had her in reach, in this moment, there would be no force on earth that could stop me from taking her until I was sated.

She swallowed hard, her throat bobbing. I watched her throat move, and my mouth and lips ached to taste her skin, to kiss the column of her perfect throat.

"Valentine?"

"I *need* you," I hissed, writhing on the bed.

Her gaze shook, wavered, running up and down my body, tender and afraid all at once. "I love you, Valentine."

She was waiting. I knew what she was waiting for. It was the farthest thing from my mind then, though. All I could think of was her, her body, her skin, her core hot and damp. The swell of her tits, the thick muscle of her thigh. Her soft, sweet, affectionate hands. I wanted her bare against me. I'd take it, if I could.

Thank god I was shackled again.

Her eyes filled with tears as I fought the demon inside me. She was still here. Even after the way I'd assaulted her and had barely managed to pull myself back, she was still here.

"Love you, Kyrie." I growled it, teeth gritted past the pain of the handcuffs against which I struggled.

She blew out a shaky breath, looked at the ceiling as if it held some secret strength. Took a deep breath, wiped at her face with both hands. Then she looked sideways at me. Her gaze was suddenly inscrutable, unknowable. There was a darkness in her eyes I couldn't fathom, couldn't decipher.

Kyrie turned toward me, slowly, moving as if through water, her eyes never leaving mine. "I love you, Valentine Roth. Okay? I love you. Always. No matter what."

Her hands slid onto my chest, palms flat against my pecs. And then she moved astride me, thighs gripping my waist. I blinked, blinked hard to clear the haunting vision-memory of a different woman in this same position, hands on my chest, core hovering over my abs, hair a curtain around her face. I blinked and heaved in a shuddering breath, jerked against the cuffs. Distorted reality twisted and resolved back into focus, showing me Kyrie in all her glory. She leaned back, sitting on me. Reaching up behind her back, she freed the clasp of her bra, setting it aside. She gazed down at me, an unknowable dark fury in her eyes.

"This is for you, Valentine. Because I love you. Because you saved me. Because you've given me so much." She was breathing deeply, not panting but merely dragging deep, calming breaths in and letting them out slowly. "Do you know me? You see me? You feel me? You do, don't you, Valentine?"

"Kyrie...." It was all the reassurance I had to offer.

It took every ounce of strength I possessed to keep still as she straddled me. Even more than it took to move off her earlier.

"Do you love me, Valentine?" She seemed so desperate to hear it, to be reminded.

I swallowed past the lump of emotion in my throat, past the raging chemical torment, aching to hold her in my hands, to kiss her skin, to taste the salt of her flesh, the sweet tang of the juices between her

thighs. "Yes…fuck yes, Kyrie. So much. You don't—
ahhh, god help me…you don't have to do this."

"Yes, I do. I do. I can't watch you endure this torture any longer."

"That's no reason. I'll survive. I survived it once.
Survived worse. I'll be fine."

That didn't help her at all. She fell forward, fighting sobs. "God, Valentine. What did she do to you?"

I shook my head. I couldn't revisit that. Not
now. Not with Kyrie sitting on top of me. Not with
this need inside me, not with the drug gripping me,
shredding me, controlling me. Even making coher-
ent sense with my words took effort, and to recount
what I'd endured would wreck me. I needed strength
for that, and I was weak in that moment.

Another wave of boiling, magma-hot sexual fer-
vor took me, sent a sheen of sweat coating me as I
fought to keep still, to keep from thrusting upward.
I could feel her, so close. So close. Her pussy was
inches from my cock, sliding against my navel. All
she had to do was lean forward just so and take me
in, and I'd find relief.

"Please, please…*fuck*, Kyrie…*please*…." I was
begging. I couldn't stop myself from pleading with
her to take mercy on me. I was barely even aware of
what I was saying.

I had no control left, none. My body writhed and bucked beneath her, and she rode it out, lower lip caught between her teeth, eyes wavering and wet.

And then...sweet Jesus...I felt her small warm gentle strong hand on my cock, and I knew her touch, knew even with my eyes closed the feel of her hand around me, and I breathed in deeply and let it out and soaked up the bliss of her touch, the glory of her body on top of me, tried furiously to block out everything else but the knowledge that this was Kyrie, my Kyrie. I knew her scent, knew the smell of her deodorant and the conditioner in her hair and the lotion on her skin, the way it all mixed together with her sweat and the unique indefinable scent of Kyrie-ness. I knew the feel of her thighs clenched around my hips, knew from the way she sucked in her breath and shifted forward that she was about to slide me inside her. I fought to hold still, to stop myself from driving up and in before she was ready, fought to let her do this, rather than take what I so badly needed. I growled in my throat and gritted my teeth until I thought my jaw would crack from the pressure.

"Open your eyes, Valentine. Look at me as we do this." Her voice was low, barely a murmur, but it cut through me.

I forced my eyelids to open, forced my gaze to hers. Eyes so blue, like polished sapphires, like the Aegean, locked on mine, love and affection and heated need of her own now warred with the darkness, with a deepening rage, with frantic misery. She knew. She knew just by looking at me, by my refusal to answer her question, what had been done to me. Perhaps not the details, but she knew.

And she knew as well that this, what was happening in this moment, would change things between us. I wanted to beg her not to do this, to let me suffer. But such was my weakness that I couldn't. Couldn't.

With a small sigh through parted lips, her bluest blue eyes on mine, Kyrie sat down on me, impaled herself on my cock. I groaned in relief, could have cried from the sweet familiar clenching wet warmth of her pussy around me. "God…Kyrie…oh god. You feel so good. Nothing…*nothing* has ever felt so good as you right now."

She whimpered as she drove her ass down flush to my hips, filling herself with me. "Roth…my Valentine." Her eyes closed involuntarily, and her head dropped between her arms as she braced herself on my chest.

"I love—I love—oh, oh *god,* Kyrie…I love you." It took everything I had in that moment to separate the insanity of need and glorious relief enough to make sense of my own mind, to get the words out for her.

She sobbed and fell forward, clinging to my neck with desperate strength, almost choking me, writhing her hips in a slow undulation. "Roth. Roth. Roth."

No one ever said my name the way she did. My last name, on her lips, during love like this, was a prayer, a whispered plea and a term of unfathomable endearment.

"Kyrie."

Wetness slid hot against my neck where her face was pressed into my flesh, the dampness of tears. Her mouth slid against my flesh, stuttered down to my chest, lips pressed in a kiss, held there for a moment as she lifted her hips to draw me out, her pussy sliding wet and slick against my throbbing, aching cock. Her hands held her weight on my shoulders, pushing me down into the bed.

And she moved. Glided down, her ass to my hips, her pussy squeezing around me. Oh, I knew that, too, the way her muscles clenched around me, the way her breathing was coming in short gasps, the way her face scrunched up and her lips fell open. She was close.

But she didn't. She held it off. Sat down firmly on me, my dick buried deep inside her, and leaned

back. Stared down at me. Debated something inter-
nally. She leaned to the side, grabbed her jeans off
the floor and dug in the hip pocket, producing a
small key.

"No, Kyrie, don't. I'm barely holding back—"

She ignored me and inserted the key into the
cuff around my wrist. The key turned in the lock,
and, for the first time in I wasn't sure how long, I
was totally free. I didn't dare move, didn't dare look
at my wrist. A twist, and my other hand was free as
well. And then, just like that, the only thing keeping
me in place was my own will.

"I trust you, Valentine." She leaned over again,
picked up her T-shirt and ripped a length of cotton
free from the hem, wrapped it gingerly around my
wrist, around the burning, bleeding wounds, and
then did the same for the other side. "I can't handle
seeing you handcuffed like this. It's killing me, baby."

"Kyrie…." I wasn't sure what I was going to say,
if I could make sense of the turbulence in my soul.

My body was trembling, a coiled, tensed preda-
tor set to pounce on unsuspecting prey. I was a live
wire, electrified, dangerous. More than anything,
I desperately needed to move, to feel her sliding
around me, to revel in the delirium of her body. But
I didn't dare move for fear of hurting her, for fear
of letting the beast free. It was a beast, this chemical

within me, a demon. It cared nothing for her, for me, for us. All it cared about was sexual release, the feverish animal desire, the hunger, the clash of bodies. But I cared. So I fought it.

Until she bent forward and I felt the silk-soft brush of her breasts against my chest, felt the lightning strike of ravenous desire, a bolt of love so hot, so deep, so all-consuming, I couldn't contain it. Couldn't hold back, couldn't do a single damned thing but thrust up into her, growling her name—

"*KYRIE—KYRIE—KYRIE….*"

—and move, move, move. My hands were alive, roaming her body, scouring her skin from nape to ass, shoulder to shoulder, touching her everywhere I could reach, caressing her knees and thighs and belly and ribs and waist and the contour of her arms and her cheeks, her lips, her forehead….

I couldn't stop touching her and thrusting, thrusting.

But being beneath her, as I'd been beneath—

With a curse, I sat up, needing to be in any other position. Kyrie sat up with me, wrapped her legs around my waist and her arms around my neck.

Her lips touched the shell of my ear. "Valentine. It's okay, love. It's okay. Whatever you need. Do what you need to do. Take me how you need to take me." She rose, lifting herself up with her arms around my neck, drawing my cock nearly out of her pussy, hesitated, holding—holding—holding, and then she slammed down hard. "You know me, baby. You know how I like it. You know what I can take. I love you. I trust you."

"God, Kyrie. I don't deserve you." I had no idea where that came from, but it felt true, and it speared my heart, seared my soul.

"Yes, you do. I'm yours. I'm here with you. I'm doing this willingly. I'm here because I want to be. You're inside me because this is what I want. Take me." Her voice shook with emotion. "*Take* me, Valentine."

I laid her down on her back, frantic, gasping, sweating, soul churning and body aching and heart crashing and melting. Her thick blonde hair splayed out on the white sheet of the bed, the blankets and comforter long since kicked aside. She kept her heels hooked around my waist, reached for me. I took a moment to absorb her beauty, to drink in the reality of her presence. So beautiful. So perfect. Lovely, delicate, strong.

I shook all over, still trying to hold back, to be gentle, to fight the madness of this chemical rage. This was *Kyrie.* My Kyrie. I couldn't—

She broke through my thoughts. "Let *go,* Valentine. This is me. It's okay. You can let go."

The last vestige of my self-control was shattered totally by her words, by the absolute sincerity in her voice.

I pulled out of her, breaking the hold of her heels around my waist. She planted her feet on the bed, staring up at me with emotion-fraught azure blue eyes tender and trusting, hands splayed on the sheet, fisting the jersey material, chest heaving, tits swaying with her breath. I let my eyes roam her body, head to toe, from the tangled mass of honey-blonde hair to the sex-smeared pink crevice of her pussy.

And then I could hold back no more.

I grabbed her by the hips, rolled her to her stomach. Kyrie knew me, knew what I wanted, and gave it to me. She drew her knees up beneath her belly, stretched her ass high in the air, thighs split as far apart as they would go, spine arched to press her chest to the mattress, arms out in front of her, fingers gripping the sheet. Her face turned to the side, watching me.

Shivering violently as I fought the urge to slam into her with merciless abandon, I gripped my cock in one hand, the other palm resting on the wide round curve of her ass. Found the hot slick wetness of her cunt, breathing in the sweet aroma of her arousal, and guided the tip of my cock into her, slowly. Slowly. It took all I had to do this gently, to keep a rein on the insanity.

"Oh—oh—oh *god*, Roth. Fuck. Yes, god yes. More." Her voice was muffled by the bed, her eyes scrunched closed tight, rapture on her face. "Harder, baby. FUCK ME. *FUCK ME*, Valentine."

I fucked her. With total abandon I fucked her, drawing back my hips and driving in hard, my flesh slapping loudly against hers, the generous muscle and flesh of her glorious ass quivering and quivering and quivering as I fucked into her again and again, groaning with each crashing, grinding thrust. And she took it, my Kyrie took it, whimpering at first, whining in her throat, holding still and just taking what I gave her.

She started shoving back into my thrusts, spine arched upward to draw her hips back in synch with my pulling out, and then she pushed with her hands and bowed her back to meet my driving cock. And now she was wailing with each meeting of our bodies, screaming into the mattress as my cock filled her, her pussy clenching around me, squeezing and gripping with involuntary spasms. I held her hips, my hands wrapped around the crease where hip met thigh and jerking her back into my thrusts, lifting her bodily off the bed to sit her on my cock, cramming myself deeper and deeper into her wet, pulsating core.

"I'm—I'm coming, Roth. I'm coming. Oh god, oh jesusfuck I'm coming, Roth. Come with me. Please, baby. Come with me. Right now. Oh*fuckfuckfuck!*" She was crying, sobbing my name, trying to thrust back but losing all muscular control as her body detonated, shattered, going limp. "ROTH! ROTH! Oh my *god*, Valentine, oh-oh-oh...."

I was absolutely mindless then, a rutting, ravenous beast of a man, pounding into Kyrie with reckless ferocity, grunting with each thrust, growling and cursing. I palmed her luscious, jiggling ass with both hands and spread her cheeks apart, sliding in even deeper yet, so deep it almost hurt, and she squealed in a kind of aching rapture as I held her like that, ass cheeks spread apart, her body bucked forward with the primal power of my thrusts.

My stomach ached with the pressure of my impending release, and my balls throbbed, tight against my body and pulsing, thighs tensed and flexing and hurting with exertion. I shook, trembled, and felt a volcanic upwelling begin somewhere in my atoms, in the nuclei of my being. Kyrie sobbed, boneless with orgasmic ecstasy, held up only by my hands as I lost rhythm, and I was gasping for breath, making a sound that was frighteningly like a sob as

I crashed into her, harder and harder and harder, her ass shaking with each slapping thrust, her sobs turning to a single drawn-out moan as she began to reach climax yet again. I felt her pussy spasming, her inner muscles beginning to squeeze around me as I felt my balls tighten until they hurt, my cock swelling and throbbing.

And now I was incapable of even thrusting. All I could do was keep her ass gripped tight against my front and grind into her. My vision twisted and distorted. I saw white. My lungs swelled until I couldn't breathe, and my vocal chords froze and my stomach lurched and flipped and sank, and my blood sang and my mind wheeled and all the earth spun around us and stopped, halted—

"KYRIE!" I cried her name as I came, my entire being exploding, my heart stopping.

I felt the relentless gush of seed shoot out of me in spurt after spurt, and now I was pulling out and thrusting in, coming still, coming again, and she was pushing back into me and whimpering my name, and I was coming again, fires of orgasm raging unquenchable inside me, white-hot and catalytic. Those fires congealed and coalesced and turned liquid, rocketed out of my cock and into Kyrie in yet another wracking spasm.

The white-out distortion of my vision cleared, and I was finally able to let Kyrie go. She collapsed forward, rolled to her back, and caught me as I fell, cradled my head against her breast.

I heard her heartbeat, frantic and pattering wildly.

Yet, even as we gasped together for breath, I knew the monster was not yet sated.

# 9

## ICARUS

ROTH AND I TENDED TO GET PRETTY WILD IN BED. IT WAS just how we were. He was a powerful man with an insatiable appetite for sex, and I was a young woman nearing her sexual prime, my appetite every bit as ravenous as his. In the months since he'd first sent for me, we'd had all kinds of incredible sex. We'd fucked in every conceivable position, in beds and on the floor and against the wall and just literally everywhere. We'd fucked sober, fucked drunk, fucked angry at each other.

That was pretty epic, actually. I don't even remember what we were angry about. One of those long frustrated days where every little thing went wrong and built up and culminated in a shouting match. I shouted "FUCK YOU!" and he'd just growled at me. And then, just like that, he was slamming me up against the sliding glass door of the hotel balcony, ripping my clothes off and thrusting into me. I'd screamed in rage, yet as he'd pulled out and pushed back into me, I'd had no choice but to wrap my legs around his waist and hold on, digging my nails into his shoulders, slamming my ass down as hard as I could in an attempt to hurt him. By the time we'd both finished, neither of us could remember what we we'd been arguing about.

All the ways we'd fucked each other, and yet none of them could even come close to the mad ferocity of what had just happened.

I'd be really, *really* sore later. And I knew we had a long, painful talk coming. Nothing had been solved. Nothing was okay yet. Roth wasn't okay.

And we weren't done yet. I could tell by the way he was still tensed, his breathing not ragged anymore but coming in long, deep pulls.

"Roth, listen—"

"Kyrie, I'm sorry—"

I put my palm over his mouth. "No. That's what I was about to say. Don't apologize. Just don't." I made sure he saw me, made sure he was looking into my eyes. I could see the wildness still lurking there, and it scared me a little. I wasn't sure even I could take another pounding like that. Not yet, at least. "Roth, baby. I love you. You think I didn't know what would happen when I uncuffed you? I knew. Okay? I knew. And it's fine."

"Did I hurt you?"

I shook my head. He hadn't. Not really. I'd be sore later, and would probably be walking funny, but it was worth it. I needed Valentine to know it was me. To know I was with him. And, honestly, I'd been worried he'd literally go crazy if I didn't do something. He'd been given an experimental libido drug, and who knew how it would affect him. He'd been in pain, literally tortured by need, and I was unable to let him remain in such wracking agony.

I collected my emotions, my worries, my thoughts, and pushed them down, pushed them away. I couldn't deal with all that, not yet. I couldn't deal with the rage I felt against the woman who'd done that to Valentine. She'd tortured the man I loved in who knew how many different ways, and the hate I felt for her was too potent to handle right then, not with Valentine in the state he was in.

"Kyrie, you should know now that when this drug wears off, I'm going to be sick. I mean it. Violently ill. Like the flu and drug withdrawal at the same time. It's—it's horrible, Kyrie."

"We'll deal with that when it comes, Roth. I'll be here. Okay? I won't leave your side, no matter what."

He clung to me, shaking. "Swear?"

"I swear, Valentine. I swear."

He rolled off me, onto his back beside me. "God, it's relentless."

"What?"

"The drug." He put a hand over his crotch and cupped himself, gripped his hardening dick. "It's crazy. I feel crazy. Literally, like I've gone mad. I can't control it, Kyrie. I can't. I can't."

I pushed his hand aside and saw that he was hardening again already. Roth had a pretty short refractory period, but this was fast even for him. "Roth. Look at me." He fixed his pale blue eyes on mine. "Just be still. Let me take care of you, okay?"

"How?" He arched his back and flexed his hips. "Take care of me how?"

"However I need to."

"You can't take any more, Kyrie. I know you. I won't let myself do that to you again. I'll hurt you for real, and I'd never—I'd never—"

I leaned in and kissed him to silence him. "I know. You're right, I can't. But there are other things, baby."

He was fully engorged by then, and I took him in my hand. I watched his face twist in pained pleasure as I slid my fingers down his length. There was no drawing it out, no making him wait for the payoff. My only goal was to bring Valentine to release as quickly as possible. I spat onto my hand and smeared my saliva onto my palms, and then wrapped both hands around his thick cock, stroking him hand over hand. He groaned, thrust up into my fists, curled his fingers into the sheets.

"Look at me, Valentine." I slowed my strokes until he opened his eyes and met my gaze. "Don't take your eyes off me, okay? Watch me. Watch me do this."

His eyes, tortured, conflicted, agonized, fixed on mine. I didn't try to smile for him, didn't try to hide my own inner turmoil. He was covered in sweat, chest heaving as he gasped raggedly, hips grinding relentlessly. His feet scrabbled at the sheet, heels digging in to push his entire torso off the bed as his cock throbbed and thickened and pulsated in my hands.

"Jesus, it hurts. I'm close, Kyrie."

"I know, baby. I know. I can feel it."

I kept stroking him faster and faster, until he was frantic with the impending climax. Wrapping my fist low around his base, I continued the hard and fast pumping, cupped my upper hand around the head of his cock and spat onto him again, providing more lubrication, and then squeezed my fist around him and stroked him hand over hand the way I knew drove him craziest. He groaned and growled and thrust into my strokes, and I knew by the way his rhythm faltered how close he was to exploding.

I leaned over him and suctioned my lips around his soft, broad mushroom head, stroking hard at his base, both hands grinding up and down his length, working with my tongue and throat.

"Kyrie, god, Kyrie…I'm gonna come—"

I moaned, humming around his cock, stroking and pumping and sucking until he was crazed and maddened, grinding hard into my mouth. I followed his thrusts, keeping my lips around his tip until I felt his stomach tense and his body arched. At the moment of his climax, I bobbed my head down to take him toward my throat, pulling his cock away from his body and angling myself to open my throat so I could take him deeper, pumping my fist around his base, working my throat muscles around his head and stroking him with my tongue. He was groaning and cursing, making incoherent sounds, gasping, and I felt the hot gush of come hit the back of my throat and I backed away, swallowing. He lowered his body to the bed, hands fisting in the sheet as he fought for control. I knew what he wanted to do.

I let go of his dick long enough to move his hands to my hair, and he immediately gripped at the roots and gently but insistently pushed my head down. I went with it, resuming my hold on the base of his cock to stroke him, bobbing my head in quick dips, sucking, taking the next warm, salty wash of come down my throat.

He groaned and pulled me up, thrust shallowly so the tip glided through my lips, and I moved my hands on him in long, soft squeezes, smearing my palms around him, and then I felt him tense in my hands and thrust hard. Opening my throat, I took him as deep as I could and felt the final spurt of his seed sluice down my esophagus, and backed away to swallow it.

Valentine went limp on the bed, and I sat up, wiping at my mouth with the back of my wrist, still squeezing and stroking his throbbing cock to milk every last spasm of his release. I watched as film of whitish come oozed from his tip and used it to smear down his length, and he groaned, gasping brokenly for breath.

"Enough…enough, Kyrie," he rasped. I let go, sat beside him, and watched as his breathing slowed. Gradually, he seemed to return to something like normal. "Stay here with me. I'm tired, Kyrie. So tired."

"Rest, Valentine. I'm here, and I'm not going anywhere."

He rolled to his left side, and I spooned up behind him, held him close and felt him drift to sleep. Uneasily, heart aching with love, mind buckling from the weight of unanswered questions, I slipped into sleep myself.

I woke to the sound of Roth gagging, heaving. The bed was empty, and he was on his hands and knees in the tiny bathroom, puking. My bag of clothing was on the floor near the bed, so I dressed quickly, hating the feeling of putting on clean clothes when I knew I was desperately in need of a shower. There wasn't any other option, though. I moved to stand by the doorway of the bathroom, bending over to rest my palm on Roth's bare back. He was still naked, and his entire body was dripping sweat. His skin was hot to the touch, his hair wet and tangled and pasted to his skull.

Gasping, Roth straightened slightly, pushing up with one hand on the rim of the toilet, visibly shaking. "Help me—help me lie down." He struggled to get his feet under him, and I supported him, helping him stumble to the bed. He covered his eyes with his forearm, chest rising and falling. "Bucket. Need a—need a bucket."

I went topside, found a big plastic bucket in a storage closet near the cockpit, and placed it on the floor beside Roth. He flung a hand out, reaching for me. I knelt on the floor, took his hand in mine, and placed his palm on my cheek. "I'm here, Valentine. I'm here."

"I don't know what I'd do without you," he murmured.

"You don't have to find out."

His stomach heaved, his Adam's apple bobbed, and I brought the bucket closer to him. He grabbed the side of the bucket, leaned into it, and gagged, dragged in a shuddering breath, and then vomited. I held the bucket in one hand and brushed the hair away from his temples with the other. When the wave passed, he rested his forehead on the rim of the bucket, gasping for breath, his stomach still heaving. He gagged again, coughed, spat, drooling, and then vomited again. Nothing came up this time but bile.

He rolled away, letting me take the bucket. "I don't have anything left to bring up," he said.

"I'll see if I can find something. Some water, at least," I said, setting the bucket on the floor beside him. "Here's the bucket in case you need it."

"Just…hurry."

I scurried into the galley, where I found Harris making coffee.

He lifted his chin at me. "How's he doing?"

"Not good." I rummaged in the small refrigerator for a bottle of water, found a package of Saltines in a cupboard. "She gave him some kind of experimental drug. Side effects are nasty. He's sicker than a dog."

Judging by the carefully blank expression on Harris's face, he'd heard us. "Should we find a doctor?"

I shook my head. "Not yet. Hopefully, he can ride it out. We'll have to see, I guess." I paused in the doorway. "Where are we right now?"

"A few miles off the coast of Crete."

I tried to pull up a map of the Mediterranean in my head. "Wait, Crete? Isn't that in opposite direction of where we came from?"

Harris nodded. "Yeah. But going back the way we came is probably the worst thing we could do. We're headed to Alexandria."

"Alexandria? As in Africa?"

He nodded. "Last place they'd expect us to go. Mr. Roth has no business contacts there, no friends. So it's a perfect place to go for that reason. We can hide out until Mr. Roth is feeling better and we have a chance to make a plan." He twisted the lid on his Thermos of coffee. "We're stopping in Crete to refuel. Little place called Sitia. We can get some fuel and food, and hopefully weather out the storm that's headed our way."

"There's a storm coming?"

Harris nodded, tapping a thumb against the side of the Thermos. His eyes wouldn't quite meet mine, a faint blush tingeing his cheeks. "Yeah. Big one, coming in from the west. Heavy wind and rains. It'll make some pretty scary waves, I'm thinking. Best to take shelter. We're really not big enough to tackle a storm, especially if Mr. Roth is sick."

I never saw Sitia. I didn't sleep. I didn't leave the room except to empty the bucket and bring him more water to drink. He spent three days vomiting, three days during which the boat rocked and pitched under the deluge of rain, three days of hell.

The passage of the storm coincided, ironically, perhaps, with the subsiding of Roth's illness. Anger boiled deep inside me, buried way down beneath the concern and the love.

After he was able to keep down some water and crackers, he fell into the sleep of the dead, and didn't so much as stir the entire trip from Sitia to Alexandria.

# 10

## CONSEQUENCES

I WAS ON THE BOW OF THE YACHT, A BLANKET WRAPPED around my shoulders. Dawn. The sun was rising up over the alien silhouette of Alexandria. Spires, tall and thin, pierced the cityscape, next to rounded towers and twisting cupolas. A high, thin, wavering voice broke the silence, calling out in a strange, chanting song.

I heard his shuffling footsteps behind me, and didn't have to turn to know who it was. "That's a muezzin."

"The singing?" I turned and glanced at him.

He had a towel wrapped around his waist, naked but for that. He nodded. "Yeah. He's calling the faithful to prayer. Five times a day you'll hear that."

We sat together, side by side, listening to the muezzin's call echo across the city. After a few minutes, the song faded, and we were left with the soft lap of waves chucking against the sides of boats. I could feel Valentine ruminate, feel him thinking, trying to formulate a thought.

"It isn't over," he said, his voice smooth and his words crisp and formal once again. "She will come for me. And now, for you. And Harris. She will come, and she will enlist the help of her father."

"What do we do?"

He let out a long breath. "I should hide you somewhere. The farthest corner of the earth. Indonesia. Russia. Tierra del Fuego, perhaps. Put you up in a tiny flat. Make sure not even I know your precise location. Post a guard and pay them enough to ensure their unwavering loyalty."

I pivoted on my butt to face him, pressing my knees into his thigh. "No, Roth. That's not happening. I will *not* be separated from you again."

"I need to keep you safe. I can't let her get hold of you. I cannot. I *will not.*" He growled the last part, enunciating the syllables with increasing venom.

"Then don't. But I'm not going to let you out of my sight. I crossed the world to find you, Roth. I risked death." I took his hands in mine. "I was shot at. Chased in a car. I watched men die. I—I probably killed at least one person myself. Just to be by your side."

He withdrew his hands from mine. "I know." His voice shook, thin and pained. "I know, Kyrie. And I—I hate myself for—"

"And I'd do it all again. In a heartbeat. I know it isn't over. I know we're in danger. I know who we're facing."

"No. You don't." He stood, paced toward the very point of the bow, gripping the railing. The towel rode low on his hips, exposing the muscular arc of his hip-bones. "You really don't. What you saw? Those men? They were…just her household staff. Not even that. A skeleton guard. Her father runs a—it isn't merely a cartel or anything so simple. It's more than that. He has an *empire*, Kyrie. Access to literally everything. A small army, and that's no exaggeration. He can wield tanks. Rocket launchers. And we've got…Harris."

"And you and me."

He nodded. "True. But I'm still weak from being sick. I can still feel the drug in my blood. And, that aside…I'm not okay." He glanced at me over his shoulder. "And you?"

"I'm no one. I'm just your girlfriend, and there's nothing I can really do, is there?" I hung my head and stared at the deck between my feet. "That's your point, right?"

"Kyrie—" He was clearly confused by the turn of the conversation, by my sudden and vitriolic self-loathing.

"It's true, and you know it." I stood then, pulled the blanket tighter around me, moved to the starboard railing, and leaned over it. "It's true, and *I* know it. I learned a few things rescuing you, Roth."

"Kyrie, that's not—"

I kept going. "I realized how useless I am. I have a degree I'll never use, and never planned to. Social work? What the hell was I thinking?  I'm not an entrepreneur like you. I don't have a specific skill set, or—or anything. I'm your girlfriend. That's all I am. I know you love me. I don't doubt that. And I'm not even doubting *why* you do. What's that stupid saying about gift horses?"

"Never look a gift horse in the mouth."

"Yeah. That. Whatever the fuck that's supposed to mean. I'm not doing it, is my point. You love me. Why, I'm not sure. I don't care. I'm just glad you do, because I love you, and I don't know what I'd do without you. You—you saved me first, Roth. I was going to starve, or go homeless, if you hadn't— done what you did. And now I'm here. I have you. I have the memory of the last few months we spent together. Seeing the world with you? God, Valentine, those months were the best of my life. But when you went missing, I realized...I was forced to ask myself, what do I *do*? And I couldn't come up with an answer."

Roth didn't answer right away. I lost myself in the movement of the water a few feet below, trying to see through the dark ever-moving ripples. I felt him beside me, but I couldn't make myself turn to face him. He didn't touch me. He just leaned over the railing beside me. That should've been a warning flag to me, but I was so lost in my own crisis that it wasn't.

"I suppose you should know. Before we left New York together, I made some...provisions. Should anything happen to me, you will be provided for. By which I mean, every single dime of my liquid assets will belong to you. The structure of my company will be shifted to streamline things, which just means selling off and combining subsidiaries, all proceeds from which will go to you as well."

"But, Valentine, I'm—"

"The only person I care about. I've arranged to have Harris provided for as well, but as much as I care about and trust him, he's still just a friend and employee. You—you're...I don't know. Family, I suppose. The woman I love. I haven't spoken to my father since the day he cut me off and cast me out. Nor will I ever. I have no siblings, no other family, no

dependents, no one. Just you." He gripped the railing and twisted his hands around it, as if he wanted
to strangle it.

"I have no plans to let anything happen to me.
I plan to live. I plan to do everything in my power
to keep you and myself alive, no matter what it
takes. My only point in telling you about the pro-
visions I've made is to reassure you. You'll never
face homelessness or hunger again. Never. As it is,
should you decide to…should you decide you wish
to leave me—if we were to break up, I mean, you will
be equally well provided for. Enough so that you'll
never have to work a day in your life, even if you
were to indulge as wildly as you could imagine."

"Roth—" I had to stop and breathe. "Let me get
this straight. If I were to dump you, tell you I wanted
to go back to Detroit and—I don't even know what
I'd do, but just hypothetically—"

"If you were to want that, I'd let you go. I'd fight
for you—I'd fight until it was clear you really wanted
to go. But if you did, I'd call Robert. He would then
set up a private series of accounts in your name,
giving you unlimited access to one point six billion
dollars." He tapped the railing with his index finger. "That account is already set up, actually, with
something like half that amount in it. It's in your
name alone. I can't access it, and once it reaches that

number, Robert's access as executor will be canceled, leaving you as the sole controlling party."

My mind reeled. "Roth, I don't—I don't understand."

He shrugged. "I don't want you to feel dependent on me. After all this trouble is sorted, I'll give you the codes and cards you need to access the money. That way, you can do what you want. You can figure out what you want. Do you want to be an artist? You can sit around all day and try. I'll hire the best artists in the world to teach you. Want to cook? Eliza can teach you. Want to be a philanthropist? Go back to school and get a different degree? Pursue a trade? I'll make it happen. Anything you want. But you won't need to ever ask me for a dime. If you stop loving me, that will still remain true."

"Why?"

He went stiff, taut, and tense. "You know." The two words were barely whispered, a low murmur nearly lost in the lap of the water and the sound of the breeze.

"Daddy."

He nodded. "Exactly." He let out a breath, staring out at the expanse of ocean. "It was an accident. I told you the truth, Kyrie. I swear to you, what I said to you was the truth. I never meant for that to happen—for your father to die. But he did, and it was my fault. When he died, I was responsible for the direction your life took. I alone am responsible."

"I don't want your money, Roth."

"Too bad. You've got it. You don't need to touch it, if you like. You can pretend it's not there. But it is there, and it's yours whether you want it or not."

I rubbed at my face. "How much did you say?"

"One point six-seven billion U.S. dollars." He waved a hand. "A rather fussily specific number, I suppose, but Robert did some kind of elaborate equation. The number is formulated to allow you to live a life of…excess, really…and never have to even think about what you're spending. Cars, houses, staff, taxes, trips anywhere for as long as you want. Unless you decided you wanted to own…god, I don't even know, dozens of fifty-million-dollar houses or something, you couldn't ever spend all that. That's how he came up with the number, he said. Assuming a specific amount of money spent per day, every day, for one hundred years."

I tried to summon words, and couldn't. "Roth. That's crazy. I don't think I can even fathom how much money that is."

He shook his head. "You can't. You really can't, Kyrie. You could spend a million dollars *every single day* for an entire year, and still burn through… barely a third of that."

"I can't even wrap my head around a million dollars, Roth, much less a *billion*."

"That's the point."

We lapsed into silence after that, both of us lost in our own thoughts.

I'd spent a lot of time deliberately not thinking about Roth's revelation regarding my father. I couldn't. There was no point to it. I loved him, and if I thought about what had happened between him and my father, I'd go crazy. I couldn't think about what Roth had told me about my father, either, about how he hadn't been totally legitimate in his business dealings. But it didn't matter. Not anymore. Not now. Daddy was dead. He'd been dead for a long time. I'd healed as much as I ever would. Knowing Roth was the one who'd pulled the trigger—accidentally—didn't change the reality of Daddy's death, didn't change what I'd gone through afterward.

So I intentionally remained in denial. I couldn't change the facts, and I didn't know what to do with the truth. So I pushed it all away, refused to think about it, and just enjoyed being with Roth. Healthy? Maybe not. But what else was I supposed to do?

And now, with all that had happened since I woke up alone in France, it mattered even less. What mattered was that I had Roth back. He was alive. We were together.

I pivoted, turning to face him. I sidled closer so I could peer way, way up into his face. He was shuttered, his face blank of expression, save for a slight pinch between his eyebrows. "Valentine?" I put my hand on his chest, reassured myself with the steady drum of his pulse under my palm. "Earlier you said you weren't okay."

He didn't turn to embrace me, didn't wrap his arms around me, didn't look down at me. "I'm not."

"Talk to me."

He shook his head. "I can't. I don't know how."

"Please, Valentine. Talk to me. Tell me what happened."

He pushed away from the railing, holding on to the metal so he was bent over, a posture of tortured conflict, pushing and pulling at once, as if he was unable to even understand within himself what he wanted to do. Straightening abruptly, he paced away from me, hands scrubbing through his hair.

"I can't, Kyrie. I can't."

I followed him. "Why?"

He didn't answer, just turned and strode past me, clutching the towel around his waist. "I can't, I just—I just can't. Okay? I *can't*."

I let him go. I stayed on the deck alone for several minutes, gathering myself. Should I pursue it?

Keep after him until he told me? Or was I supposed to let it go?

I had an inkling as to what had happened to him. A sinking feeling in my stomach. A knot of fear. The handcuffs around his wrists and ankles. The fact that he had been handcuffed naked to a bed, unable to escape. The fact that she'd given him an illegal, experimental drug to force his libido into overdrive....

The facts added up to a horror I wasn't sure I knew how to handle.

But I had to find out. I had to know what she'd done to him. The anger I felt within me was bubbling to the surface, becoming ever more potent and frightening in its intensity. Pushing the rage away, I descended to the staterooms, found Roth in the shower. His huge, powerful frame was too big for the tiny space, and he was slumped to the floor; hunched over, head between his knees. The water was running cold, and his skin was reddened from being scrubbed.

I shut off the spray, unfolded a towel. "Valentine. I'm here. It's okay. Come on out."

His blond hair was wet and plastered to his skull, his arms wrapped around his knees, hands fisted in front of him. "I need a moment, Kyrie."

I crouched beside him. Touched his shoulder

and felt my heart crack when he flinched away from me. "Roth, please. It's me. Okay? Just come out of the shower at least."

He unfolded himself slowly, gingerly, shakily. I wrapped the towel around him, gently rubbing his skin dry, shoulders, arms, chest, waist, legs…. I hesitated, and then dried off his backside and then his front, realizing in a general sort of way what he'd be feeling if he'd been subjected to what I feared he had. I finished drying his hair, and then wrapped a clean, dry towel around his waist. He stood still through it all, not reacting even slightly. I wanted to cry at his limp lethargy.

We'd showered together dozens of times, and we always dried each other off. He loved watching me rub his body with the towel, all over, and I always did it the way I just had, and usually by the time I got to his hair, he'd be aroused, even if we'd just had sex. The fact that he wasn't even looking at me… my stomach revolted, my chest tightened, my heart ached.

Harris always seemed to know exactly what needed to be done and he'd left a pile of new clothes on the bed, boxers, jeans, a T-shirt, a zip-up hoodie, thick socks, and sturdy hiking boots. I helped Valentine dress, feeling sicker and sicker with each passing moment. When he had the jeans and T-shirt on, he slumped to the bed, sitting on the edge and staring at the floor between his bare feet.

"What do you want, Kyrie?" His voice was low, distant.

I sat beside him. "Tell me what happened. Tell me—tell me what happened, Valentine. Everything."

"Why?"

"I have to know."

He didn't answer for a long, long time. I sat in silence, waiting, not touching him. Eventually, he heaved in a deep breath, let it out, and began. "I know for a fact I locked the doors before we went to bed that night. I set the alarm. I remember doing it. You fell asleep, after we…after. I put you in bed, but I wasn't tired yet. I stayed up for a while, answering some emails from Robert. When I finally felt tired enough to sleep, I shut everything down. Put our phones on the chargers, locked up, turned on the alarm. I remember…I woke up for a split second. I felt a pinch in my neck. I managed to open my eyes long enough to see a man I didn't recognize standing over me, a syringe in his hand. Then I felt this cold-ness rushing through me. I fought it, Kyrie. I fought it so hard, but I couldn't do a damned thing. I went under. Everything went black. And when I woke up, I was cuffed to the bed where you found me." He swallowed hard, held his head in his hands, palms at his temples, fingers curled into his hair. "As soon as I opened my eyes and looked around, I knew where I was. I knew who had me."

"Gina."

"Yes. Gina Karahalios. I'm assuming Harris filled you in on what he knew?" He glanced at me, and I nodded. "Well, I'm guessing by now you understand me well enough to know I'm not precisely forthcoming with information about my past. I only told Harris enough to allow him to keep tabs on the situation. Enough time had passed that I had grown complacent, I suppose. I should have known better."

"How long?"

"How long what?"

"How much time had passed?"

He tilted his head, resting his elbows on his knees. "Ten years. Almost to the day, actually. It's what, late September now? I made my move to get away from Vitaly's operation on August twenty-eighth. I remember the date exactly. It was a Tuesday. I had everything planned out. Money saved in a dozen banks around the world. A boat ready. I was going to sail to Istanbul, and go overland from there to France, and then take a train to London, fly from there to New York. They'd never find me. No one would ever find me. Only...I didn't count on Gina. She knew somehow. Not the details, but she'd sniffed out the fact that I was planning on leaving. And she wasn't about to let that happen. She was possessive of me. Insanely so, actually. I knew that, but I thought if I slipped away, she'd eventually get over me." He paused, breathing slowly and deeply, staring at the wall as if seeing the events of ten years ago. "I knew how crazy she was. I'd seen it. It was part of why I was leaving. We were at a club one night, Gina and I. I'd just closed a big deal. Sold a dozen crates of AKs worth maybe half a mil to this small-time Israeli coke dealer for over two million. We were celebrating. Gina went to the bathroom, and I stayed behind at the bar, drinking. This girl came up to get some drinks, saw me, and started chatting me up. Innocent enough. Wasn't even really flirting. I made sure to seem uninterested, but not rudely so. I said maybe half a dozen words to her. Barely looked at her. We talked about the damn weather, for god's sake.

"Well, Gina returned and saw us talking, assuming the worst, I suppose. I don't know. She came up, took her seat beside me, and the girl left. I thought that was it. Didn't think about it again. I fell asleep late. Or early, I guess. Gina was always an early riser, no matter what time we went to bed. So I woke up midmorning, and she was gone. No big deal, right? I made some coffee, had a bagel and lox. Went to take a shower, and—Jesus, I can still see it. The girl from the club. Her hands were tied to the shower head, and she'd been…tortured. Fuck, it was horrible. She'd had her throat cut eventually, but not before Gina had done a lot of other…things, to her. It was fucking horrible, Kyrie. Just for talking to me. And no one could do a damn thing about it. I went to find Gina and confront her, and she acted like she didn't know what I was talking about. By the time I got back to our room, the body was gone, no sign that she'd ever even been there. There was no police report, no missing persons report, no obituary. Nothing. For all intents and purposes, the girl had just vanished. People knew, though."

I wanted to cry for him, but I didn't dare. "God, Valentine. That's so…awful."

"I couldn't prove anything to anyone. No one had seen her taken—no one would even say a word about her. And Gina played innocent. But later that night, she made a point of telling me that I was hers. She had this little smile on her face the whole time we were—" He cut off, waving a hand.

"Valentine, it's okay. We're together now. I love you. That's all that matters."

He nodded. "Yeah." A long pause. "Anyway. The point is, I tried to leave. And she sent a guy after me. Not just to kill me, though, but to make me suffer first. If he'd just shot me from behind, I would never have had a chance. But he tried to cripple me first. Stabbed me in the back. We fought, and I won. I made him tell me who'd sent him, and why. He told me. And I put a bullet in his skull. That's something I'll never forget, either. I got away, and thought that was it.

"I ended up in New York, used the money I'd saved to buy a house on Long Island. Flipped it. Did all the work myself. Sold it for a profit, did it again. Bought an apartment complex building in the Bronx, fixed the units up, rented them out. Had a business going within a few years, making serious money. Legitimate money. Diversified. Hired someone to keep the real estate business going, started buying companies out, improving them, and selling them off. Then I met your father…and by that time, I hadn't heard a peep from Gina or her father. I thought they were history.

"And then, ten years later, I woke up handcuffed to the bed in Gina's estate on Oia."

I slid off the bed, knelt between Valentine's knees. Took his hands in mine. "Valentine? What did she do to you?"

He squeezed his eyes shut, tried to pull his hands away. Spoke through clenched teeth. "She…you know what she did."

"Tell me."

His chest was heaving, veins standing out purple in his neck, on his forehead. "You really want to hear me say it? Fine. She stripped me naked, handcuffed me to the bed, and groped me. Got me hard. Fucked me. I wouldn't let her make me come, though, and she got mad. She'd put a cock-ring on me, so my erection wouldn't go away. Couldn't. I did everything I could. I tried to stop it. Jerked on the cuffs so hard my wrists started bleeding. I was so hard it hurt. So hard for so long. I wouldn't let her make me come. So she…forced that pill into me. Two of her goons pried my mouth open and put the pill onto my tongue. Forced my jaw closed and pinched my nose closed so I had to swallow to breathe. I damn near choked. But she got the pill into me. A few hours later, she came back. And this time…well, you saw how I was. It turned me into a monster. I still fought it. I fought it for—for you. I knew it was wrong. The need, it was *wrong*. It wasn't me. But I couldn't stop it. I couldn't stop my body from reacting to the chemicals. I tried, Kyrie. I tried. *Fuck*, I tried."

His voice broke. His shoulders shook. He tucked his chin against his breastbone and shuddered, and his hands clenched around mine, turning to fists around my fingers, crushing me. I let him, swallowed the cry of pain. A groan left him, scraping out between grinding teeth. "She took what she wanted. She got on top of me, and she raped me. Made herself come on me again and again, and I tried to hold back even though it hurt."

He paused.

"She took what she wanted from me for herself, but it wasn't enough," he continued. "She wanted to break me. But I held out. Refused to come. I don't know how. Then the pill wore off. You saw what happened, the side effects of the drug leaving my system. I went through that. She came back, found me covered in vomit. Couldn't have that, of course. She couldn't fuck a puke-covered man, so she had her goons uncuff me. I tried to escape. I puked all over one of them, and managed to get his gun in the process. I shot him. But I couldn't even stand on my own. They cleaned me off. That hurt rather badly." He paused again, rubbing at his face, then began again. "I wouldn't take the pill the second time. I'd killed one of her men, and it had taken two of them to administer the pill the last time. So she decided to…have some fun. She water-boarded me. Poured water into my mouth. Up my nose. It's like drowning, but worse. Panic. You can't breathe, and she knew just when to stop so I wouldn't actually die. And then she'd start all over again. She used a moment when I was gasping for breath to put the pill into my mouth, and then she kept pouring water down my throat and forced me to swallow it. Even after I'd swallowed it, she kept water-boarding me. Over and over and over. Just to hurt me. Because she enjoyed it." He finally opened his eyes and looked down at me. "And then you and Harris rescued me."

"Valentine...." I didn't know what to say.

"I never gave her the satisfaction she wanted. If you hadn't rescued me, I would have succumbed. She would have broken me." He ducked his head, closed his eyes. "She did break me. I didn't give her what she wanted from me. I didn't let her make me come. But she still broke me."

I withdrew my hands from his, reached up, and took his face in my palms. "No. She didn't. You're not broken, Valentine."

"Yes. I am. I am." He jerked his face from my hands. "Look what I did to you. I had you pinned to the bed. I nearly—I nearly did to you what she did to me. I *did* do that to you. Just because you didn't fight doesn't mean—" He choked, gasped, started again. "I forced you. I *brutalized* you."

I couldn't stop the tears. "No. Valentine, no." I shook my head, gripped his face. "Look at me, Valentine. Please."

He twisted his face out of my grip, closed his eyes, and refused to meet my gaze. "It won't happen again, I promise." He murmured the words, syllables dropping from his lips like cold, hard pebbles.

"Valentine, no. Look at me. That's not how it was."

I was lying a little, though. That hadn't been my Valentine making love to me, hadn't been my Roth fucking me. That had been someone else, something else. He hadn't forced himself on me. He'd stopped. But what we'd done when he was in the throes of the drug, that hadn't been us, either. I couldn't figure out what it was or how I felt about it, but it wasn't us.

Roth wouldn't look at me. Wouldn't touch me. Wouldn't let me touch him. I put a palm to his cheek, trying to be gentle and tender. He flinched away.

And that scared me.

"Valentine, please...don't pull away from me now. Please don't."

He didn't answer. Didn't even acknowledge my words.

"Look at me, Valentine. *Please!*" He shook his head. Panic ran hot in my blood. "*LOOK AT ME!*" I screamed.

He flinched, and his eyes went dull. He went slack. Unresisting. "Okay, Kyrie. I'm looking at you."

I sobbed. "I'm sorry, Valentine. I'm sorry. I'm so sorry. I shouldn't have—" I fell to the floor, weeping. He didn't touch me. Didn't comfort me. Didn't say a word. I forced myself to stop and sat up. I looked at him. "You didn't brutalize me, Valentine. You didn't force me. You didn't take anything I didn't give."

"Okay." His voice was flat.

"Roth?" I stood up, stumbled back, spine to the wall. "Valentine?"

He blinked, glanced at me. "Yes?"

"Say something."

"What would you like me to say, Kyrie?" No intonation, no inflection, no Roth.

I'd lost him. He was gone. I shook my head, knelt down, and crawled toward him. Put my hands on his knees. He looked down at me indifferently. "Roth? Please. Don't do this. Don't pull away from me. This is me, okay? I'm sorry I yelled at you. I'm just…I'm scared. I'm confused. I'm angry. Not at you, at her."

"It's fine. It doesn't matter."

"It does matter, Valentine. It's not fine."

"Okay."

I wanted to scream at him again, tell him to wake up, to come back to me, but I couldn't. I fell backward onto my butt, fighting tears, sobbing, chest heaving. I sat for a long time, just watching Roth. He in turn sat staring into space, motionless, blank. Eventually, I stood up, wiped at my face, and moved to the door.

I twisted to glance back at Roth. "You're letting her win. You're letting her break you. I love you,

Valentine. I'm here. I'll fight for you. I'll fight for us. But if you give up, what is there to fight for?"

I moved topside, found Harris behind the wheel, feet propped up, a cigarette smoldering between two fingers, a paperback in the other hand.

When he saw me, he set the book face down. "How is he?"

I could only shake my head. "Not—not good." I couldn't bring myself to tell Harris what had happened. I assumed he would guess pretty close to the truth.

"Give him time."

I shrugged. "I guess."

"I've been waiting to decide what we should do, where we should go next. We should be safe here for a while, but they've got contacts all over the world. They'll get wind of us here soon enough. We need a plan."

I felt cold and empty. "Just...just take us back to New York. If the bitch wants us, she can come get us."

"Kyrie, I don't think that's—" I leveled a look at him, and the expression on my face was all he needed. He held up his hands in surrender. "Okay. Okay. New York it is."

# 11

## THE MANHATTAN PROJECT

THE RELIEF I FELT AS I SET MY BACKPACK DOWN IN THE master bedroom of Roth's Manhattan tower home came in a thick, hot, choking wave of tears. I dropped the bag to the floor, staring around at the familiar room. Wide bed, white duvet tucked in neatly at the edges. The wall opposite the bed slid open to reveal a floor-to-ceiling television that could double as a computer display. A set of double doors leading to a walk-in closet larger than most middle-class single-family homes. The door beside that leading to the bathroom, another expansive universe of dark marble and spotless glass and polished metal, modern lines and sleek curves and soft lighting. The wall facing outside was entirely glass, the whole wall designed to slide open to make the huge corner balcony and bedroom into one mammoth indoor-outdoor space. The balcony where Roth had told me the truth regarding my father's murder. The balcony where everything I'd ever known had changed.

I turned away from the balcony. Roth stood in the doorway, unmoving, staring blankly over my shoulder at the skyline. "We're home, Valentine."

He nodded. "Indeed we are."

He'd been nearly catatonic the entire way here. Countless hours on the boat, from Alexandria to Istanbul. A terrifying twin-engine prop-plane ride from Istanbul to Paris. From there a tiny jet, barely bigger than the prop plane, four comfortable seats, no flight attendant. Just Harris, Roth, myself, and the pilot, who spoke no English and was given a fat envelope full of Euros to fly us out of a private airfield in the countryside outside Paris. No names were exchanged, no questions asked, no flight pattern filed. Hours of yet more flying low over the Atlantic. No one spoke. Harris had a laptop on which he typed nonstop the entire ride. Roth stared out the window, blinking slowly every few seconds, taking deep sighing breaths, index finger tapping at his lips. No one slept.

Now I stood in the center of the bedroom, facing Roth, searching for something to say. For something to do. Kiss him? Tell him I love him? Drop to my knees and suck him off? Leave? Go stay with my friend Layla? Find a hotel? Stay in one of the guest rooms?

No. None of that would work. I'd told him I loved him. I'd tried to kiss him. Somewhere in the Mediterranean, partway to Istanbul. Middle of the night, moonshine gleaming through the porthole, bathing us both in silver light. Both of us were awake, unable to sleep. I rolled over, tucked my head against Roth's chest. He hadn't wrapped his arm around me. Hadn't even responded or registered that he knew I was there. I leaned up, kissed his jaw. Nothing. Kissed his cheek. Nothing. Kissed his lips. They were dry, cracked, chapped. No response, just a blank stare at the ceiling. I was worried and afraid. Was this the drugs still? Or was it psychological trauma? I didn't know, and didn't know what to do about it.

Now, standing in the center of the room, I felt everything well up inside me. All the emotions I'd buried deep, over and over, began to boil over. The fear I'd denied myself. The panic I'd not allowed myself to feel. The pain at what Roth had endured. The sick-to-my-stomach unease at the way Roth had fucked me on that boat. The look in his eyes. The feral hunger, the brutal power. The way he'd taken me, nearly forced me. And then the way I'd stuffed down my own deep fear of him, my rage at Gina. The way I'd pretended as if him fucking me was okay. Even though I knew—*knew*—it wasn't Roth. It wasn't the man I loved taking me, giving me pleasure. That was a drug, raping me despite my consent. That was some chemical-addled monster riding me, using me. But I'd done it for Valentine. He had been in agony. Crazed. And I'd missed him. Needed him. I'd hoped, naïvely, that my love would be enough. That my feelings for him would bring him back to himself somehow.

I'd been wrong.

And now…?

I was exhausted, physically and mentally. I couldn't stand up anymore. I tried. I locked my knees and clenched my teeth and sucked in deep breaths, in and out, in and out, in through the nose, out through the mouth. Dizziness washed over me. My breath came in panicked gasps, refusing my efforts to breathe evenly and regularly. My stomach twisted and rose up into my throat, hot and knotted into a rock-hard lump. I'd been as strong as I could be, for as long as I could. Now I couldn't hold it in anymore. I couldn't hold back.

My knees gave out, and I collapsed to the floor on my hands and knees, choking on my sobs. They were quiet at first, little squeaking rasps in my throat, but then my voice caught, a sob lodged in my throat, and I couldn't breathe. My arms trembled, unable to support me any longer. I felt carpet against my forehead, chest burning, lungs aching with my inability to breathe. I fell once more, this time to my side, and I curled up. Something broke inside me then, and the silent heaving shattered, and a sob became a wail. I covered my face with my hands, tucked my forehead against my knees, heels to my buttocks, and wept.

Moments turned to minutes, and I couldn't quiet myself, and didn't try.

I felt the ground topple and tumble beneath me, felt hands beneath my neck and hip, rolling and lifting, and then I was airborne, and the familiar scent of Roth filled my nostrils, the achingly sweet sensation of his chest at my cheek, and we were on the bed and he had me cradled in his arms, clutched close.

"Kyrie…Kyrie…." His voice was a raspy, grating murmur, thick with emotion and pitched low, barely audible. "I'm here, love. I'm here."

I twisted against his chest, looked up at him. His eyes were wet. Roth. My Valentine, the powerful, indomitable Valentine Roth…was crying. For me? For himself? For us? He didn't wipe the tears away as they trickled down his cheeks. One tear…two. Three. Four. Unchecked. His eyes were red, unblinking, staring out over my head. His chest rose and fell as if he was fighting a battle he knew he couldn't win.

I touched my palm to his cheek. "Valentine?"

"I fucked it all up. I gave in. I tried to fight it. I knew it was you. I knew what the drug was doing to me was wrong, but I couldn't fight it. And I knew you'd do anything for me. Anything. And you did. You—you took everything I could do to you. I hurt you. I—violated you. Us. I did that to *us*."

"It wasn't you, Valentine—"

"I couldn't stop."

I sat up straighter, stared into his eyes. Looked deep into myself. "Valentine, listen. Please listen. What happened on the boat? Nothing happened that we haven't done before, right? Did I ask you to stop?"

"No, not after—"

"Exactly. It wasn't entirely you, and I get that. But I love you. I love you so much. I don't hate you. I don't feel violated by you."

"I know." He had to pause to breathe, to swallow, to blink. "And I love you. But…what happens now? With us?"

He was supposed to tell *me* that. "I don't know."

"I feel like…like something is broken between us."

"No." My voice was so small, I wasn't sure Roth heard me. I said it louder. "No, Roth. You can't think that way. You can't let her win. You love me. I love you. That's all that matters."

"Is love enough?"

"It has to be," I said. "It *has* to be. She can't win, Roth. She can't. We can't let her." I sucked in a deep breath, let it out slowly. "I didn't risk death and see men killed and cross the world to find you, only to lose you like this. Only to lose *us* to her fucked-up games."

"Every time I close my eyes, I'm there in that room. I haven't really slept since then. Not really. Every time I do, I dream of her. Of being waterboarded. Of being raped. Of feeling her on me, feeling her skin. I see her hair, and her fake breasts. I feel her fingernails on my skin. I probably have scars from her nails digging into my chest. I feel it all over again, all of it. I can't sleep. I can't even try."

"God, Valentine. How could she? *Why?*" I let the tears slide freely down my cheeks.

He shrugged, faking an insouciance I in no way believed. "Because she could. She wanted me. She felt she owned me." He rubbed at his chest. "She's a fucking animal."

I couldn't help it. I touched my lips to his chest. Tenderly, with butterfly gentility, I kissed his skin, the scars where her fingers had left marks on him. I leaned over him, not straddling him, just lying beside him and kissing his chest. All over, inch by inch. I smoothed my palms over his skin, tracing the ridges of his ribs, the furrows of his muscular abdomen, kissed his neck. He was tensed all over, unmoving, not breathing.

"Kyrie…."

"Yes, Valentine. It's me. It's me. Look at me. Feel me. It's me." I kissed his cheek. The corner of his mouth. His forehead. Beside his nose. His eye, so gently, feeling the lid flutter beneath my lips. Then the other corner of his mouth. "Did she do this, baby? Did she kiss you this way?"

He shook his head. "No," he whispered, barely audible.

I kissed him, feeling the chapped surface of his mouth against mine. "These are *my* lips against yours. Do you feel me? Do you know me?" I pulled back, and his eyes were closed, expression taut and pained. "Open your eyes, Valentine Roth, and look at me. See me. *Me*."

His eyes flicked open, haunted cerulean the same shade as the Mediterranean fixing on mine. "Kyrie. I see you, darling. I see you. But…."

"What? But what?"

"When you kiss me, when you touch me, it hurts. I feel her. I focus on you, but all I feel is *her*." He shot up off the bed, strode shirtless across the room, and touched the panel beside the door to the balcony.

The entire wall of glass slid soundlessly aside into a pocket, letting in the blare and honk and shout and laugh and clamor of Manhattan dozens of stories below. The sun was setting, framed between the endless towers of glass and mirrored steel. Roth stood gripping the railing of the balcony in both hands, a familiar posture. His shoulders slumped, his head hanging.

I stifled a heart-wrenching, gut-wracking sob as the man I loved walked away from me, every line of his body hard and conflicted and taut. I stared at him, watched him, and refused to look away until exhaustion took its toll, pulling me under like a riptide.

I woke to the sounds of the city, a breeze wafting over me. The bed beside me was empty. Night had fallen long ago. I sat up slowly, stiff and sore. My heart ached. I didn't even get that moment of forgetting, the split-second illusion that everything was okay. I wanted that moment; I needed it. I glanced at the balcony, saw Roth sitting in one of the chairs, feet up on the railing, still shirtless in a pair of blue jeans, barefoot. I stood up, stretched the kinks out of my back and neck. I was still wearing the same clothes I'd been wearing in Alexandria, despite several days of travel. It didn't matter, though. Not then. Not in that moment.

I smelled him as I approached him, the Scotch on his breath. He peered up at me as I slid between the back of his chair and the wall, and took the seat beside him. He had the bottle in one hand, a rocks glass in the other, a bucket of melting ice on the table, along with a second glass, empty and clean. I took the empty glass, clinked four cubes of ice into it, and pried the glass from Roth's hand, poured until it was nearly overflowing.

I took a sip, hissed and winced at the burn, then took another sip, which went down more smoothly. A third sip morphed the burn into a warming glow. We sat drinking Scotch in silence, in the relative darkness of night, Manhattan ever wakeful and busy and endless around us.

The bottle was three-fourths gone, and I suspected he'd been out here drinking most of the night. I didn't know what time it was, and I didn't care.

"'M a little sloshed, I'm afraid." His voice was slurred, a low stumbling growl from beside me. "A lot, actually. Probably couldn't stand up even if I tried."

"That's okay." I took another long sip. "I might join you."

He took a drink, ice clinking and clattering. He twisted his head sloppily to gaze at me. "Why are you still here?" He enunciated his words very carefully, precisely, his accent bleeding through more strongly than ever.

"Because I love you. I chose you. Remember? You brought me here. You made me yours. And then you told me your secret. And even knowing that you killed my father, I still chose you. I couldn't stay away then, and I can't stay away now. I won't. Not just can't, Roth. *Won't.* I won't abandon you, especially not now. How could I claim to love you if I walked away now? You need me, now more than ever."

"Never needed anyone before. Not anyone. Father kicked me out, disowned me. And damn him, I survived. Nearly didn't, a few times. Nearly got myself killed more than once. I hadn't a clue what I was doing when I started running guns for Vitaly. I got into that by accident, you should know." He glanced at me, blinked blearily. "I never intended to get into that. I started out like I told you, buying fishing boats and real estate, that sort of thing. And then I was out for drinks with a man who was rumored to have several apartment blocks in Moscow for sale. We were in…Kiev? Maybe Kiev. And he—this man, he asked me if I wanted to make a quick and easy ten grand. Well, of course, who doesn't? And when he said all I'd have to do was take a suitcase from Kiev to Istanbul, I knew it was no good. But I'd just had a sale fall through, a big one. And I owed money. I'd borrowed, so I owed. I needed that ten grand. So I did it."

Roth took another long drink, emptying his glass, then set the tumbler down on the table between us.

"I met Gina two weeks later," he continued. "In Athens. She took me home to her apartment. I remember standing outside the door of her flat in Athens, wondering what I was getting into. I'd seen the craziness in her eyes already. You couldn't miss it, even then. Two drinks together, and I knew she was dangerous. But I went into her apartment with her anyway. Later, after we'd fucked, she lay beside me and looked at me. I remember what she said. I remember it verbatim. 'You know, Val, now that you've fucked me, you can't ever leave me. I won't let you.'"

He blinked and lifted his hand to his mouth as if he'd forgotten that'd put down his now-empty cup.

"Gina, she was fucked up in head, in the things she wanted us to do. In bed, I mean. I'm quite honestly too drunk to be tactful right now, so I'm sorry. She wanted to tie me up. She wanted to blindfold me and do all sorts of nasty shit. Not really true BDSM, just…she demanded total control. Wanted total subservience from me, sexually and otherwise." He ducked his head, staring at his knees. "I went along with a lot of what she wanted. Most of it. I drew the line at a few things. She got off on pain. Giving, and receiving. I'd let her hurt me, but I wouldn't hurt her. I wouldn't let her peg me. She went mental when I said no to that. I gave her control, though. I let her have it. It killed me, deep down. I hated it. Hated her more with every day that passed.

"Every time I did what she wanted, it was because I was afraid of her, afraid of her father. Not of her physically, but of of her unpredictability. Like, if I didn't do what she wanted, I went to sleep nervous. I could wake up hogtied. I did once, actually. Went to bed after an argument and woke up hogtied. Slipped me a mickey in my drink, but I was already drunk and angry and didn't feel it. Woke up tied hand and foot, hands to feet behind my back. She left me like that for hours. Because I wouldn't…god, so filthy to think of now, but she wanted me to felch her. I wouldn't. Fuck no, I wouldn't. Bad enough argu-ment, I worried I'd just never wake up. She'd slit my throat in my sleep." He shot a sidelong glance at me. "Does my need for control make sense now, love?"

I thought of the times he'd given me control sexually, let me do what I wanted to him. Now, hearing this story, it made so much more sense. Made the trust he'd shown me that much more heady. I could only nod, trying to hold back emotion. "Yeah. It makes a lot of sense. Makes me love you even more for letting me have control the way you have."

He nodded. "That was hard. That day in the shower? You remember that? What you did with your finger? I always, always drew the line at that. Letting her do that kind of thing to me. I never would. It was just...my personal line. And she hated it. It made her so, *so* angry every time. But I let you do that. I gave that to *you*. Because...I knew you. I understood you. I knew you wouldn't hurt me, wouldn't embarrass me. Wouldn't demand something you didn't think I'd mind giving."

"Never, baby. I love you. I love you so much."

"I know." He watched me empty my glass and pour another. "Catching up quick, aren't you, love?" In all the time I'd known him, he'd never sounded so English. I'd heard him sound formal, almost stuffy, precise, arch and crisp. I'd heard him sound gruff and harsh and vulgar. But this? This was a side of Valentine that I never knew existed.

"Yeah, getting there," I said.

Silence sat thick between us. And then he twisted his head to look at me, a strange expression on his face. "I'd kill for you. You know that, right? When they come, I'll kill them. All of them. As many as they send."

I swallowed hard. "I know. I wish we could just… sell everything. Take your money and go. Buy a big boat and live out there. Like we were. Just you and me. They'd never find us. I'll live that life with you."

He shook his head. "I wish we could, too. But Kyrie, I've—I've put this off long enough. Hidden from them long enough. Avoided. Pretended I didn't know they were watching and waiting. I have to end this." His gaze cleared, the haze of alcohol burning away under the intensity of his expression. "Let me hide you. Send you with Harris somewhere they'll never find you. Let me handle this. Handle *her*. I'll take care of things, and then we can—"

"No." I stood up. "No, Valentine. Not happening. I'm not leaving your side. I don't have anywhere to go. I have no one and nothing but you. I'm staying."

"What about Cal? And Layla?"

I shrugged miserably. "I love them. Of course I do. But my brother? Cal has his own life. He doesn't know anything about any of this, and it's better that way. He's a college kid. He plays beer pong and hazes new frat pledges and studies for midterms. And Layla? I don't want her involved. I go anywhere near her, all of this could spill over and put her in danger. She's my best friend. Closer than a sister. And I just can't put her at risk."

Roth nodded. Stood up, put his hands on my shoulders for balance. "Okay, then."

I waited, but he didn't say anything else. "Okay? All that, and all you have to say now is 'okay'?"

He frowned down at me. "What do you want me to say, Kyrie?"

"I don't know." I turned away, watched the red taillights and white headlights streaming in opposite directions far beneath me. My voice was small and broken. "Anything. Tell me you love me. Tell me it'll be okay."

His silence was long and fraught. "I can't tell you it'll be okay. I won't lie to you."

I turned in place and put my back to the railing. I waited, watched him. His eyes were lucid and searching me. He was still drunk, but in the dark, depressed, hopeless stage. "That's it, then?"

"I'm drunk, Kyrie. I haven't slept in days. Haven't showered in longer. I'm a mess. I'm fucked up. I don't know what I'm feeling or how to deal with it. I'm scared to sleep. I'm scared to touch you. To let you touch me. I'm…useless right now."

I let out a long, tremulous breath. Summoned my courage. My determination. "Come on." I took his hand, led him inside.

He followed me, let me pull him into the bathroom. He stood still, eyes narrow and hooded, watching me as I gingerly unbuttoned his pants. "What are you doing, Kyrie?"

"You're taking a shower, and I'm going to help you. I need one, too. Let's take this slow, okay? One moment, one hour, one day at a time."

I lowered the zipper, tugged the denim down. I knelt, helped him step out, let him steady himself with a hand on my shoulder. He stood before me in a pair of gray Calvin Klein boxer briefs, muscular, toned, and beautiful. I turned on the water, set it to the hottest it would go, and let it steam up the bathroom. I stood in front of him, still in my jeans and T-shirt. I wanted him to reach for me, to help me out of my shirt, out of my pants. But he didn't. He just stood there, and my heart broke a little. I peeled my shirt off slowly, never taking my eyes from his. I unbuttoned and unzipped my jeans, stepping out of them. I waited in my bra and underwear, watching as his chest filled and lowered with deep breaths, his eyes moving over my body.

Not looking away from his conflicted blue gaze, I reached up behind my back and freed the hooks of my bra. Shrugging out of it, I let the undergarment fall to the marble. Tugged the waistband of my panties down with my thumbs, let the underwear fall to the floor, and stepped free. And then I was naked in front of him, and his hands were twitching at his sides, his brows lowered, muscles heavy, fists clenched, chest heaving.

I waited.

He took a step toward me, and my heart lifted, my pulse beating just a little harder. "Kyrie…."

"Roth. I'm here. I'm yours. Don't be afraid."

"I'm not afraid," he growled.

"Then touch me. Prove it."

"I have to prove myself to you?"

I shut down the hurt. "No. That's not what I meant. You won't hurt me. I won't hurt you. I'm not her. You're not there anymore. You're with me. You're safe." I stepped toward him. Put my hands on his waist, smoothed them up his back, trying to block out the pain in my heart at the way he flinched at my touch. "It's *me*, Valentine. You can trust me, you know that. I love you. I just…I need you to love me back."

He blinked, squeezed his eyes shut, spoke through gritted teeth. "I'm trying, Kyrie. I'm fucking trying, okay?"

# 12
## HOME

*VALENTINE*

THE WAR WITHIN ME WAS A FURIOUS ONSLAUGHT OF NEED versus fear versus memory versus nightmare. She stood naked in front of me, tanned taut skin, lush curves, long blonde hair sleep- and wind-mussed, eyes reddened and wet with tears. She was trying to hide her emotions from me, trying to be strong for me, but I could read her like a book. She couldn't hide from me, and I hated that she felt like she had to. She needed me. She wanted me. What had happened between us on the boat… had fucked her up, no matter what she said. But she was soldiering on. Forgiving me. But yet…she doubted. I felt it. I saw it in her.

It hadn't been right. She'd done it for *me*; she'd given herself to me because she'd seen my need. But that hadn't been me. Hadn't been *us*. It was something I couldn't wrap my brain around, something I couldn't adequately define or explain to myself.

And now here she was, naked and willing. Telling me she loved me. Begging me to touch her. To love her. And Jesus, I wanted to. *Needed* to. I needed her. I had to remind both of us of who I was. I had to know Gina hadn't somehow stripped me of my capacity for love and gentility and passion; just as importantly, I had to know she hadn't robbed me of my strength or my masculinity.

But I felt fear. Deeply rooted, powerful, gripping, paralyzing.

Fear isn't manly. When I ran from Gina and her father, I had some money and my name. I never used a fake name. Never pretended to be anyone other than myself. Yet when I ran from the Karahalios clan, I was running not just from the specter of death, from what Vitaly wanted me to do, from what Gina wanted me to do, but from my own lack of control with Gina. I'd acquiesced to her in so many ways. I'd given in again and again. I'd done things, let her do things I hadn't wanted to. All because I had been afraid. More than I'd ever reveal to Kyrie, or even admit to myself. I had buried all that as deep as it would go once I was free of Gina, and I'd left it there, buried and denied, for almost a decade. And now it was all coming up. Coming back. Scenes from the past flashing before my eyes.

I was paralyzed.

Not just by what Gina had done to me while I was cuffed to that bed. I could get over that. I'd resisted her. She hadn't broken me. I held on, held out.

No, the real nightmares came from the memory of nights in years past, nights I'd spent wondering what Gina would make me do next. I'd been just a kid. Not a virgin when we met, not by any means. Not innocent, but in no way prepared for the madness and insatiable cruelty of a woman like Gina. I'd been afraid of her. Damn right, I had been. Still was. Evil I do not fear. Death I do not fear. Violence and blood and torture I do not fear. The unpredictable blood lust, the cruelty for the sake of sadism, and the way she savored fear, delighted in agony, relished manipulation and madness—*that* I feared.

So, standing there with Kyrie naked and waiting for me to be her man—the man I was, the man I had been and should be, all I could feel was the fear of bygone days. Remembered fear. The feeling of filth on my skin after Gina finally left me. Wanting to scrub my skin until it bled to get the film of self-loathing off.

When I finally escaped to New York, I hadn't touched a woman for more than a year. Couldn't look at a woman, couldn't bear to be touched, kissed, or spoken to unless it was for business. And the first time I did finally take a woman, it had been an escort. A prostitute. The terms had been laid out ahead of time. There would be no date. No illusion of romance. She would not speak. She would not touch me. If she wanted me to stop, she would say my name: "Mr. Roth." At which point she would receive half-pay and would leave immediately. The first time, I'd been a bastard. I paid her triple. I hadn't hurt her, but I'd been gruff, harsh, demanding. I'd done what I needed to do to relieve the ache, and then I sent her home. I hadn't spoken a word. It had been brusque, cold, and cruel. The next time, with the next prostitute, I'd forced myself to go slower, to be kinder, gentler. As time went on, I learned a balance. I established my demands at the outset. Made it abundantly clear that this was to be a one-sided transaction, nothing more. It was about me taking what I needed and being done. Then one of the escorts broke the rules. She kissed me. She touched me. She'd refused to pretend to come. They all pretended; I knew that, and I didn't care. This one, she didn't pretend. She let me do what I wished, and then she'd…kissed me. Asked me if I wanted to try again, but this time not for business, no money changing hands. Just a man and woman in bed together. She wanted to come, too, she said.

I went with it. I didn't follow her lead, but instead of merely taking what I wanted, I paid attention to her physical cues and tried to make her come. In so doing, I discovered a deeper pleasure. Something hotter and more intense than my own orgasm. Making that escort—whose name I never even asked—feel pleasure gave me something, did something to me.

When the night ended and the girl finally went home, I sat on the balcony of my high-rise, thinking. Reflecting. And I decided to embark on a quest. Instead of taking pleasure, I would give it. Under my terms, under my control. So I sent the escort a check for half a million dollars and a note thanking her for teaching me a valuable lesson.

And then I met Kyrie.

There had been other women in the years between that first meeting and sending Kyrie the first check. But when I made my decision, when I knew without a doubt that I had to make her mine, I stopped seeing anyone else. I cut ties with the escort service. Erased all the phone numbers of willing and discreet women I had on call. Over a year, not a single touch, not a look. By the time I had Kyrie sleeping in my guest room, I was crazed with need. I'd built up Kyrie in my mind. Made her into this… goddess. This was a woman who would change my life, a woman without compare. I made her into something no person could ever live up to.

And then…Kyrie did the impossible. She not only lived up to my expectations, but she shattered them. Defied them. Surpassed them and made me need her all the more desperately. God. And then I told her my secret, expecting it would be the end. She'd left. I'd wallowed in despair. But she came back, and she pushed me. Gave me life back. Healed me. Made me believe in love.

I'd told her I loved her, but I hadn't known what love was. I *needed* her. *Wanted* her. But love? What was that? I didn't know.

She'd taught me. She was still teaching me.

Her voice in the present shook me out of my silence. I'd been lost in my thoughts for who knew how long, the water from the shower sending steam billowing around us.

"Roth?" Her voice was soft, hesitant. She held out her hand to me, an invitation. "Come in the shower with me. We don't have to do anything. Just be near me. You don't have to do anything or say anything. Just…*be* here with me, okay?" The resignation in her voice sliced deeply, cut me down where I stood.

I was failing her.

I was still in my underwear, but she pulled me into the shower anyway, and I let her. She adjusted the water so it wasn't scalding, and then backed under the spray, facing me, letting the hot water stream down her back and onto her hair, plastering the blonde locks to her skull and pasting them to her cheek. She tilted her head back and ran her hands through her hair, scraping it backward, letting the water run over her face and into her mouth. I couldn't look away. I watched as she spat a mouthful of water out and watched as it merged on her chest with the sluicing rivulets from the showerhead above. I watched as she twisted in place, letting the hot water beat on her perfect skin till it was pink. I watched as she found the shampoo, my eyes following her curves as she bent to take the bottle out from beneath the bench, and I watched as she lathered the shampoo into her hair.

I was cold, getting wet from the mist and the steam without being under the hot spray. My boxer-briefs were wet, molded to my skin.

I watched, but didn't touch. A thousand thoughts boiled in my mind: Did I *deserve* to touch her? Had I violated her? Had I raped her despite the fact that she'd been willing? Was that possible? It didn't make sense, but there it was. I felt as if I'd somehow violated the woman I loved. Broken her trust, hurt her. Broken something between us.

And yes, I felt the stigma of what Gina had done to me. The shame, the helplessness. Shame, too, at the fact that even now, through the guilt and the confusion and the fear, I knew that the sex we'd had on the boat, when I was in the grip of the drug, had been the most wildly intense sex we'd ever had. And I think Kyrie knew it, too, adding to her internal conflict.

But there she was, telling me she needed me. Telling me she wanted my touch. By hesitating, by allowing doubt to rule me, I was letting Gina win. I was giving in to weakness by letting my fears and doubts keep me paralyzed.

Kyrie deserved more from me.

She rinsed the shampoo from her hair and worked in conditioner, and then began lathering shower gel onto her skin. She started at her shoulders, worked down her arms, her waist. I swallowed hard, watching her.

Her sensual beauty cut through my fears, her blatant need for me shredded my confusion, and the vulnerability in her eyes slashed away my doubt.

She swept the soapy washcloth over her breasts, scrubbing at the pink tips, sliding her slippery palms under one breast, and then the other. My throat swelled shut, and my heart began to beat. For the first time in a scrambled frenzy of days, I felt my pulse hammer hard, felt heat in my skin, felt desire hardening me, and I wasn't afraid of it.

I had to take back some semblance of myself.

*I am Valentine Roth,* I told myself. *I am in control. I will not be reduced to a weakling by the likes of Gina Karahalios.*

I forced myself to believe it. I felt it, and clung to the flimsy scrim of determination.

I met Kyrie's pale blue eyes with mine, letting her see into me, not hiding the roil of conflict, not hiding the hunger, the need, the fear, the uncertainty.

It was all there, but I was in control of it.

I had to be.

I clenched my fists and released them, letting out a slow breath. I pushed down the sopping-wet boxer-briefs and kicked them aside. The wet fabric hit the marble wall with a *slap,* hung there for a moment, and then slid to the floor. Kyrie's eyes widened, and her nostrils flared, and she froze in place, the washcloth hovering at her belly.

I took a step toward her, finding my voice. "Don't stop now, Kyrie." My voice was low, a growled murmur. "Keep washing yourself for me."

Her lower lip trembled and her mouth slightly parted, her eyes freighted with the same weltering myriad of emotion that boiled in mine. She ran her tongue along her upper lip, not a seductive move, but one of doubt. I stood mere inches from her, the peaks of her breasts a hair's breadth from my chest. If she took a deep breath, our flesh would meet. But she didn't. She wasn't breathing, and neither was I.

This was, we both knew, a moment that would define us.

It would either remake us, or it would destroy us.

She touched the washcloth to her stomach, moved it in small circles, her eyes on me. I could see the hope blooming in the blue pools of her gaze, and it was such a delicate flower, so fragile, such a slight thing, needing a gentle touch to foster it into life. I moved to stand beneath the stream of the water, and her gaze raked over my body, head to toe and back to my crotch. Under her gaze, I felt myself twitch, harden, and burgeon into full erection. She blinked hard and squeezed the washcloth, put a dollop of shower gel onto the white fabric and squeezed and wrung.

And then she extended her hand toward me. "I think I'm clean," she said, her voice tremulous.

I felt the washcloth touch my chest, and if I wasn't breathing before, all capacity for breath left my body in that instant, feeling the washcloth on my skin, feeling one of her hands on my chest, slathering the soap across my skin. Her other hand slipped up to slide across the ridge of my shoulder, resting with her thumb near my clavicle and her fingers at the base of my neck. The washcloth arced over my chest, down my side to my hip. Her head tilted up again, her eyes fixing on mine, and then she leaned in, slowly, slowly, eyes lifted to mine, watching my reaction. The water rained down hot, scouring away the soap. Her lips touched my skin, and my heart stopped beating. I felt it stutter in its rhythm, and then she kissed me again, sliding her lips over my heart, and it resumed beating with the gentle warm slide of her lips, pounding harder  than before. I blinked against the water on my face and watched her kiss my chest over my heart, once, twice, three times. She slid the washcloth around to my back and ran it up and down, up and down, all over my back, leaning in against me and kissing my chest, my shoulder, the hollow of my neck, slow kisses, careful kisses, switching from hand to hand, caressing my back with the soap and her hand and the washcloth.

My throat was thick, a hard lump lodged there.

Kyrie let the water rinse away the soap, and she moved around behind me, and I felt her breasts slick and soft and wet and firm against my back. Her hand moved over my chest, over my sternum. I leaned back, pressing my back to her front, and she breathed against my ear, her lips at the shell of my ear, not whispering or kissing, just there, breathing, a presence. The washcloth moved to my hip, across my belly to the other hip.

God, the touch of her lips, the soft heat of her flesh against mine, her presence, calm and comforting, the love and the hope and the determination exuding from her…I soaked all this up and let it spread like a healing salve over the wounds within me.

I sat down on the bench, and Kyrie moved around to stand in front of me. My hands rested on my thighs. We spent a long moment in the hot stream of water, my gaze roaming from her face to her breasts and down to her core, to her thighs, hers moving over me in the same way, as if relearning my body, my features, as if seeing me for the first time.

"I need—" Kyrie began, but couldn't finish, her voice giving out.

"What, Kyrie? Tell me." I looked up at her.

"Your hands. On—on me. I need you to—to touch me. Please. Anywhere. Just…hold me—touch me…." Her voice shook, cracked. "*Please.*"

As if her plea was a key unlocking invisible shackles around my wrists, my hands lifted and came to rest on her hips. She breathed out, a gasp of relief. Her eyes closed, and I could feel her trembling all over. Nerves? Fear? Need?

It was all three, I sensed.

I slid my palms up from her hips to her waist, and she rested her hands on my shoulders. I ran my palms across her back, smearing the water on her skin, tasting shower spray on my lips. I closed my eyes, and felt myself falling forward. Falling. Falling. My mouth parted, and my lips touched her flesh, hot, silken, wet, the skin of her stomach under my mouth. A kiss. Her voice scraped out in a breathless moan, almost a sob. I moved my hands back down her spine to hold her hips once more, and my lips slid up her flesh to kiss her ribs, and then between her perfect breasts, and now my hands were holding her to me, cupping her ass. I wasn't aware of grabbing her there, but I had, at some point, and she was leaning into me, into my kiss. I massaged the muscle and flesh of her ass, kneading, caressing.

I rested my head on her stomach and let out a breath. "Kyrie. God, my Kyrie." It was a prayer of relief.

"Yes, Valentine. *Yours.* Your Kyrie."

"Why?" I kissed her again, right between her breasts, and then looked up at her. "*Why?*"

She knew what I was asking. "Because you made me yours. Because I *want* to be yours. I love knowing I belong to you." She cradled my head in her hands, fingers curling in the hair at my nape, thumbs grazing my cheekbones, my ears. Tipped my face back, so I was looking up into her tumult-rife blue gaze. "And Valentine…you're *mine*. You don't belong to her. You belong to me. Don't you?" That last was equal parts plea and demand and declaration.

"*Yes….*" I breathed. "I do. Completely."

I was gazing up at her from between her breasts, and now she took a deep breath, swelling her chest and letting it out. Her eyes remained on mine as she shifted, twisted her torso just slightly, and now her nipple brushed across my face, slid down, and fit between my lips. I took the taut peak into my mouth and tasted her, and my eyes fell closed, my hands still splayed on the firm, generous bubble of her backside.

The taste of her skin, the heat of the water, her hands on my face and in my hair…my universe had shrunk to these things.

I gave in, letting my need take over.

Letting my love take over.

I twisted, pulled at Kyrie's hips to bring her to a seat on the bench, and I moved to my knees in front of her. Our faces were at eye level then, and she spread her knees apart, pulled me into the "V" between her thighs and wrapped her arms around my neck. Crushed me to her, our bodies clasped together, my arms going around her waist, hands on

her back, in her wet hair. Water splattered on us, still
hot. Time was forgotten. Everything was forgotten
as she palmed my cheeks and our eyes met, hers wet
with tears, mine wavering and vulnerable.

She kissed me. Or, I kissed her. Both at once,
perhaps.

It was not a deep, endless kiss. It was a burst of
passion, a momentary eruption of need between us.
And then I removed my lips from hers, bent, and
kissed the slope of her left breast, and then the right,
and then took her right nipple into my mouth. I
felt rather than saw her head tip back on her neck,
and she held tight to my skull with shaking hands,
fingers trembling in the wet plaster of my hair. The
other nipple then, a reverent kiss, tongue sliding
gently over the pebbled peak. And downward, a kiss
to her belly.

"Roth…?"

I didn't answer. I couldn't. My mouth was busy
kissing, sliding my lips across her wet skin, kissing
her hip, the crease near her thigh. The muscle of
her quadriceps, then in and around to the soft inner
skin. I knew by taste and by touch the sweetness and
silk of her core, knew indelibly each fold, each and
every millimeter of flesh. She shivered, sighed, and
let her thighs fall apart. Giving in.

Trusting.

How could she still trust me? But she did, and I wouldn't question it.

But I would earn it.

My thumbs traveled delicately from the apex of her vagina down the slick warm crevice of her opening, down the seam, parting her ever so gently.

A kiss, at first. Just a kiss.

She sighed, a deep frantic breath.

"I love you, Kyrie." It was a murmur, a muttered admission. Barely audible, perhaps drowned by the noise of the shower.

She knew. But I had to show her.

Nearly falling backward on the bench, holding on to my head, she flicked her eyes open and craned her neck to look at me, a panicked need on her features. "What did you say, Roth?"

I looked up at her. "I said, I *love* you."

She seemed to melt somehow, inside. "Oh, Valentine. Valentine. My love." Her eyes spilled tears, and she swallowed hard.

I kissed her other thigh then, as I had the first, outside to inside, my thumbs caressing her soft, damp skin. She breathed out hard, sucked in a breath, and clung to me. The next time my lips touched Kyrie's flesh, they pressed against her opening, and my tongue parted her and slid in. She gasped, and I tasted her essence. She clutched my head, my face, and I swept my tongue up and in, lapping at her, parting her further. The marble was hard beneath my knees, but I didn't care. The water was still hot but beginning to cool off. I didn't care. I tasted her, my thumbs keeping her spread apart for my tongue. I found the small, hard nub of her clitoris, and I tasted that as well, and this time she whimpered, her fingers curling feverishly into my hair. I flicked my tongue against her clit again, and again, and her hips moved in time with my tongue.

I slid the middle finger of my left hand down the seam of her pussy, and then in, pushing in, and in, and she leaned back and lifted her hips, expelling a harsh breath. I delved into her slick warmth with one finger, curling up and in, sliding out, then back in. Kyrie's grip on my head tightened, and she pulled me closer, sucking in a breath and letting it out with a moan.

"Valentine, oh god. That feels good, baby. Keep doing that."

I glanced up at her as I slid my tongue against her clit, and her eyes met mine. Her gaze was hooded, heated. I held her stare as I slipped my ring finger in beside the middle, and then found the rippled rough patch of skin high inside against the inner ridge, caressed it, suckling her clit between my lips.

She bucked against me, whimpering. Pulled my face against her core, and I tongued her in a slow rhythm, speeding up with tongue and fingers as her writhing turned frantic, as her gasps turned desperate. When her ragged breathing and bucking hips reached a frenzy, telling me how close she was, I slowed nearly to a stop.

"No, *no*, Valentine, don't stop, *please* don't stop. I need to come. I need you to make me come. Let me come, baby, please."

"You'll come when I'm ready to let you come."

She moaned in protest. "Now. Please. I'm right there!"

But I didn't let her. I stopped entirely, withdrawing and shutting off the water. Unfolding a huge white towel, I wrapped Kyrie in it, lifted her into my arms, and carried her to the bed. I laid her down gently and used the excess fabric to dry her off head to toe. Her skin was flushed, her cheeks reddened, her breasts rising and falling rapidly, her knees pressed together. Her eyes were wide and tender and vulnerable and desperate. She arched her spine off the bed, rubbing her thighs together. She reached for me, sitting up.

"I need you," she murmured.

"I need you, too," I responded. "More than you could ever know."

Kyrie tugged the towel out from underneath herself and handed it to me, watched as I dried myself and then tossed it aside. I crawled onto the bed, scraping my palms across her tits and down her belly, and then I gripped her thighs. She let out a sigh, spread her thighs apart for me. She reached for me, sliding her fingers into the wet hair above my ear.

When I moved my face nearer to her core, she shook her head. "No, Valentine. No more of that. Please. Just make love to me."

I paused, hesitated, and she sat forward, taking my face in her hands. She tugged at me gently but insistently until I moved upward, leaning over her. "You don't want me to—"

She didn't let me finish, her palms still on my face. "No. I don't need that. All I need is you. I just need *us.*"

All I could do was kiss her. It wasn't just a kiss, though. It was more. It was a plea. An admission of need, a declaration of love.

When you live with someone, your relationship inevitably moves past the honeymoon, exploratory stage where each touch and kiss is new and thrilling. It becomes more intense in some ways, though. The newness fades, replaced by familiarity. You know how she'll respond. You know, just by the way she looks at you, that she wants you. You don't need the buildup, the kiss that moves into desperation, the slide of palm over skin that becomes a caress and then a frantic removal of clothes. You don't always need the foreplay. You look at each other, and you know. You just *know*. You reach for each other, and you merge. Rhythm is instinctive. You breathe in synch. Your hips meet, hands find flesh, foreheads touch, eyes flutter and flicker and lock. You slide into her. You don't need to look or guide yourself in, you just fit. You match. She lifts her hips just so, and you're there, and she lets out a sweet sigh of love as you fill her, and then everything fades and you find your rhythm and your completion together, and you don't need to say a word.

Kyrie and I had that. Months of traveling the world together gave us the kind of intimacy and familiarity with each other that usually takes years to develop. I knew her reactions; I knew just by the expression on her face when she needed me. We made love silently much of the time. No words, no frantic cursing. Just bodies moving in perfect synchronicity.

I think her favorite moments, however, were the times when I took her exactly the way I wanted her, when I didn't ask her what she wanted, when it wasn't sweet or tender or thoughtful. When I just *took*. She loved those moments. She blossomed in those moments—she came alive, responded with fervency. She not only took what I gave—or rather, succumbed to my giving—but she pushed me, demanding more, the flames of fierce sexuality fanning hotter and hotter.

She needed that now.

Darkness fallen around us, the sounds of the unsleeping city loud beyond the window. We both needed to know, regardless of the hell we'd endured, regardless of what was still coming, that Kyrie was mine, and I was hers, and we would have each other and be okay.

So I kissed her. To reclaim us.

I kissed her and tasted the fear on her lips, tasted the tears, and breathed in the tortured doubt. I kissed her, and it wasn't a sweet kiss. It wasn't a slow-burning kiss. It was fiery and demanding. I let the desperate determination saturate me, let my bone-deep need to retake control bleed out of me, and I knew she tasted it on me, felt it, breathed it.

I was lying on my back, and she was on her side next to me, her breasts crushed against my ribs and her mouth demanding on mine. I gave her all of me in the kiss, let my hands catch in her hair, clutch her skull and press her closer, press her into the kiss, the kiss…. It expanded and deepened and unfolded, fracturing into a million scintillating pieces, neither of us breathing yet not needing to, needing only the kiss, our lips and our mouths and our heartbeats and our hands. Her palm strayed across my chest, arced down my waist, and never ever before had I felt the ache of touch, felt the burden of needing her so fiercely. I could only kiss her and swallow my fears, drown my nightmares in the sweetness of her lips and the influx of her breath in my mouth as we both broke to gasp and blink and clutch at each other.

The city outside our tower was silent, forgotten. Muted.

Stars, atoms, pain, orbits, politics, enemies…all faded into nothingness.

There was only Kyrie. Only her mouth devouring mine, her hair cascading around my face, tickling my cheekbones and pooling on the pillow.

I had to hold her. My hands hungered for her. I found her skin, feathered my touch across her spine, around her shoulders, down her waist and the ridges of her ribs padded by lush flesh. I curved my palm around her hip, caressed her ass and her thigh and her arm and her hand on my cheek, and the kiss stumbled and tripped and burst open into something beyond kissing, moving from starlight to nova, from incendiary explosion to atomic detonation.

She was touching me as well, her needing fingers tracing my biceps and my chest and the arc of my hip and then descending to my legs, the hair on my thigh and the curled thatch of hair around my cock, and now her hand wrapped around me in a slow, hesitant caress. I gasped, breaking the kiss, my heart hammering at the feel of her hand on me.

A stroke then, a sweet gentle downward sweep stoking the fires in my belly. The frenzy of my heart-beat becoming tympanic thunder, and her teeth pulled at my lower lip and her knee slid onto my thigh.

This was a ferocious yet fragile thing between us.

Kyrie's hand left my cock, and her knee pressed into the mattress on the other side of my body, and the "V" of her spread thighs cradled my waist. She was above me, and I was panting and panicking, instantly weak and gasping and frantic, fists in the sheet and eyes squeezed shut.

"—Breathe, Roth…breathe for me. Come on, baby. It's okay. It's me. It's me. Look at me, baby. Look at me. Can you open your eyes?" I heard her voice, but all I could feel was the weight of Gina on me, all I could feel was the helplessness, shackled for her pleasure, at the mercy of a woman who had none.

Palms on my cheeks, thumbs beneath my eyes, wiping gently. Lips on my cheekbone, my jaw. "It's me, Valentine. It's Kyrie. Open your eyes and see me. Look at me."

I heard her voice. I knew it was Kyrie. But the panic didn't allow me to respond.

I fought it.

*I am Valentine Roth, and I am in control.*

Shaking all over, trembling, gasping raggedly, I forced my eyes open. Saw through the waver of unsteady vision the perfect beauty of Kyrie St. Claire. Not Gina. The weight of her body on top of me was familiar, beautiful. Her hair was blonde and thick and still damp, hanging to one side. Her eyes were blue, deep cerulean, loving and concerned. This was Kyrie. My Kyrie. I made myself stare at her, drank in the beauty of her, soaked up the reality of her here with me. Let her presence sink in, let the truth of now replace the fear of what had been.

I forced my fists to unclench from the sheets, and Kyrie took one of my hands in hers, threaded the fingers of her right hand through my left, the back of my hand against the pillow by my head, her weight resting on our joined hand. And then her left hand merged with my right, and she was leaning over me, hair a curtain blocking out the world.

"You see me, baby?" Her voice was so small, tiny but insistent.

"I see you."

"You know me? It's me."

It was still hard to breathe. I couldn't look away. Didn't dare. The endless blue ocean of her gaze held me, and I willingly let myself drown into her.

"Don't look away from me." She drew her knees up, shins to the mattress, calves under her ass.

"Never." I felt my rabbiting pulse turn to hammering thuds as she lifted her hips.

She writhed on me, sliding her core over my hardening cock. She held my gaze, moving her body in a sinuous rhythm, bringing me to raging erection with the slow, wet slide of her pussy. I couldn't breathe and didn't need to, because she was kissing me and giving me her breath.

"Ready, my love?" She stilled, hovering over me, the tip of my cock nestled between the lips of her pussy.

"Yes…yes."

"Look at me, baby." Her brows drew down, and her mouth hung open.

"I am." I stared up at her, my hands tangled in hers, her breasts swaying so her nipples brushed my chest.

"I love you," she said.

It was a frozen moment in time, the momentary pause before we joined, before our bodies merged, her eyes on mine, the sound of her voice echoing in my ears. And then, before I could respond, before I could summon the three syllables roiling within me, she impaled herself on me.

Kyrie ducked her head and bowed her spine out, letting out a breathy moan and grinding her hips against mine, burying me deep, deep, deep inside her heavenly slick warmth.

I let her move. I let her glide and stroke and moan and grind and slide. I held her hands and stared up into her blueblueblue eyes, and I didn't dare even breathe. She shook, and fought for breath. She shuddered, hovering over me, my cock drawn almost out, her eyes boring and drilling into me, demanding that I *see* her, see her, feel her, feel the cracks between us filling, feel the broken linkage binding us together repairing.

I saw.

I felt.

But I couldn't move. Not like this. Not with her above me. It was a war within me. The wounded portion of my psyche refused to be buried, refused to be ignored, and this, weighted down by the woman I loved, this was not okay. I wasn't over it, I wasn't healed, and pretending wasn't going to work.

I was a man in control. Of myself, of my surroundings, of those whom I employed. Of my life, my emotions, my reactions. I didn't allow anything into my life that would threaten my control. I refused. For ten years, I refused. And then I brought Kyrie to my home, brought her into my tower and let her into my life. That was the beginning of the end of my control. She had a way of worming under my control, wiggling into every crevice of my life, of my soul, of my mind, and taking over. My control, where Kyrie was concerned, was nonexistent.

Being held hostage by Gina, having every scrap of control taken away from me, that had left a deeper scar than I cared to examine. Not just mentally or emotionally or sexually, but in every aspect of my life. Of my sense of self.

I had to reclaim it, but I didn't know how.

Kyrie was a woman who should never be sad. Never feel pain. Never ache, or be lonely, or afraid. She was too beautiful, too perfect, too lively and strong and wonderful for such negativity. Life engendered pain. Living, if you did it properly, left you vulnerable to pain. I'd spent ten years not living. Alive but moving through life empty of vitality, full of purpose but devoid of that spark which makes life worth living. Kyrie had given me that, and I now saw her own spark guttering, darkening, wetted and tamped down.

I couldn't let that stand.

I owed her more than that.

I could foster the spark within her. Fan it into flames, and warm myself on its heat.

Sometimes, I think, when you don't know how to take another step for yourself, you have to focus on someone else, and take the step for them. Live for them. Be strong for them, even when you have so much within yourself in need of healing.

Kyrie collapsed forward, buried her face in my neck, her hands trapped between our chests, her palm to my heartbeat, and she sobbed, her entire body convulsing as she climaxed. "Valentine… *please*…." She lost her voice then, choking and gasping. Her hips drove downward, and then she drew forward, hesitated, fluttered her hips ever so gently, and then pounded down, crying out into my neck. "God, oh god, oh god, Valentine—*fuck,* I need you. I need you. Baby, please, please, I need you."

I slid my palms down her spine, closed my eyes, and drew a breath filled with the scent of her skin and the damp, clean odor of shampoo from her hair. I drew in the scent of Kyrie, filled my hands with the curves of her ass. I breathed her in, caressed her flesh, felt her shuddering above me, heard the plea, and felt the paralysis break.

I lunged upward to a sitting position, Kyrie still impaled on me, and I wrapped my arms around her neck, nipping at the tender hollow at the base of her throat, at the fragile sweep of her neck. Kyrie whimpered, clung to me, snaked her arms around my neck and crushed me closer as I pivoted us together and slid to the edge of the bed. She gasped in surprise when I stood, cupping my hands under her ass, supporting her perfect weight with my hands and with the tension of our joined bodies. Standing, her legs wrapped around my waist, her arms around me, her face buried in my throat, kissing, sucking, biting.

I felt the clench of her pussy around me and reveled in the pulsing squeeze of climaxing muscles. I had to move. Had to fill, and retreat. Had to hold her as if to merge every inch of our bodies, every atom and molecule of our beings.

"Kyrie…." I ground my hips up against hers, and felt her begin to move with me, a juddering grind of her body down mine, meeting my upward thrust with a slow downward stroke of her own.

"Valentine. God, yes. This."

"I love you, Kyrie. I love you." Heat billowed within me, a surging tidal wave of fiery need spreading through me, setting me alight from toes to fingertips, scalp to soles, soul to mind to heart, all of me igniting as we found a mutual rhythm together. "You feel this? You feel how we fit together?"

"Yes!" She gasped, sobbed, lifting her face from my neck and gazed up at me with wet eyes, red-rimmed eyes. Her hair was unbrushed and wet and tangled, her skin damp from the shower.

She had never been more beautiful to me than in that moment.

I cupped the pale flesh and muscle of her ass, lifted her up, and then slammed her down onto me as I thrust up with all the power in my body. She cried out wordlessly, hanging her head and grinding onto me.

A glimmer of moonlight shone through the open doorway and reflected off the mirror in my closet. Kyrie rolled her hips against me as I strode across the bedroom and into the closet. She whim-pered raggedly as I set her down and pulled out of her.

"Wha—what are you—what are you doing?" she demanded. I grabbed her shoulders and turned her in place to face the three-way mirror. "Oh."

"Look at yourself, Kyrie. Look how beautiful you are. Look at us together. Watch us," I told her. "Don't look away."

I slid my hands over her breasts, cupping them, lifting them, kneading their fullness. I pinched her nipples with the thumb and forefinger of each hand, rolling her thick, sensitive pink buds until she gasped. I took one of her hands in mine and moved our joined fingers together down, down, between her thighs.

"Let me see you touch yourself, darling. Let me see you put your fingers in your pussy," I growled in her ear, sliding my middle finger and hers into her opening. "Let me see you get your fingers wet."

Kyrie sucked in a sharp breath as our fingers slipped into her pussy, and I curled my digit inward, scraped high on her inner wall, finding that spot and guiding her touch.

"Just like that, Kyrie. Keep touching yourself. Don't stop." I withdrew my fingers and watched as she rubbed herself. "I want to watch you come, just like this. Come for me, Kyrie. Make yourself come."

I pressed two fingers to her clit and massaged her in a slow, gentle circle, and felt her hips move, a slight flutter to match my circling touch. Her mouth fell open and her eyes went wide, and I sped up, pausing every now and then to pinch her clit between my fingers, to flick it, rub it, and then move in ever-faster circles around it. Her free hand reached up to clutch at my head, her eyes not on mine in the mirror, but on our hands moving at her sex, at the way her hips began to grind and gyrate. Her tits began to sway and bounce as her motions became more and more frantic, her thighs trembling, her legs falling open wider.

"Put two more fingers inside yourself, Kyrie," I ordered, my lips moving against the shell of her ear. "Fuck yourself with your fingers, my love. Let me see you do that."

"Oh, oh…*ohhhhh,* god, Valentine." She slipped her index and ring fingers into herself, her digits curled to rub against her G-spot. "I'm close, I'm so close."

"Are you watching?" I demanded.

"Yes…yes, I'm watching."

Her knees began to dip as I swiped faster and faster around her clit and her three fingers fucked harder and harder inside herself, and her eyes began to flutter, her breath coming shallow and harsh.

"I—I'm coming, Valentine, oh…Jesus, I'm coming—" She broke off, teeth clenched together, her entire body straining, and now she was screaming through gritted teeth as an orgasm tore through her.

I bent at the knees then, pulled my fingers away from her clit and grabbed her hips, jerked her ass backward. She planted her palm on the mirror, her eyes flicking up to mine. Shaking all over, still tensing and moaning with the aftershocks, she leaned forward, opening herself for me. I gripped my cock in one hand and dragged it against her clit, pushing until she rocked forward with a groan.

"In me...I need you in me, Valentine."

"You need my cock, don't you?"

"I do, god, Valentine, I need it so bad."

I pulled the tip of my dick between her slick labia and drove up into her tight, wet opening, growling as I felt her still-quaking inner walls squeeze immediately around me. Bare inside her, our eyes locked in the reflection of the mirror, I pushed deep inside her, until my stomach met the solid, round expanse of her ass.

"*Ohhhhh*...yes, yes, baby, YES!" she gasped, her voice rising to a shout as I drew back and rammed back into her.

"You like that, don't you, Kyrie?" I gripped the crease of her hips in my hands as I glided my throbbing cock out so I nearly lost her heat, and then pulled her ass into my thrust, growling with pleasure when the generous mound of flesh jiggled.

"I love it...fuck, I *need* it."

"You need it, do you?" I pulled back again and thrust deep, hard.

"YES! I need it so bad." She squeezed her eyes shut briefly as I set my favorite rhythm, pulling out

slowly and fucking in hard and fast. "I need you...
*you*, I need this...shit, oh god that feels so good—I
need us."

One hand flat against the mirror to prop herself up, bent nearly double, her tits swaying and
bouncing with each slapping clash of our bodies, she
opened her eyes as wide as they would go and kept
her gaze locked on mine.

"Touch yourself, Kyrie. Right now, while I'm
fucking you, touch your clit. Make yourself come
again."

I watched as she slipped her other hand between
her thighs and put two fingers to her clit, catching
her lip between her teeth and immediately finding
the rhythm she needed.

And now, her fingers moving in synch with the
rhythm of my driving hips, her brows lowered and
her breath came faster and faster, and she started
pushing back into me, slamming her ass into my
thrusts, harder and harder. Her gaze flickered down
and then to the side, watching us in profile in the
side mirror. I looked in the opposing side mirror,
and now we both watched, watched my thick, wet
cock sliding out of her pussy and then burying into
her body, watching her whole body rock forward
with the power of my thrust, her tits swaying forward, my balls slapping against her taint.

Her fingers moved in a blur then, and I felt her pussy clamp down, felt her body coil and tense as she prepared to come. As soon as I felt her begin to come, I slapped her ass hard, synching the crack of my hand on her flesh with driving, relentless fucking,

"*Oh*myfuckingGOD!" Kyrie cried out at the smack, arched her spine up, writhing as I drilled into her, giving in to my own rising urge to orgasm.

"That's not my name," I growled.

"Oh…oh my fucking Valentine?" It was part statement, part question, breathless as she came.

"That's better." I jerked her backward into my thrusts, our eyes meeting in the central mirror. "Is this what you wanted? Is it, love? You want me to talk to you? Tell you how good you feel? You want me to tell you how perfect your sweet little pussy feels when you squeeze my cock like that? You want me to tell you how much I love fucking you? I can't live without this. I can't, darling. I won't."

"You don't have to. Keep fucking me, Valentine. *Please.* Please keep fucking me. Just like this. Fuck me forever. Fuck me until I beg you to stop."

"Would you? Beg me to stop?"

"Never. I'll only ever beg you for more." She put both hands on the mirror now and pushed back to meet my thrusts, to fuck me back. "Just like this, Valentine. Don't ever stop."

"I won't. I promise. I love you too much. I love *this* too much."

"You—fuck, Valentine, you're so big. So big it almost hurts. It hurts so good, though." She caught her breath and started over. "You remember the last time you fucked me in this closet?"

A flash of memory seared through me as I neared climax: Kyrie, bent over against the mirror, hands on the glass, feet wide apart just like now, a vibrator in her asshole, her wide round ass jiggling and bouncing as I fucked her harder and harder, her screams filling the room, tangling with my own growls.

"God, that was incredible," I said.

"Yeah, it was," she agreed. "But...this...this is better." She met my rhythm, and I felt myself losing control, grinding hard and deep, and she rolled her hips against me, her eyes piercing mine. "I want to feel you come, Valentine. Come for me. Right now, baby."

Heat billowed through me, pressure in my balls tightening and ratcheting until I was growling and groaning, my hips flush against her ass, my cock buried deep and pushing in to go deeper.

"I'm coming, Kyrie." I pulled out, on the verge of detonation, and then slammed home. "Kyrie... god, my love...I'm—I'm coming—" She rocked with me as I exploded inside her, shouting as I came.

"You're my everything…." I gasped, groaning as another wave of seed flooded out of me and filled her. "This is…everything. My god, Kyrie…I love you so much…I need you…I love you—"

Her eyes wavered with the intensity of the moment, our gazes locked as I thrust one last time, unleashing a final burst of come within her. "I love you, Valentine."

We stilled then, my cock still buried inside her, both of us shaking. I pulled out, and she straightened, twisting in my arms. Our mouths crashed together, our arms and hands and legs trembling, our hearts beating in mutual frenzy, our tongues tangling. We broke apart, gasping, and Kyrie took my hand, led me to the bedroom. I let her go as she crawled on the bed, her ass waving side to side with a sultry sway, and even though I'd just come, I was twitching with renewed need. She rolled to lie on her back, knees lifted, thighs parted.

"God, you're so beautiful," I murmured. "So beautiful. And all mine."

"Say it again, baby. Tell me I'm yours."

I stood at the foot of the bed, drinking in her beauty, thickening into erection as I stared at her. "You're mine, Kyrie."

"Yes. I'm yours." She reached for me. "Come here, Valentine."

# 13

## FILLED

VALENTINE CLIMBED ONTO THE BED AND KNELT BETWEEN my knees. I brought my heels flush against my thighs, opening for him, staring up at him. His skin was coated in a sheen of sweat, his abs tensing with each gusting breath. His huge, strong, gentle hands rested on his knees, and his blond hair was damp and tangled, his beard thick.

With the beard he looked even more like a Norse god, six feet, four inches of toned muscle and bronzed skin. Although, in the months since we'd left for our world tour, he'd put on weight and lost some of the carefully honed perfection of his physique, not having regular access to a gym. I liked him better this way, though. The too-long, unkempt hair loose just above his shoulders with the untrimmed beard made him look even more rugged, and the loss of tone made him softer to snuggle against, made him seem even bigger. He was still a ripped and bulky giant of a man, but one less perfectly presented. More of a real living and breathing man with flaws rather than a polished and meticulously sculpted paragon of male beauty.

Now, naked, sweaty, breathing hard, his cock growing huge and hard and still gleaming with the essence of our lovemaking, he was a different kind of perfect. The obvious emotion in his eyes, the way he passed his hand through his hair with careless roughness, the way he stared at me as if nothing and no one else existed…it made my heart melt.

He still wasn't totally okay. He wouldn't be for a while, I didn't think. But he was here. He was with me. He loved me.

"Okay" was a relative and often meaningless term, I was learning. Had I been okay during the years following Dad's death? Not really. I'd been the farthest thing from okay the day I'd walked into my dark, empty, cold apartment with a handful of over-due bills and one mysterious check.

Was I okay now? Not really. Nothing was solved. Nothing was fixed. I'd seen things I'd never forget, things I knew I'd dream about, nightmares from which I'd wake up screaming. But I had Valentine, and he was refusing, as I was, to let it bury him. He'd pushed through his doubts and fears, refused to succumb. He'd taken back the part of himself I was worried he'd lost.

"Kyrie." His voice was low, a rumble of distant thunder in the darkness.

"Love me, Valentine. Just…love me." I reached for him, wrapped my fingers around his thick cock, rubbed my thumb over the broad head, and stroked him until he was pushing into my touch.

I pulled him toward me, a gentle urging. He let me guide him, shuffling forward on his knees until I could feed his massive erection into myself. He surged forward, filling me, and I fought the urge to close my eyes, needing instead to see into him, to watch him, to know his every expression and reaction. He caught my heels in his hands and lifted, fitting my feet into his underarms, hands resting on my shins. A thrust, then, slow and soft, a long inward glide to bring our bodies flush. Another. A third, and then he was moving into me with increasing speed, and I felt his huge hardness inside me, filling me, stretching me, and I kept my eyes on him, watched his muscles tense and flex and go slack, watched his belly tighten as he thrust, watched his face morph expressions: need, hunger, focus, desire, appreciation, lust, love.

He was going slow, holding back. I held still and let him move for both of us.

Silence, except for the background of Manhattan, a wash of sound I didn't even register. Just us, together. Him, breathing and moving, the wet sound of our sex, his eyes hooded and fixed on me, moving from my eyes to where we were joined, watching himself slide into me, pull back, slide in. I slid my heels up and over his shoulders, urged him closer, used the power in my legs to pull at him until he was leaning over me.

He growled at me, and leaned over me, leaving me no choice but to be curled in on myself, or let go my hold on him with my legs. I released him and let my legs fall to the bed, and he leaned back, burying himself fully inside me. His palms skated over my thighs, down the length of my legs and back up, smoothing along my calves and the tender underside of my knees and then the backs of my thighs. He wasn't thrusting, but held himself motionless, pulling back from the urge to climax.

He wrapped his hands around the backs of my knees, held me there, my knees slightly bent, feet flat on the bed. I watched him, saw the determination in his eyes.

I sucked in a sharp breath as he pulled out with excruciating slowness and then fluttered the tip of his cock against my clit, rubbing against me in a way that sent sun-hot waves of wildfire scorching through me, making me curl forward and lift my hips off the bed.

"Oh god, Valentine. I'm—I'm gonna—"

"What, Kyrie? You're going to what?"

"Come…."

"Good. Come for me, love." He gripped his big shaft in one fist and pushed the head of his dick against my throbbing clitoris, rubbing in slow forceful circles. "Come for me, Kyrie. Come…right… now."

I came. I had no choice. The low growl of his command, the feel of him against my sensitive little bundle of nerves, the look on his face, and the need in him to be in control…he owned me. He commanded me, and I obeyed. I came hard, writhing up off the bed, and in that moment he pushed into me, eliciting a scream from me as my tensed and squeezing pussy was speared open and filled by him.

"Oh, *fuck*, Kyrie. Fuck, you feel so good. So fucking good." He pulled back slowly and thrust in hard, the way he liked to do, and I screamed again, my climax burning hotter and hotter within me, leaving me no choice but to fuck against him and scream and scream and scream as he moved inside me. "So tight. So perfectly tight around me."

"Please, Valentine...please come with—with me," I begged him.

He groaned and fell forward. I wrapped my legs around his waist and my arms around his neck, holding his nape with one hand and his head with the other, clutching him to me and rocking into his thrusts. And then, without warning, I rolled us so I was on top of him, straddling him. He tensed, his eyes flicking open, and I watched him fight the memory of being restrained in this position. I looked down at him, rocked my hips and ground my ass against him, burying him deeper.

"Feel me, Valentine," I whispered. "You feel that?"

I lifted my hips until he was totally free of my body, bracing my weight with a palm on his chest. His eyes moved, sought mine, and his hands fisted into the sheets. I slipped him into my opening and slowly slid myself down around him, groaning a sigh as he filled me, feeling each inch of his thick, hard cock.

"I feel you, Kyrie," he growled, and his hips moved, thrusting himself up and into me.

I writhed on him, seating him deeper, and then rose up, fluttered my hips to feather his tip just barely inside me, teasing him, daring him to move more, move harder, to take this, to take me.

I felt him break through the pain and fear that came with being straddled and begin to fuck me in earnest. For himself now, rather than for me. I was still crazed with the aftershocks of my climax, and each thrust made me gasp and shriek, caused me to involuntarily grind against him, meeting him thrust for thrust. His fucking became wild then. He lifted my breast to his face and sucked my nipple between his teeth, his hips driving hard and fast, relentless, crazed.

He suckled my tit and fucked me hard, and I held him against me and clutched him with my legs and took it all, loved it all. I wanted to feel him come apart above me and in me and all around me. I needed to feel him take his pleasure and milk it all from him.

"Kyrie, I'm there. I'm coming, Kyrie."

"Yes, Valentine, come for me. Come inside me. Shoot your come in me. I want it. Right now, baby. Right now, my love." I leaned over him, rocking back and forth as hard and fast as I could, wild myself now with his breaking orgasm. I felt his rhythm stutter, felt him let my nipple fall from his mouth, then heard his groan against my breasts, his face buried between my tits, his hips drilling against mine with crashing force. I urged him on, whispered his name over and over.

He shook beneath me, stared up at me, all the universe shrunk down to this one moment. "Kyrie…." he breathed.

I kept my eyes locked on his as he exploded inside me with a shout, jetting hot wetness deep inside me, over and over. He filled me with his come, and the sensation of him losing control inside me had me quaking and shaking, an orgasm of my own rocketing through me, a slow, deep, burning pulsation that began in my bones and my gut and spread through me like wildfire.

"God, *yes*, Valentine, yes, I love you, I love feeling you come. Give it all to me. Give me every drop." I crushed my tits between us and bit his shoulder, kissed his temple and ground myself against him, needing him deeper and deeper so I could come with him. "Don't stop yet, love. Come inside me some more."

He palmed both globes of my ass and moved with me, our bodies pressed together from head to toe, merged and enmeshed and tangled together, our legs twined. Buried inside me, he could only grind his hips to milk his climax, in so doing drawing more from me.

Finally he rolled with me, cradling me against his chest and drawing the blanket over us. "I love you

with everything that I am, Kyrie Abigail St. Claire."
His words were a low murmur.

I was already nearly asleep, but I heard him. "I love you more than that."

"More than everything?"

"Yep."

A silence as we both drifted toward sleep. "I believe you," he mumbled.

I woke up on my side, Roth's hands roaming my torso, cupping my tits, and then digging his fingers down and down into my core. Before I was even fully awake, he was pushing into me, and I was murmuring a sleepy protest of surprise. But then he was in me and I was waking up, and his fingers were skillfully bringing me to life. He surged into me, and I reached behind my head to hold his face against my neck, gasping as he thrust into me with a steady rhythm.

No foreplay, no drawing it out. No multiple orgasms. No words exchanged. Just dawn flushing the shadows from the corners and alleys and glass-and-steel canyons, horns blaring and voices shouting and laughing, engines revving, and Roth deep inside me, fingers on me, mouth on me. Just our lazy morning love, his breathing coming in pants and gasps, mine in whimpers.

We came together, hard and fast, less than five minutes after he entered me.

I fell back asleep with him still inside me.

I woke up with the sun high, the sheets rumpled at my hips, Roth's eyes on me from where he sat on the balcony, dressed in shorts and nothing else, a mug of tea in his hands.

"Hey, baby," I said, sitting up.

"Good morning, beautiful." He gestured at the bedside table. "There's coffee for you there."

I grabbed the mug and sipped greedily at the still-steaming coffee. "How'd you know when I would wake up?"

He grinned. "If we have dawn sex, you always wake up again around ten, ten-thirty. You think I don't know your patterns by now?"

I smiled at that and wrapped the flat sheet around my chest, moving to join him on the balcony. He snagged me as I passed in front of him, making me giggle and hold the mug away from us as coffee sloshed over the side. "You're making me spill!"

"What a tragedy." He pulled me down onto his lap, and I wiggled my bottom against him to find a comfortable position, and then we settled in to drink, neither of us needing to speak, just enjoying the morning and each other's presence.

Once I'd finished my coffee, he stood up with me, parting the sheet and patting me on the ass. "Go take a shower, my lovely, sticky girl."

"You made me sticky," I said.

"Yes, I did," he said with a grin.

"Why don't you join me?" I suggested, looking up at him with an innocent expression.

"Because if I do, we'll never leave this room. And as much as I would like to spend the next few days fucking you until you can't walk, we have an enemy looking for us."

I sobered at that thought. "And this is the first place she'll look."

He shook his head. "She already knows we're here, no doubt."

"What are we going to do?"

He nudged me toward the bathroom. "Go take a shower. I've got some ideas, but I need to run them by Harris."

Worry had me frozen in place. "I'm scared, Roth."

His expression darkened, and he held my shoulders in his hands, eyes going hard. "She fucked with the wrong man. Kidnapping me was a mistake. Trying to have *you* killed? Threatening you?" His voice was razor sharp and ice cold. "That was the wrong thing to do."

"What are you going to do?"

"Finish this." The malice in his eyes made me recoil in fear.

I touched his bare chest with my palm. "Valentine…just don't—please, don't do anything rash. Be careful. Okay?"

His brows lowered. "I think we're past that point, my love. Well past it."

"Just make me one promise, then, please?"

"If I can."

"Don't try to hide me, and don't leave me behind. No matter what."

He didn't answer for several moments. Eventually, he backed away, out of my touch. "There will be blood, Kyrie."

I swallowed hard. "I know." I refused to let him retreat from me, no matter the circumstances. I circled my arms around his neck and put my cheek to his heartbeat. "*Promise me*, Valentine."

Minutes passed. "You have my word."

# 14

## THE VIPER STRIKES

I STEPPED OUT OF THE SHOWER, DRIED OFF, AND WRAPPED the towel around my chest. Roth wasn't in the bedroom, so I assumed he was in his office. I dressed in jeans and a T-shirt, brushed my hair out and pulled it back in a ponytail, not bothering with makeup.

Still no Roth.

Something in the pit of my stomach churned: something was off.

I padded down the hall in my bare feet to his office, finding it empty. Not in the gym. "Roth?" I called out. "Where are you?"

No answer.

I checked the kitchen, the dining room, the larger industrial kitchen, the foyer and sitting room, and finally, the library. The library was a huge cathedral of a space, shelves lining the walls from floor to ceiling. There were two floors of shelves, nooks and crannies with overstuffed chairs and reading lamps and small tables. I moved through the library, checking each reading nook, and then ascended to the upper floor. My skin tingled, my stomach heavy as lead, blood running ice cold in my veins. Something was very, very wrong. I should go back to the private quarters, remain behind the biometric lock separating the rest of the house from Roth's rooms.

*Wait for Roth,* the thought hammered at me.

But I didn't listen. I moved from stack to stack, hands trembling, barely daring to breathe.

The last nook I checked, in the farthest corner of the upper floor, was one with a huge black leather chair with a matching ottoman. Usually the chair faced toward the library, but as I approached, I saw that it had been turned away to face the corner. A hand was visible, resting on the arm of the chair. The hand was slim and feminine, the nails long and painted cherry red.

"Kyrie." The voice was low and smooth and sultry, lightly accented. "Do join me."

I backed away, two steps, three. But then stopped, frozen, as the visible hand retreated and reappeared, this time holding a compact pistol.

"Don't make me end this too quickly, my dear." The barrel of the pistol pointed at the other chair, which had been dragged over from another nook. "*Now,* Kyrie."

On shaky legs, knowing I'd made a mistake, I circled around and sat in the chair she'd indicated. Facing me was Gina Karahalios. I didn't need an introduction to know it. She was tall and poised and beautiful. Long black hair pulled in a twist over one shoulder, skin naturally tanned and artificially wrinkle-free, eyes dark as shadows and colder than ice, glinting at me in amusement. She wore a green dress, expensive, cut to cling to her curves, the neckline scooped deep, a string of fat black pearls draping her neck and nestled in her falsely enormous cleavage. A Chanel handbag sat on her lap.

I swallowed my fear and tried to keep the tremble from my voice. "Gina. What do you want?"

She smiled, a predatory curve of artificially plump lips. "A lot of things. But right now, you. And I have you."

"Where is Roth?"

"Val, you mean?" She winked at me. "He's dealing with a...distraction."

"Do what you want to me, but leave him alone."

She laughed, a bell-like sound of hilarity. "Oh my. How very original of you. I don't think so, though. I'll do what I want with you, and then I'll do what I want with *him*. I'm afraid much of it will hurt rather a lot."

"Why?"

"Why?" She peered at me from beneath thickly mascaraed lashes. "Because I always get what I want. I want Val. And I want you to suffer for daring to touch what is mine."

She reached into her Chanel bag and withdrew a small metal cylinder, which she screwed onto the barrel of her gun.

"He's not yours, Gina. He never was, and never will be. And if you lay a hand on me, all you'll succeed in doing is making him even more angry."

Her hand shifted slightly, and the gun popped with a short, sharp bark. A hot, piercing pain slammed into my knee, and I screamed, clutching my leg, watching the blood gush, thick and bright.

"He's so very sexy when he's angry, don't you agree?" She sounded so calm, as if we were two girlfriends talking about a mutual crush.

I could only scream breathlessly, the agony blasting through me and stealing oxygen from my lungs, the pulse from my veins, thought from my mind. I heard the *click* of a cell phone camera, and looked up through tears to see Gina touching the screen of a pink-and-diamond encased iPhone, and then heard the telltale sound of a sent message. She slithered up off the chair, smoothed the front of her dress, tugged the scooped neckline down to better prop up her cleavage, and then moved to kneel beside me. Raising her cell phone, she held it up to get a downward angle, capturing the agony on my face and the bloody wreck of my knee, pressed the barrel of her pistol to my temple, and then—*click*—took a selfie.

I watched her send it to Roth.

I couldn't move, couldn't speak, couldn't even breathe. The pain was excruciating, beyond anything I'd ever even imagined. I couldn't even sob.

Gina stood up again, smoothed and straightened her dress, placed her cell phone in her purse, which she then hung on her shoulder. She turned to me. "Come along."

I stared at her. "You—you sh-shot me."

She gave me a *well, duh* look. "And that won't be all I'm going to do to you. Oh no. Not even close." Gina touched a long, cherry-red fingernail to the bottom of my chin, lifting my face. "But...if you cooperate with me, I'll in turn make sure *I'm* the only one who will touch you. Do you understand?"

"I—"

"What that means, in case you're too stupid to follow, is that if you make trouble for me, if you cause me to repeat myself, I'll let one of my boys...

play…with you. You won't enjoy that, I assure you."
She tapped me on the nose. "Now. Come along."

"How am I supposed to—"

Gina rolled her eyes at me. "It's *one* knee. You
have two. Now *let's go,* you silly little cunt. I have
things to do."

I gritted my teeth, bit down on a scream as I
struggled to my feet. Or, foot. I couldn't put any
weight on my knee, but I had no choice except to
hobble as best I could toward the stairs. Gina followed behind me, gun barrel pressed against my
spine, urging me to go faster. Getting down the
library stairs was raw torture. Inch by inch, step by
step, I fought, trying not to scream, not to sob, not to
show weakness. This woman was a viper, the kind of
animal who would smell fear and prey on it.

I would not be prey.

She shoved me toward the front door, where
a bulky, swarthy, short man in a trim black suit
stood with some kind of compact machine gun in
his hands, waiting. I happened to glance to my left,
toward the formal sitting room, and I fell to the
floor, a sob catching in my teeth.

Eliza. Eyes open and staring, a crimson pool
spreading beneath her skull. Roth's kind and devoted
housekeeper was dead.

"Eliza? Eliza, no. No. Nononono." I crawled toward her, fingernails scrabbling at the hardwood floor, heart breaking in my chest.

I was grabbed around the middle and lifted off the ground. A hand pawed at my breasts, but I didn't even notice as I focused on Eliza, sweet, quiet, competent Eliza.

Dead Eliza.

Within me there was a hard, cold knot of rage, already in place and building, put there by the chase across France, by Roth's kidnapping, by the turn my life had taken, all at the hands of this woman. Rage at the hell my man had endured. All that rage was only intensified by the sight of Eliza.

I thrashed, kicked, bit, and screamed, heard grunts of pain as I connected with flesh.

"Knock her out, Tobias."

A blow struck the back of my head, a lance of dizzying pain knocking the breath from me, narrowing my vision to tunnels. Another blow, and then a third, each harder than the last, and finally blackness swallowed me.

# 15

## MERCENARIES

*VALENTINE*

It took every ounce of self-control I possessed to let Kyrie shower by herself. I stood in the doorway of the bathroom for several seconds, drinking in her lush, glorious nude beauty as she adjusted the water and stepped in. I wanted to shove my shorts off and go in there with her, shove her against the marble wall and fuck her senseless, and then dry her off and take her to bed and fuck her again and again, until we were both so spent we couldn't move.

Instead, I wrenched myself away and went up to the roof. Harris was there, sitting in the pilot's seat of the chopper, smoking a cigarette and thumbing rounds into a clip.

He saw me coming, lifted his chin at me. "Mr. Roth. Glad to have you back."

I let out a sigh. "I owe you, Harris. More than I can ever repay."

He shook his head. "No, sir. You don't. That girl, she's something else. Haven't known her long, but she's like family. So are you. I don't want a fucking dime from you. Not for that. I took care of her because it was the only thing to do. I helped her go get you because it was the only thing to do."

I shrugged. "All right. But I still owe you my life. So you need anything, *anything,* ever, it's yours."

Harris's eyes were frozen emeralds. "Get the fuckers."

"That's why I'm up here, Harris. I can't leave her. I promised her. But…I can't just sit here and wait with my thumb up my ass. I have to do something. We have to get them. Strike first."

Harris clamped the butt of his cigarette between his teeth, set the clip he was filling aside, and reached down behind his seat to pick up a long, flat black case. He laid the case across his knees and opened it, revealing a Remington MSR. It was a military version, not the stripped-down and simplified civilian version.

"Holy shit, Harris. How'd you get your hands on one of those?" I asked.

He shrugged. "Know a guy."

"All right, fine. Keep your secrets, then." It was supposed to be a joke, but it came out flat. I rubbed my temples with my middle fingers. "You have a plan?"

He nodded. "Yep. Find 'em, start killing."

"Your plan might need some fleshing out, possibly."

He closed the case, set it behind the seat once more, and resumed thumbing shells into the clip. I realized, belatedly, that it wasn't a clip, but rather a magazine, and the shells were 7.62 NATO rounds. "Yeah, maybe."

There was an explosion of concrete at my feet, accompanied by a distant *CRACK*.

"Shit!" I ducked behind the body of the chopper. "Someone is shooting at me!"

"No shit." Harris was already flipping switches, bringing the aircraft to life. "We have to get out of here, Mr. Roth."

As he said that, a bullet hit the windscreen of the helicopter, splintering it, followed by another round to the seat just behind Harris's head.

"I can't leave Kyrie here!"

"They're not trying to kill us. We'd already be dead if they were. She's locked in your quarters. We'll circle around and find the shooter, and then swing by to grab her." He pointed at the seat. "Now get the fuck in the helo!"

Something buzzed angrily past my face, going through both open doors of the aircraft, accompanied by a *CRACK*. The helicopter was roaring, the rotors a blur overhead, creating a downdraft so powerful I could barely stand up under it. My gut churned as I slid into the passenger seat, the chopper leaving the ground even before I was fully seated.

I stared at the door leading down to my quarters; I was leaving Kyrie behind. I'd promised her I wouldn't, but here I was, doing it. Another round hit, pocking the body, and another one, hitting the nose. We were being driven away, I realized, as the roof of the tower fell away.

"I don't like this, Harris," I shouted. "They're herding us away from the building."

"No shit. Don't see much option unless you want a bullet through the skull."

Harris had the engine at full bore, the nose angling down to push us aggressively forward, away from the building at a speed reckless for an urban area. The crack of the rifle was no longer audible, and if we were being shot at anymore, the shooter was missing. Or, more worrisomely, they'd successfully driven us off the roof and didn't need to shoot.

Harris circled my tower several times at a distance of a few blocks, scanning the rooftops, but if he saw anything, he wasn't letting on.

And then my phone chirped, letting me know I had a message. My stomach roiled as I brought the device out of my pocket. The message was displayed on the sleep screen. It wasn't a message, though; it was a picture.

Of Kyrie.

She was in a chair in the library, clutching her leg, which was a bloody wreck. She'd been shot. Her face was a mask of shock and agony.

Hellish rage boiled inside me, red filling my vision, blocking out the world, blocking out thought and reason. "Go back," I growled.

"We can't—" Harris began.

My phone chimed again, and another picture winked into life on the screen beneath the first. This one was a selfie, clearly taken by Gina. She had a suppressed Walther PPK held to Kyrie's temple, her lips pursed, glee in her eyes. You could just barely make out the bloody mess of Kyrie's knee at the bottom of the photograph.

I showed the photos to Harris, who glanced at them briefly, then returned his attention to piloting the helicopter.

His lips compressed into a thin white line. I could see his knuckles whitening as he gripped the controls. "Fuck."

I didn't bother responding. Harris jerked the chopper around violently, slewing the nose back toward my building and throttling forward. As we neared my rooftop, he pointed behind my seat. "There are a couple of cases back there. Grab one."

I twisted around and grabbed one of the pistol cases, opened it, and pulled out the pistol contained within, a Glock .357. There was a preloaded spare clip, which I tucked into my back pocket. As I checked the load on the other clip, Harris had the helo flaring over the rooftop. I leapt out while the skids were still two feet in the air. I was through the door within seconds, ignoring the spit of a round cratering in the doorframe, ignoring Harris's shouts to wait, ignoring the suppressed bark of Harris's MSR as he popped off several rounds.

I took the stairs three at a time, ran through the door and into the hallway beyond my private quarters. Up into the library. I slid to my knees in the spot where I knew the photo had been taken, my favorite spot in the upper back corner, with the antique overstuffed leather chair. There was only a blot of darkening, drying blood where she'd been.

No note. No other evidence, except the casing on the floor near one of the stacks.

Harris was waiting for me by the front door, staring at something off to the left, in the formal sitting room. I felt my feet dragging, as if knowing I would find something horrible, and didn't want to get within sight of it. I glanced at Harris, and saw the sorrow on his face, then his cold, calculating, murderous rage.

I'd seen and done a lot of nasty shit in my life.

Nothing could have prepared me for the sight of Eliza, dead on the floor with a bullet through her skull. I fell to my knees beside her, my jeans slipping in the tacky blood. "Eliza. God, no. No. Eliza!"

"Come on, man. We gotta move." Harris was pulling at me, lifting me up.

"They killed Eliza, Harris."

"I know." His voice was too calm, too quiet. "That woman was like a mother to me, Valentine. Trust me, we'll get these fuckers. We'll fucking slaughter every last goddamn one of them. But first, we have to go. We have to move."

"We can't leave her here, Harris."

"We won't. I've got a contact in the city who can take care of things. Clean up the mess, take Eliza someplace where we can bury her in private after all this is over. Okay?"

I let him push me into motion, and we headed back up to the helicopter. I was in a daze after that, my mind cycling rapidly through all the worst scenarios. Gina had Kyrie. She'd shot her.

"I've never hurt a woman before, Harris." I spoke softly into the headset. "I've never once done anything to physically harm a woman. Not even when Gina begged me to do shit to her. But…I'm going to kill her, Harris. I'm going to put a bullet in her fucking head."

"You won't get any judgment from me on that score, boss. Shit, I'd pull the trigger myself."

Long minutes of silence, then: "Where are we going?"

"Airport," Harris said. "We're meeting Henri in Paris."

"Henri?"

"Yeah. He called me late last night. Karahalios burned him out. Torched the whole building his bar was in. Sent a couple of guys to his personal residence. Obviously, that didn't work out so well for Karahalios's boys, and now Henri is out for blood."

"I'm sorry that he's involved."

He glanced at me. "Didn't have much choice. They were gunning for us, and I didn't know who to trust. I had to stash her somewhere safe while I worked out transportation to Greece."

I nodded. "I know. I get it. I just don't like it. He's retired. He shouldn't have to be in this shit."

"Or any of us, for that matter."

"Yeah." I brought up the pictures on my phone, keeping the rage stoked. "How do we find her?"

"Henri brought some gear with him. I think he can probably track that phone number, unless she's got some kind of encryption on it. We'll find her. I promise."

My phone chimed as we landed, indicating a text message: *Val, my dear. I know you well enough to know you're planning to rescue your little slut. Don't. You'll only make things worse for her. Much worse. Stay away until I summon you.*

Harris's phone beeped twice, and he glanced at it briefly, then at me. "We have to stop in Harlem," Harris said, banking the chopper.

The stop in Harlem was brief. Harris found a landing pad on the roof of a building I owned, and left on his own. After a forty-five-minute wait, Harris returned carrying a huge black duffel bag and rolling a battered Samsonite suitcase. I helped him lift the bags into the chopper, and they were both very heavy. Weapons, clearly.

From Harlem we went to my private hangar at LaGuardia. Harris had obviously called ahead to have the Gulfstream prepped and a flight plan logged. The hours to Paris were the longest of my life. I spent the entire flight on edge and impatient, rage billowing through me with every breath.

A Mercedes was waiting for us when we landed, and Harris slid into the driver's seat, guiding the vehicle away from the airport and into the narrow streets of Paris. Thirty minutes from wheels-down, we were stopped outside a hotel and Henri was sliding into the rear seat, buckling his belt and speaking to Harris in French too rapid for me to follow. Harris nodded and then responded, pointing at me, indicating my phone. Henri took my phone from my hand without a word. He pulled a laptop from a backpack and connected a cord from the phone to the computer, then began rapidly tapping the keys.

"Wish I could say it was good to see you, Henri," I said. "Sorry about your bar. I'll buy you a new one when this is over."

"*Non.* I do not want your money, boy. I want the bitch dead. I want Vitaly dead. I can rebuild my own fucking bar. You know as well as I that you do not retire from this business. I was a fool to think I could." He glanced up at me over the rims of his reading glasses. He looked like an innocent, kindly grandfather, until you looked into his eyes. "But it *is* good to see you."

"Thank you for what you did for Kyrie."

"It is nothing. She is a beautiful girl. And one with real spine, *oui?* She did not faint away when things got messy." He tapped a few more times. "The bitch is arrogant. No security on her phone at all. This will be easy to find her. She is in transit, I think. Over the Atlantic."

"You saw the photos and the message?" I asked.

He nodded. "*Oui.* I did." His gaze met mine, direct, hard as granite and merciless. "You must decide, Roth. Do you accept her instructions to keep Kyrie safe? Or do you take whatever steps are necessary to take her back, and so risk her life?"

I wiped at my face with both hands. "What would you do?"

Henri was silent for a few moments, closing his laptop and storing it in his messenger bag. "She is an evil woman, Gina Karahalios. A spawn of the devil himself. She has no mercy. She has no intention of sparing Kyrie, nor you. I think, if it were me, if this were my daughter or granddaughter, I would not stop until I had her back, dead or alive. She will not live long in the hands of the Karahalios bitch. I think you know this."

I nodded. "Yeah, I agree." I ground my teeth together, and then blew out a breath as I decided. "We take her back."

"At all costs." Henri made a phone call, speaking in what sounded like French-accented Russian, and then hung up.

"Now. A private airport, and a flight to Sofia. I have several…acquaintances meeting us there."

"Sofia?" I blinked, processing. "As in Bulgaria?"

Henri's lips curled in a faint smile. "*Certainment.* One of my oldest friends lives there. He knows some people who can help us, no questions asked. Only need…oh, a hundred grand, U.S. Maybe two. Easy."

"Cash?" I asked.

"That is preferable, I think." Meaning, *Obviously, you idiot.*

"I brought cash," Harris put in, setting a destination into the car's GPS. "We'll have enough."

"These friends of yours—" I began.

Henri cut in. "Not friends. They are not the type you would be friends with, I think. But they are professional. Previously Spetsnaz, I believe, although I am not sure." He shot me a piercing glance. "You trust me, Roth?"

"With my life. With Kyrie's, more importantly."

He nodded. "Well, then. These men will do."

Enough said.


We landed on an airstrip in the countryside an hour's drive outside Sofia itself. The airstrip wasn't really big enough for the jet Harris was flying, but he brought us down and stopped us just short of the end of the runway. An old blue Mercedes van waited for us, smoke-filled, stinking of fish and body odor and stale cigarettes. The driver said nothing. Henri said nothing. No one said anything, not for the entire hour-long drive into the city. Henri and Harris carried the various cases of weapons with them, while I carried the briefcase full of cash that Harris had, somehow, had the foresight to procure.

I was falling back into a world I thought I'd left behind. Sullen, unwashed, unnamed drivers, acrid cigarette smoke curling in the thick air of a van. Suitcases full of weapons and cash. The complex cultures of southern Europe: Bulgaria, Macedonia, Albania. Dark purposes you didn't think about too closely, acquaintances whose real names and INTERPOL records you *definitely* didn't want to know about.

Kyrie had been sucked into this world as well now. Our interlude in Manhattan had made me believe, if only for a few hours, that we were okay. That I'd be okay. That I could take on the Karahalios clan and win without any casualties on my side.

I'd left Kyrie alone only for a moment. The talk with Harris was supposed to take five minutes, tops.

I was going to get him moving on finding Gina before she found us.

God, I'd been such a fool. And Kyrie had paid the price.

I pushed the guilt and the rage out of my mind. I had to, or I'd be useless. I had to focus.

We met Henri's acquaintances in a bar in the eastern end of Sofia. There were five of them, one of them an older man about Henri's age who carried himself with the same air of calm, cold capability that Henri possessed. The other four were younger. Mid-thirties. Hard-eyed, lean, and muscular, dark hair and days' worth of beard growth, smoking an unbroken chain of cigarettes. All four of them could have been from anywhere in Europe or Russia, even the Middle East, possibly, and as we sat down with them, I overheard them speaking to each other in at least three different languages. I didn't speak any language fluently except English, but I could recognize and pick out words and phrases of most of the common European languages. I sat silently, sipping cheap Scotch and letting Henri and Harris do the talking. I was long out of this world, and I knew the best thing I could do right now was let the others get things moving. Henri, especially, was a man to whom you listened when he spoke, whose directions you followed. He'd made it to old age in a profession that you didn't so much retire from as survive, and he knew the kinds of people we'd need on our side if we were going to have a chance of getting Kyrie back.

Harris and Kyrie had been lucky when they found me. Gina had been careless, arrogant. She'd assumed sweet, innocent, American Kyrie wouldn't have a clue about how to find me, much less get me back. She hadn't counted on Harris. But now… now she would be on high alert. I had to assume she knew where we were, that she was tracking our movements.

Henri and the ex-Spetsnaz boys conversed for several minutes. Then one of the mercs gestured at me with his cigarette. "You are Roth. I know you. I have heard of you."

I lifted an eyebrow. "Doubtful."

"No. You work for Vitaly. Many years ago."

I sighed. "That I did."

He nods. "I know this. Now he takes your girl? He is not a good enemy to have, I think."

"Not him. His daughter."

"Bitch." The man spat on the floor, a gesture of contempt or disgust. "Even worse."

"Agreed."

"My cousin, he meet her at a bar. Athens. She fuck him. Then she kill him."

I nod. "That's her M.O."

He dragged on his cigarette, exhaled smoke out of his nostrils, and rolled his lips to spew the rest. "Your girl. She is dead, I think."

"Not yet." I pointed at him with my glass. "That's what I want your help with. Get her back alive."

"It won't be easy."

Another one of them spoke up. "Or cheap."

I glanced at Harris, who very subtly lifted a shoulder. I finished my Scotch. "Name your price."

The four conversed in undertones, and then the one who claimed to know me tapped the table with a middle finger. "Fifty thousand each. U.S. dollars. Up front."

I looked to Harris, who lifted his chin slightly in agreement. "Fine. But half now. Half after I've got her back."

"No guarantee of her alive, now *or* then." He shrugged. "With that bitch, there is no guarantee of anything."

I squeezed the glass in my fist, and then forced myself to set it down before I shattered it in my hand. "True. But still. Half now, half after. Regardless of… what happens."

"*Da.* This is good." He lit another cigarette with the cherry of his previous one.

Henri had his laptop open on the table. He swirled red wine at the bottom of his glass, and then set his reading glasses on the table. "She is back in Greece. One of their little island places. The approach will be difficult."

"*Nyet.*" The one who seemed to be the spokesman waved a hand in dismissal. "A little boat. Very fast. No problems. But security? *That* is the problem. Getting out is the problem. I don't want Vitaly to come look for me when this is done."

"No witness." The man on the end, silent up until now, sought me out with his gaze, watching for a demurral.

I shook my head. "Whatever you need to do. I don't give a fuck. But Gina is mine."

"I would not go anywhere near her. Not for any money." He shrugged. "Maybe with rifle, from a thousand meters."

The spokesman shook his head. "Still too close."

I tapped the tabletop with my palm. "Enough. What's the plan?"

The next few hours were spent coming up with a workable solution. Ingress and egress routes, worst case scenarios. Supplies needed. Calls were made, brief, hushed conversations in half a dozen languages. We separated once plans were in place with an agreement to meet at the same airfield at which we'd landed, at dawn the following day.

Sleep was impossible.

I'd managed to avoid worry by keeping my thoughts on the present, on our plans. But with the lights out in a smelly hotel room in Bulgaria, all I could think of was Kyrie. In pain. Afraid. Alone. All I could do was imagine all the ways Gina would find to torture her, just to get back at me. To lure me in. We were walking into a trap. I knew it. Harris knew it. I think Henri knew it. The other four? They were paid enough to not care.

The mercenary had spoken the truth, though, as had Henri.

Kyrie was likely as good as dead.

# 16

## PAYMENT DUE

I WAS IN AN EMPTY ROOM, NAKED, MY WRISTS BOUND IN front of me with zip-ties, and my hands bound to my feet, which were zip-tied as well. It was a painfully uncomfortable position, my torso pulled forward so my knees dug into my stomach, leaving me unable to straighten my legs or my back.

The room was bare stone, big gray flags of stacked and mortared rock. Old. Very old. Subterranean. Lit by a single bare bulb wired to the ceiling. I was gagged, a bitter, foul-tasting sock shoved into my mouth, duct tape across my lips.

Hours had passed. Or maybe just minutes. Days, perhaps? I had no way of knowing. There was no window, no indication of daylight. The room was cold, so cold I shivered nonstop. Hunger and thirst

had long since become familiar aches. But yet, ironically, I had to pee. I'd been holding it for what felt
like days. I refused to pee on myself, but I didn't see
much choice. I couldn't hold it forever. I was lying
on my side, the hard cold ground digging into my
shoulder, hip, and knee.

After tying me up and gagging me, Gina and her
silent goon had left me here. I expected immediate
torture, rape, and death. But no. They just left me
here to shiver and rot.

Just as that thought entered my head, I heard
a key in a lock, and the door creaked open. Gina
entered, a thin, cruel smile on her lips. She was
dressed for the club, it seemed to me, wearing a
short, tight blue dress that revealed more than it
covered, clicking over to me on Louboutin high
heels. Her hair was bound in a ponytail high on her
head, the end hanging over one shoulder. Her nails
were long sapphire-blue talons. She held a Christian
Dior purse. I noticed all this, registered the high-
end brand names as if they mattered. I watched her
approach, worked hard to keep the fear from my
eyes, my breathing slow and even and regular.

My knee throbbed. Gina's goon had wrapped
my wounded knee while Gina explained that she
wouldn't want me to bleed out before she'd gotten
some fun out of me.

"Kyrie, darling." Gina crouched in front of my face, dragging a finger through my hair, pulling a lock out of my eye and placing it behind my ear. She set her purse on her knees, opened it, and withdrew a black folding knife. "Sorry to leave you for so long. I've been monitoring Val's attempts to reach you. So far all he's doing is drinking that vile Scotch of his with some friends. He plans to come for you, of course. I'm counting on it. So I'll have to have my fun with you now, before things get really exciting." She turned toward the door and snapped her fingers. The goon came in, dragging a young blonde girl. "She's going to be part of the fun. Her name is… what was it? Lucy?"

The girl wasn't bound or gagged. She was clothed and showed no sign of blood or bruises. She was clearly terrified, though. Rightfully so. "L—Lisa. My name is Lisa."

"Ah, yes. Lisa." Gina stood up slowly, unfolding to her full height in a smooth, sinuous motion that reminded me of a spitting cobra rearing back. "Feel free to scream, sweetheart. No one can hear you."

"What? What are you—what are you going to do to me?" Lisa backed away from Gina…right into the chest of the goon.

"Me? Nothing." Gina quirked an eyebrow at the man, and a lecherous grin spread across his ugly face.

"Tobias, now…he's been talking about his plans for you since we picked you up."

"Please…p-please…don't hurt me. What do you want from me?" Lisa tried to worm out of Tobias's grip, but in vain.

His hands were circled around her biceps, and she might as well have been struggling against the bulk of a mountain. He pressed his nose to her ear, latched onto her earlobe with his teeth. Lisa froze, head tilted sideways, clearly wanting to pull her head away but knowing she'd risk ripping her earlobe if she did so. She couldn't even scream, panic choking her, as he bit down hard enough to draw blood.

"We only want you, girl." He licked his lips after speaking, his voice guttural and thickly accented. "You are nothing. Only example."

"Oh, shut up, Tobias. Just get on with it." Gina moved around behind me, one hand clutching the knife, the other latching into my hair.

I screamed through the gag as she dragged me upright by my hair, chunks coming out at the root. I had no way to even try to balance myself, but once I was sitting on my haunches, Gina crouched behind me and kept one hand on my hair, making sure I didn't fall over.

"This is for you, Kyrie. This is what's in store for you." Her voice slithered against my ear. "I want you to watch." The point of her knife touched the hollow behind my ear. "If you close your eyes, I'll cut off your ear."

I swallowed hard, tasting bile and horror and the bitter gall of the sock in my mouth. I didn't dare close my eyes, but it took every ounce of willpower to keep them open. Being forced to watch what Tobias did to that poor girl…it was a living nightmare I would never forget.

I sobbed past the tape.

Eventually Tobias stood up, buckled his belt and wiped his bloody hands on his pants leg.

He glanced at me. "You are next, bitch."

He licked his lips, knelt in front of me, reached down between my legs and shoved his fingers hard against me, missing my entrance and gouging hard enough to nearly break the skin. I curled forward, almost fell, and screamed through the gag.

He laughed. "Just a bit of fun, this little bitch." He gestured at the ruin that was Lisa. "You? I'm going to have *hours* with you."

Gina whispered in my ear. "A little secret about Tobias? He's really fucked up in the head. He can't get off until they're dead. He can go for hours. It's sick, really. But he's very useful."

Tobias grabbed Lisa by the ankle, jerked open the door, and dragged her out by the foot. I heard her moaning, protesting, crying, and then the wet impact of a foot on flesh. The moans stopped.

The door closed, and Gina stood to move in front of me, bending over and ripping the duct tape off in one fast motion. I spat out the sock, gagged, and then vomited all over her Louboutins. She watched dispassionately. There was no warning, just the flash of her hand and the sudden burst of pain as the back of her knuckles cracked across my cheek. And then she was kneeling in front of me, her breath on my face. She had my hair in her hand, gripped tight at the scalp. I held my breath, refused to let myself think or fear or react.

Her other arm reached around behind me, her nose an inch from mine, her eyes on mine. "These were my favorite heels, you little cunt. Now I have to change."

She moved to stand behind me, and I felt a tugging at my hair, felt her knife hand moving. Gina rocked back on her feet and stood up, the length of my hair clutched in her hand. I stifled a cry at the sight of my hair in her fist, cut raggedly from my head. Opening her hand, Gina let the long blonde strands flutter to the floor at her feet, into the puddle of my vomit.

She wasn't done yet, though.

I ground my teeth together, gritted them against the pain as she grabbed a hunk of hair at the crown of my scalp and scraped it from my head. I choked on my screams, trembled to contain my need to thrash, to fight. It was just hair…it was just hair. It would grow back. But *fuck* did it hurt, the razor-sharp blade slicing into my scalp as she got the angle wrong, scraping across my head, slicing, cutting. She didn't stop until every last strand of hair was gone, leaving me shaved as bald as a brand-new military recruit.

She stepped back, glancing down at her hands, which were coated with smeared blood and hair, and then back to me. "There. Not so beautiful anymore, are you? It's a start, at least." She titled her head to the side, assessing me. "Your features are still too perfect, really. I mean, you *are* a very beautiful girl. Or at least, you *were*. You won't be when I'm done with you."

I didn't respond. I just stared at her, chewing on a strand of hair stuck between my front teeth. I wanted to say so many things, curse her out, beg her to stop, tell her she would regret this. But I said nothing. I let my hate and my malice speak for me, gleaming from my eyes.

Gina leaned forward, slicing between my wrists, hitting skin as she parted the plastic of the zip ties.

My feet next, leaving me unbound and bleeding from cuts on my scalp, wrists, and ankles. I wanted to lunge at her, tackle her, but I didn't. I would bide my time. Find the perfect moment.

Clearly wary as she cut me free, Gina took three quick steps backward, away from me, watching me. "Too cowardly to attack even now, I see." She grinned. "Well, it will still be fun. I had hoped you would go for me. I would have enjoyed cutting you to ribbons. But, oh well. This way I get to enjoy the fun a bit longer."

I stayed in place, chest heaving from the struggle to endure the agony.

After a moment of staring at me, Gina kicked the base of the door with one foot, holding her hands in front of her daintily, as if she'd merely gotten them dirty. The door opened, and she stepped through, handing her knife to Tobias.

"Here. Clean this for me. I'm going to change." The door slammed closed, and I heard her speaking to Tobias. "Leave her alone for now, Tobias. I mean it. You can have her when I'm done, but not before. If I find you've touched her, I will be *very* displeased."

I still had to pee. And for some reason, I still held it. I wasn't sure why. It gave me something to focus on besides the fear and the pain, perhaps?

My bladder was screaming, my knee throbbing, my scalp burning, wrists and ankles aching. Blood streamed down my face, down the back of my neck, the cuts on my head still oozing. I was dizzy from hunger, throat parched, tongue thick and dry.

I wanted Valentine. But I also hoped he would stay away. If he came for me, she would kill him. She was going to kill me anyway. I knew Valentine would come for me, even though he had to know it would be a trap.

I sat up eventually and struggled to my feet, testing my knee. I could hobble slowly, but any weight on the leg had me crying and near to collapse. I moved in slow circles around the room, limping, limping, limping. Keeping the rest of my body loose, ignoring the pain, ignoring the increasingly desperate need to pee.

I was going to die in this room. I was going to be raped, tortured, and then eventually killed. I should just accept it. But I didn't.

I couldn't.

I would not let them do to me what they'd done to Lisa. I would attack, make them kill me first. That would be better. Better than being raped.

*Valentine. Save me, Valentine,* I thought. *Please. Please.*

Even raw terror can't keep you awake for ever. I dozed fitfully, jerking awake and then nodding off again.

Time passed, whether in hours or minutes or days, I couldn't tell.

The door opening jarred me from a daze.

A bulky shape filled the opening briefly, and then the door quietly closed behind Tobias. I watched him approach me on silent feet. He stood in front of me, staring down at me, black eyes leering, crazy, hungry.

"I'm not supposed to be here. But she won't know. It won't matter." Tobias knelt in front of me. Reached out, ran his palm over my scalp. "Nice."

I kept absolutely still. Noticed the butt of a gun in a shoulder holster, visible beneath his suit coat.

"Lie down," he ordered.

I remained sitting.

He reached into the pocket of his pants, withdrew a small folding knife. Opened it. Touched the blade to my left nipple. "I say, *lie…down*."

An idea formed in my head. A desperate, doomed idea, but something. It would probably get me killed, but at this point, that was better than enduring what Tobias hand in mind for me. So I moved to my back, keeping my knees pressed together. The aching pressure in my bladder was at critical mass. I couldn't hold it much longer.

Tobias set the knife down beside me and unbuckled his pants and let them fall to his knees. I kept my eyes on his, rather than subjecting myself to the sight of his dick. He leered at me. Gripped his dick in his hand and stroked himself. Rubbed it against my knee. Shuffled forward, knocked my knees apart, and then slammed the inside of my upper thigh with his fist hard enough to leave a bruise. Did the same to the other side. I stifled a cry, forcing myself to remain still. I forced myself to let him get closer. Forced myself to keep my legs open. I kept my eyes on his ugly, straining face as he bent over me, lips curled into a greedy, anticipatory smile.

I felt him at my entrance, thick and hot, but not quite hard. Apparently I wasn't bloody enough to really excite him; he punched me, a fist to my cheek, a brutal blow that rocked me backward, made me dizzy. His dick hardened then, and then he hit me again on the other cheek. A third punch, and I felt my nose break, blood sluice down my face.

Now he was fully erect and poised at my entrance. His grin was hungry, evil.

I choked on my tears and breathed through the pain as Tobias prepared to thrust into me.

"I like it when you scream," he murmured, his breath hot and fetid on my face. "So scream loud."

*VALENTINE*

We met at the airstrip and flew from there to Athens, where Henri and his friend split away from the main group without a word. Harris had guided the rest of us to the Marina Zea, to a dock where a rusting fishing vessel bobbed, waiting for us. The captain was a wizened little Greek with skin the color of walnut shells and weathered to a similar texture.

We waited for an hour, then two. Finally, Henri and his friend returned, and I noticed both of them had changed shirts and now smelled of soap.

Henri nodded at me. "Gina's shadows are now ghosts. We go now, she won't know we are coming."

Bags of weapons and Kevlar vests and boxes of ammo were broken out as soon as we reached open water, each of us gearing up. We detoured, stopping at a little fishing village, where Henri's nameless friend and Andrei—who was armed with Harris's MSR rifle—departed in a helicopter. I glanced at Henri, an eyebrow lifted in inquiry.

"Andrei is an expert sniper. My friend is an experienced pilot." Henri gestured at the rising aircraft.

"We have a helicopter, a favor from my friend. Now we have support in the sky."

It was a long trip, and I nodded off uneasily as the old fishing vessel plied the waves, traveling east and south, through the lowering darkness and into the night.

A quiet word in Greek from the captain, and we were all awake immediately, collecting our gear and moving to the stern. Alexei and Matteo pushed the Zodiac into the water as the fishing vessel drifted to a stop. The two mercenaries held the boat in place as the rest of us climbed in, and then we pushed off, the powerful outboard motor buzzing. I heard the splash of an anchor, and the fishing vessel's lights winked out, leaving us to slip across the Aegean in the moonlit darkness. No one spoke a word.

Dawn stained the sea with a pink glow. I sat in the back of the Zodiac, fighting panic and nerves and seasickness as the tiny boat zipped across the water, lurching up over waves and crashing back down. I had a Steyr AUG bullpup assault rifle in my hand, spare magazines in the pocket of my tactical vest, a pistol in a hip holster, and a Kevlar vest beneath my clothing. Harris was beside me, similarly attired and armed, as were Henri and the other three mercenaries.

The island loomed in the distance. A quarter mile away, Matteo cut the motor and handed out paddles. We pulled through the water silently now, Henri and Harris kneeling in the bow with assault rifles aimed at the island. I heard the distant *whump-whumpwhump* of the helicopter skimming over the water on the other side of the island.

As we approached the shoreline, the crash of waves against the rocks became a roar. Alexei lifted his paddle from the water, gestured at us with his four-fingered left hand—his pinky finger was nothing but a stub—and we all stopped pulling. Sasha cut his paddle into the water, angling us toward to a fold in the rock face of the island. Once the rubber bow of the Zodiac bumped against the rock, stopping us, Alexei tied the mooring line to a rusted ring driven into an outcropping of rock.

He gestured up at the rock face. "This used to be a fortress in centuries past. There is a stair in the stone. We go up."

Staring up, I could well believe there used to be a fortress here. I'd seen a satellite image of the island: it was a finger of bare rock thrusting up out of the Aegean with a narrow beach on the south side, along with a small natural bay. High above, was a massive house built directly into the rock itself, a glass-and-steel structure constructed over the ruins of the ancient fortress.

We were on the north side of the island, facing a nearly sheer vertical slope of bare rock. It seemed impossible to ascend, but I watched as Alexei slung his rifle around his back and climbed up with the agility of a billy goat. Looking closely, I could see a narrow set of grooves carved into the ancient stone. It couldn't be called a "staircase," but it would allow us to climb up unnoticed. It took us an hour to scale the face, and as we topped the rise behind the mansion, I heard the helicopter nearing, the thump of rotors loud now.

*BOOM!* The MSR cracked, shattering the glass window beside the front door.

Men streamed out of the building, wielding Uzis and AK-47s, shouting at each other. They saw us, then, and opened fire, sending rounds whizzing and snapping at us.

The MSR boomed again, and I watched a man tumble forward. *BOOM!* A second body dropped. Alexei darted forward, spraying bullets in short bursts. He leaped through the space where the window had been, boots crunching on glass, and I could see him pivoting, scanning—*crackcrackcrack*—then shouts were cut off, and bodies hit the floor. I was

right behind him, then passing him, my MP5 rattling nonstop, jarring against my shoulder.

Kyrie was here, somewhere. I had to find her. I
had to find her. Reason left me, then, and I took off
running.

Voices behind me called out for me to wait, but
there was no waiting. Shapes moved in front of me
and I cut them down. I pushed through door after
door, heedless of the danger, spraying rounds at anything that moved, kicking bodies out of the way as I
sought the entrance to the lower levels. My actions
were automatic, instinctive, rage-fueled. My only
thought was to find Kyrie. There was nothing else.
I didn't care what happened to anyone, even myself,
as long as I found her.

Alexei called out, gesturing to me. "Here! The
stairs down."

I shoved past him, bounding down the steps
recklessly. Alexei followed behind me more cau-
tiously. We descended a winding staircase down into
the fortress, moving through narrow hallways and
into empty rooms, a labyrinth leading us downward
in a series of concentric circles.

At one point, we came to a T-intersection, and
Matteo pushed ahead of me, rounded a corner to
the left, rifle to his cheek, firing. Blood sprayed, and

he was rocked backward, clutching his throat. Alexei pulled him back around the corner even as Matteo gargled and went still. Alexei rolled out around the corner in a crouch, fired, and pulled back hastily, wiping at his forehead with an uneasy, disbelieving bark of laughter. A bullet had creased his face, missing his temple by a fraction of an inch.

I peered around the corner, saw daylight through a doorway. A man stood in the doorway, a rifle aiming at me. He fired, the bullet cracking into the wall beside my head. I aimed at his torso and squeezed the trigger, and he dropped.

Silence, then, apart from the helicopter circling in the distance.

The doorway led us out onto a balcony carved into the rock face itself, the Aegean blue and turbulent fifty feet down. Another open doorway loomed to our left, a black mouth leading further downward into the bowels of the ancient fortress.

Sasha, Henri, and Harris headed back up, searching the rest of the rooms once more, making sure there were no surprises waiting.

I heard the *crack* of a pistol echo up the staircase. A momentary pause, and then *crack…crack… crack…crack.* It was a big pistol, by the sound of it. Silence. Then one more booming report.

My throat tightened, and my gut churned. My heart pounded; Kyrie was down that staircase somewhere.

I knew it. I felt it.

But was she alive?

# 17

## THE FORTRESS FALLS

Just before Tobias pushed into me, I lunged up off the ground, wrapping my legs around his neck. I ignored the screaming, wrenching agony in my knee, the haze of blurring pain of his blows, and clamped my thighs around his throat, squeezing with every ounce of strength I possessed. He thrashed, kicked, punched, and I silently accepted the pain, each smashing punch rolling into the mass of torment that was my entire body.

And then...I cut loose, let my bladder unleash all over him. I felt my urine splatter against his chest and my legs, then arched my hips up so the stream hit his face. He was bellowing, thrashing, cursing in whatever language he spoke, fighting me. I held on, held on, gritting my teeth against the pounding, tearing pain in my knee, even as the relief of my now-emptied bladder swept through me.

Abruptly, I released him and reared back, lashed out with my good leg, felt my heel connect with his face, and kicked again. And again, and again, as viciously as I could, letting my rage take over. I rocked forward, struggling, groaning, and made it to my feet. Tobias was cursing, gagging, but more surprised than really hurt. I had mere seconds before he would be up on his feet, bashing me with his huge fists. I stomped on his crotch as hard as I could, and then grabbed the butt of the pistol from his shoulder holster and hopped backward, stumbled and nearly fell. Bumping up against the wall, I gripped the gun in both hands, finger resting on the trigger, the gun held out in front of me at arm's length, the way Harris had showed me.

*BANG!*

The pistol jumped in my hands, nearly jerking out of my grip. Tobias flinched and grunted, red staining his chest. I brought the barrel back down, not bothering to aim except for the center mass, like Harris had told me.

*BANG!*

Another red circle beside the first. Tobias was groaning, cursing, gasping, crying.

This time, I aimed. I centered the front sight over his crotch, squeezed the trigger…and then changed my mind. Adjusted aim upward, hesitated, held my breath, and squeezed. His head exploded, and my stomach heaved, rebelled, lurched. I let the pistol hang in one hand as I leaned to one side, dry-heaving, nothing in my stomach to bring up except bile.

I set the gun on the ground and quickly stripped Tobias of his pants and tugged them on. They were way too big, but I used the belt to cinch them around my waist, tying the end of the belt around itself near my hip and rolled the cuffs up around my ankles. Gagging at the sight of the gory mess that was his head, I rolled his body to one side, struggling with his bulk, and worked his blazer off one arm, then let him flop back down and worked it off the other side, then donned the coat myself, buttoning it to cover my torso. It was wet with blood at the shoulders, lapel, and collar, but at least I was covered.

Next, I loosened and untied his necktie, gagging at the stench and the sight of brain matter. I dry-heaved again, fought it, shoved it down. I wrapped the tie around my knee and knotted it as tight as I could stand it, choking back the sobs of agony. But once it was tied, the throbbing in my knee lessened slightly, enough that I could hobble to the door. Remembering the way Henri had stood behind the door of his bar, I positioned myself to the left of the opening, so the door would hide me when it opened. I waited, standing on my good leg to spare my wounded knee. Something hard and heavy weighted down the pocket of my appropriated coat; I dug it out and found an extra clip for the pistol. Not knowing what awaited me, I exchanged it for the partially depleted one.

The door flew open and hit me, knocking me into the wall.

"TOBIAS! What the fuck are you doing?" Gina was shouting even as the door was still swinging open. "They're here! We don't have time for—" She stopped when she saw Tobias's body. "Shit. *Shit.* SHIT!"

I was hidden behind the door, waiting, the heavy silver pistol held in both hands. I settled my weight on both feet, teeth clenched against the pain, involuntary tears of physical anguish streaming down my face. Blue-lacquered nails clicked against the edge of the door, pulling it away from me.

As the door swung away and revealed me, I brought the pistol up, blinking away the tears of pain, and fired as soon as the barrel was aimed at center mass.

Gina jerked as the bullet hammered into her, and then twisted in place, clutching her side where the round had hit her. Expensive blue silk went dark with blood.

"You?" she mumbled, her voice faint with shock and pain.

"Me, bitch." I fired again at her torso.

She stumbled backward, bumped up against the wall. Rage swept through me, blinding me, taking over. The gun was exploding, jumping in my hands as I shot her, once, twice, a third time, a fourth. Gina's entire body was a mess of red now. She slid to the ground, eyes glazed.

"That was for Valentine," I said.

I blinked, felt the gun heavy in my hands. Saw in my mind what Tobias had done to Lisa. What he'd tried to do to me. What Gina had done to Valentine.

I ran one palm over my scalp, feeling blood and scabs and stubble. "This is for me."

*BANG!*

The wall was covered in crimson, my final shot going through her skull and pitting the wall behind.

She was dead, finally dead. And yet…it seemed almost anticlimactic; a single squeeze of a trigger, and she was dead.

My knee gave out, my strength ebbing, and I slumped to the floor on my hands and knees, coughing, sobbing.

*Valentine.*

*They're here,* she'd said.

I couldn't give up now.

*Get up,* I told myself. *Get UP!*

I forced myself to my feet, hopped and hobbled to the door, swung it open and limped through it. I lost my footing, and had to lean against the wall for support. I groaned through clenched teeth at each step away from the doorway, stumbling along a dark, low, ancient corridor lit by dull yellow bulbs in wall sconces every few feet. I saw a stairway ahead of me, a bright rectangle, indicating daylight.

I heard gunfire chattering. Automatics rattling, pistols barking. In the distance, a slow and rhythmic *BOOM…BOOM…BOOM…BOOM,* a heavy rifle.

The stairs would be my downfall. There was no way I could make it up that many steps. My knee was bleeding through the pant leg, aching and burning and weak. I was dizzy, thirsty, starving, my entire body throbbing with a million points of pain. Blood was salty on my lips, sticky at my nose and mouth, drying and tacky on my neck and head.

I heard a step above me, a voice shouting in… Greek, maybe? Or Russian? I wasn't sure. Prone on my stomach on the stairs, I craned my neck and peered up, saw sunlight on a gun barrel, a silhouette of man standing at the top of the stairs. I'd made it too far to give up now. I still had the pistol in my hand, I realized, so I rolled to the side, brought my gun up and struggled to aim. The barrel wavered, and I squeezed the trigger. The explosion was deafening.

He ducked backward out of sight as my gun went off, and this time the recoil jerked it out of my hand. It arced over me and landed on my back with a sharp impact to my spine, and then tumbled between my body and the stairs. I scrambled and twisted to reach it, but my strength was waning, fading. I felt it, scrabbled for it, felt the cool wood of the butt against my palm.

But he was there already, right above me, two steps up. He had a machine gun pointed toward the floor. I rolled to my back and lifted the pistol one more time, sobbing with desperation as he lifted his machine gun. But instead of shooting me, he swiveled his weapon around behind his back and bent toward me. The sun was a blinding orange ball framed by the stairway entrance, making it impossible to see anything but shadows and silhouettes.

I was going to die, now.

"Good thing you missed," a deep, sweetly familiar voice said.

I blinked, dizzy and confused, and tried to focus on the figure above me.

Valentine?

It was my Valentine.

I sobbed and collapsed to the steps, relief sapping me of any remaining strength.

I felt myself lifted into Valentine's arms, and this was familiar now, his brawny arms cradling me against his chest, his gorgeous pale blue eyes worried and fearful and reddened and leaking tears as he gazed down at me.

"Kyr—Kyrie." His voice broke. "What did they do to you, my love?"

I blinked slowly, feeling darkness threading through me. "Should see—you should see the other guy." I even managed a smile.

He smiled back at me. "My girl. You're safe now, love. You're safe. I've got you." His lips trembled as he pressed a kiss to my forehead. "I'll never let anything happen to you again, I promise. I promise."

That was all I needed. I let go of consciousness, let darkness pull me under.

## *VALENTINE*

I felt something hot and wet under my hands as I cradled Kyrie's head in my palm. I felt tears slide down my cheeks at the sight of her battered face.

She was alive, though.

Her hair had been shaved off, leaving her head covered with nicks and cuts. Blood trickled past her ear, down her forehead and along her nose. Her face was bruised, her cheeks swelling, black eyes forming. Her nose was broken, blood oozing from her mouth, chin, and throat. She was wearing a man's trousers with a belt tied around her waist, and a blood-stained jacket. She was naked beneath the blazer. She stank of urine. She had a .45 Smith and Wesson in one hand, which I gently pried from her grip.

She was limp in my arms, head lolling.

Alexei was stealing down the stairs, rifle swiveling. I let him go. He could take care of things down there.

"Valentine." Alexei, from the bottom of the stairs. "You must see this."

I refused to let her out of my arms, so I descended the stairs with Kyrie, carefully angling her head through the doorway at the end of the hall.

Tobias was on the ground, two bullet holes in his chest, and the back of his head blown off. And then there was Gina, her torso riddled with bullets and a hole between her eyes.

"She did this." Alexei gestured at Kyrie with his chin. He crouched, sniffed, wrinkled his nose. "Clever girl. Brave. Very, very tough."

I could only nod in agreement, my throat too thick to speak.

I could read the scene as well as Alexei: Tobias's underwear pulled down around his knees, the stench of urine, his soaked shirt and hair, his broken face, the blood on Kyrie's feet. I could see the respect in Alexei's eyes as he glanced at her, unconscious in my arms.

He moved past us, rifle at his shoulder. I heard scattered pops of gunfire here and there. Harris and Henri were undoubtedly mopping up above. Alexei popped his head into a few doors here and there as we ascended, making sure they were all empty. He paused in one, stopping in shock, and then backed out, anger on his face.

"It is good for that pig down there that your girl kill him first." He gestured into the room. "He was a monster, I tell you."

I glanced in, and saw what had, at one point, been a girl. My stomach heaved, and I had to turn away.

We made slow progress back up through the dark labyrinth, up and up and up to daylight. There we found the helicopter waiting on the landing pad on the far east side of the island. Andrei lay prone in the open door of the chopper, MSR at the ready, scanning for threats. Henri's friend, the helo pilot, was refueling the chopper, courtesy of the Karahalios family.

Henri emerged from the smashed window, stepping over bodies. "All is clear."

Harris wasn't far behind him, trotting over to me. "Kyrie? Is she—?"

"Alive. Roughed up, but alive."

"And the bitch?" Henri asked.

"Dead," Alexei answered.

"You?" Harris asked.

I shook my head. "Nope." I lifted Kyrie slightly. "Her."

Harris frowned, looking her over. "Did they…?"

I knew what he was asking. "I don't know. I don't think so, but I'm not sure." I moved toward the helicopter, shielding her from the downdraft as the rotors began to whirl and whine. "Let's get her out of here."

Andrei had his rifle cradled in his arms with casual familiarity. "Matteo?"

Alexei shook his head and then twisted in place, gesturing with a thumb at Sasha, who emerged from the house with Matteo's limp form over one shoulder. Alexei provided a brief explanation in Russian, gesturing sharply at his throat with a middle finger. Andrei dropped his rifle and cursed viciously in Russian, pacing back and forth in front of the helicopter, and then slid to a crouch, shoulders shaking.

Alexei glanced at me as if in apology. "His brother." He pointed to Sasha. "My brother." Then he gestured at all four of them, his finger moving in a circle. "Cousins."

"I'm sorry," I said, not knowing what else to say.

He only shrugged. "You go. Take Matteo with you." Alexei motioned for Sasha to follow him. "Fishing man will return us to Athens. We meet you there for payment of the rest."

Andrei laid Matteo in the back of the chopper, and then shrugged out of his shirt, leaving his arms bare with just the Kevlar vest over his chest. He covered his brother's face with the shirt.

He scooped the rifle back up, glancing at Harris. "Rifle is mine."

Harris nodded easily. "Sure."

I held Kyrie on my lap, her head resting on my shoulder, lolling with the motion of our takeoff.

A few minutes into the flight, Harris leaned over to me. "You know Vitaly will find out what happened," he said, shouting into my ear over the noise of the rotors. "He had to have had video surveillance on a place like that."

I nodded. "I know."

"This isn't over, Roth."

"It is for now."

"Where do we go from Athens?" Harris asked.

I spent a few minutes thinking. "Buy me the biggest yacht you can find. I don't care how much it costs. Staff it and get me security. I want the fucking best, Harris. Men whose loyalty cannot be bought or questioned." I glanced down at Kyrie, wiped at the blood on her face with my thumb. "Tell Robert to streamline everything. Sell off the subsidiaries, everything that's not vital. Make it so I can run it all remotely—so I'm not needed in the day-to-day operations."

Harris already had his encrypted satellite phone out and was dialing.

I planned on vanishing, going off the grid for a long, long time. Vitaly would be looking for us, I knew that. Let him look.

By the time he found us, I'd be ready for him.

# 18

## HEALING

I woke up slowly, taking stock. The last thing I remembered was Valentine's face peering down at me.

Gina. Tobias. Lisa.

Memory assaulted me, and I sobbed.

"Sshh." Valentine's voice, murmuring in my ear. His chest was beneath my cheek, his arm around my shoulder. "You're safe. I've got you, Kyrie."

"Valentine?" His name came out in an incoherent mumble.

"Yes, love. It's me."

"You came."

His chest rocked, as if he was stifling a sob of his own. "Of course." His hand smoothed over my scalp, ever so gently. "Of course I came for you. Nothing could keep me away."

"Hurts."

"What does?"

"Everything."

He rubbed my arm with his hand. "I know. We're almost there."

"Thirsty." A straw touched my lips, and I took a tentative sip. Cool, clean water wetted my lips. I took a greedy gulp, letting the water soak into my mouth, wetting my tongue. I swallowed it, and then some more. "Where?"

"We're in the air right now. We'll be in Athens in a few minutes."

"You…are you okay?"

"Me? I'm fine. Not a scratch."

I tried to summon something to say, but everything hurt. I took another sip, and thought of something he should know. "Tobias. He—he didn't. I—he tried. He was going to. I stopped him. I—I killed him."

He let out a breath of relief. "You did good."

"I peed on him." The admission actually made me laugh, for some reason. It wasn't funny, though.

"I know."

"I killed Gina, too. I shot her…so many times. I couldn't stop. She was so evil." I felt dizzy, tired. I was exhausted. My face hurt. My broken nose hurt. My knee throbbed. My ribs hurt, too, thanks to

Tobias. At the time, none of the pain had registered, and afterward, everything else had been throbbing too badly to notice. "Tobias…she brought in a girl, an innocent…girl. An American girl. She made me watch while Tobias…*god*…." I couldn't finish, shivering, stomach roiling at the memory.

"I know, love. I know. We found her." Valentine kissed my temple. "Shush, now. It's over. You're safe now. Rest, all right?"

"I like it when you sound English." I wasn't sure where that came from.

Sleep pulled me under.

I woke again, and this time I didn't hurt as much. I felt light, as if I could float, yet my brain seemed heavy and sluggish. I opened my eyes to bright sunlight, the way things are always a little brighter at sea. I felt the rocking of a boat beneath me, gentle but constant, the deep side-to-side rolling motion of the sea. I'd spent enough time on boats with Roth, on rivers and at dock and out to sea, that I could recognize the motion anywhere.

There were floor-to-ceiling windows running around the room, polished chrome between each pane, blonde-colored wood trim beneath, matching the floor. The bed I was on was a California king on a pedestal against the back wall, set in the center of the room. The glass ran three hundred and sixty degrees, providing a view of the sea in every direction. The sun shone off to my left, bright orange and resting on the horizon. Sunrise, it seemed. The sea was calm, tinted orange-pink.

I swallowed, my throat dry. Rolling my head to one side, I saw a panel on the wall beside my head containing buttons and sliding switches. They were all conveniently labeled: *lighting*—with three sliders all at the bottom, indicating that they were off; *wall tint*—and a single slider, at the bottom; *ceiling tint*—with a single slider toggled up. I glanced up, and saw that the roof of the room was flat black, opaque. I stretched out and slid the ceiling tint switch down, and the roof's opacity faded to transparent, showing me the sky, orange-red now, a few clouds appearing as gray twists across the horizon.

Where was I? Was this a boat? Clearly it was, since there was nothing in any direction but ocean. Looking out past my feet, straight ahead, I could see the bow of the boat. A man in black fatigues stood at the bow, and as I watched, he turned in place, revealing a machine gun of some kind slung across his chest. Another identically dressed man approached and the two conversed, each of them scanning the horizon in all directions as they spoke. One of them laughed and slapped the other on the back, and then retreated from the bow, moving astern.

Footsteps thudded on stairs, and Valentine appeared beside the bed. "Kyrie? You're awake!"

I worked myself into a sitting position, feeling the distant twinge of aches dulled by medication. "Those men out there—who are they?"

He sat beside me on the bed and gathered me in his arms, settling me on his lap, his pale blue eyes assessing me head to foot. "Our security. There are six of them. Three of whom were with me when we rescued you. You'll meet them all later, though. How are you feeling?"

I nodded against his chest. "Groggy, but okay."

He nodded. "You've got some pretty potent meds in you right now." He took my hand in his. "I brought a doctor on board, someone Henri knows. You needed knee-replacement surgery, as well as stitches to your scalp. You also needed your nose set. You had some bruised ribs, black eyes."

I nodded, and my head swam. I stilled, and burrowed against Valentine. "Dizzy. I'm kinda thirsty." I looked up at him, saw the worry in his eyes. "I'm okay, Valentine. I am. If you hadn't come when you did, though—"

He shook his head, interrupting me. "I didn't protect you. I left you, and she got you."

That's right. He had left me. I blinked at him.
"Why *did* you leave me? Where did you go?"

"I was gone for five…for five fucking minutes.
I went up to the roof to talk to Harris. I had some
plans to discuss with him. They must have been
waiting. Someone shot at me. Not trying to kill me,
just…driving me away. Getting me out of the way so
Gina could…."

"She was waiting in the library. The house was
empty. I looked for you after I got out of the shower.
But I found her instead. I knew…going into the
library, I knew I should turn around and leave. I felt
it. But I—I didn't. I was stupid. I went anyway. And
there she was." I swallowed hard against the lump
in my throat, and Valentine pressed a button on the
wall panel, speaking into an intercom, requesting
water be brought up to us. "I should have listened to
my gut. If I had—"

"No. You should have been safe in my home. I
thought you *were* safe. It was only supposed to be
five minutes. I'd be back before you got out of the
shower." He pinched the bridge of his nose, shoulders heaving and sinking as he fought his emotions.

Boots pounded on the stairs outside the bedroom, and then a man entered the room. He was
tall and lean, his eyes mocha-brown, his features
weathered and hard-bitten, but attractive in a lupine

sort of way. He had a scar running down the side of his face, going up into his close-cropped black hair. He had a machine gun hanging by a strap from his shoulder, one hand resting casually on the stock, two bottles of water in his other hand. He handed the bottles to Roth. "I am glad you to see you awake, Miss Kyrie." He grinned and did a two-finger salute, and then retreated down the stairs.

When he was gone, I took the bottle Valentine had opened, and drank slowly. "He seems nice."

Valentine shook his head, laughing. "Nice? That's not really an applicable word to use for a man like him."

"What does that mean?"

I noticed Valentine's accent was thicker than usual, his normally carefully cultivated tone lacking its usual drawing-room polish, as if a façade had been dropped. "It just means that Alexei is...many things. Nice, however, is *not* one of them."

I didn't try to decipher what that meant. I scooted over on the bed, making room for Valentine. I patted the bed. "I need to be closer to you."

He slid downward to a lying position, keeping me on his chest, in the sheltering warmth of his arms. I pressed my face against his throat and inhaled his scent, felt his heart beating beneath my palm.

I slept again.

When I woke, I was still on Roth's lap, cradled against his chest, his arm around my shoulders. He had a cell phone in his other hand, a huge thing almost the size of a tablet, and he was tapping at it with one thumb.

"Help me to the bathroom?" I said. He tossed the phone to the side, slid off the bed, and scooped me up in his arms. "No. Let me stand. I need to try to stand up."

Roth ignored me, descending a wide but steep set of stairs to a lower level of the boat. I sighed and let him carry me. There were floor-to-ceiling windows here too, but the ceiling was lower, the same blonde wood as on the floor above. To the right of the stairs was a long white leather couch on one wall, perpendicular to the windows, facing a huge TV screen. Ahead, a short corridor led past the TV to a full bar with stools, the window wall facing the bar so anyone sitting on the stools would have a view of the sea behind them. Left of the stairs was a doorway, leading to the bathroom. The bathroom, of course, was as luxurious as any of Roth's I'd ever been in. Marble and glass and blonde wood, windows looking out over the ocean, soft lighting. He sat me on the toilet and helped me arrange the oversized gray T-shirt of his that was all I had on.

You know your man loves you when he helps you go to the bathroom.

When I was finished, he took me back to the bedroom, setting me on the bed with exquisite tenderness. I loved his protectiveness, even though I knew I'd need to exercise my knee soon.

I flexed the knee back and forth, testing it. "So. This boat? The security?" I glanced at him. "You want to fill me in?"

Roth picked up his phone and spun it between his thumb and forefinger, sitting cross-legged on the bed, facing me. "You were out for a week. You had a nasty fever for a few days. You were severely dehydrated. She had you for almost three days, you know. That's how long it took me to get to you. Three *fucking* days." He wouldn't look at me. "Once I got you back, I knew I'd never go back to New York. I'm in the process of selling off the tower and a huge portion of my subsidiary businesses. I'm selling all the estates, except for the vineyard in France. Harris acquired this yacht for us, and here we are."

"But we're safe now?" I asked.

His features darkened. "No one will ever harm you again. I promise," he growled. "On my fucking life, I swear it."

That wasn't the same as a reassurance that we were safe. "But?"

"But her father is still out there." He traced a vein on the back of my hand, following it up my forearm. "He's…not as psychopathic, but…far more calculating. He's tirelessly vindictive. His daughter is dead. Two of his estates were attacked. Thirty-some of his men have been killed." He paused. "Kyrie, you just…you don't know Vitaly. He's not going to let this go."

"So we're running from him?"

Roth frowned. "You need time to heal."

"And then what?" I pushed the sheet off my legs and stared at my knee, seeing the bandages covering the recent surgical scars. "We just live on a boat forever?"

Roth smirked at that. "*Boat?* Kyrie, my love, this is one of the largest super yachts ever built. You've only seen the smallest fraction of it. This bedroom and the level down there? It's the…penthouse, basically. Our private quarters at the very top. There are a dozen guest cabins in the decks below, staff quarters for almost fifty people, an industrial kitchen, and a formal dining room. A gym, complete with an Olympic pool. It has its own helicopter landing pad, as well as a hidden launch for a smaller boat. Now, because of our unique situation, I've only staffed it with a six-man security team, a skeleton crew to run the ship, and a small staff to run the kitchen and clean. Everyone has been screened a dozen different ways, and of them, only Alexei has access to our quarters up here."

"Where's Harris?" I asked.

Valentine hesitated. "I've given him some time to himself. He's earned it." He sighed. "It feels a bit odd without him around, but he needed some time off."

I shrugged. "Okay." It wasn't okay, though. I would miss Harris, a lot, for one thing.

Roth frowned, seeing my discomfort. "What?"

I couldn't quite meet his eyes. "I don't want to spend my life running, Valentine."

"Neither do I. And we won't. I just…I need time. *You* need time."

Silence extended between us for a length of time I couldn't measure. "Valentine? Eliza…?"

It was several moments before he could speak. "I've known her most of my life."

"She said she'd worked for you for twenty years, but then you said when your father kicked you out, he left you with nothing. I'm not sure I understand."

"She was my father's employee first. I think I told you that. Well…she was assigned to me. I was too old for her to be considered a 'nanny,' but she was my personal…I don't know. Servant? I hate that term, because it wasn't like that. She was my friend. My parents were not really…accessible sorts. My father had billion-dollar accounts to manage, ultra-high-profile clients to entertain. My mother had charities to run, parties to throw. Our house was always filled with important people. Parliamentarians, European politicians, presidents and prime ministers and royals. Hollywood A-listers. Heads of banks and international corporations. And me? I was just their son. I was expected to make an appearance, show them my best manners, and then retire to my rooms. And Eliza was all I had. She wasn't that much older than me. Forty-eight to my thirty-seven. When you're fifteen, sixteen, an eleven-year age difference is a lot. But she was my friend. My only friend."

He trailed off, going silent for a while, remembering. Eventually he continued, and I remained silent, grateful for this rare peek into Roth's past. "When my father…sent me out, as he phrased it, she'd been working for him for eight years, five of those as my personal…whatever. I was twenty-two when I moved to New York—when I escaped Gina and Vitaly, I suppose I should say. Five years exactly from the day my father sent me out, I hired Eliza out from underneath him."

"So what you told me originally—"

"Not entirely the truth, no. Once I had things going in New York, I called Father's head of staff,

Gregory, and asked for Eliza's contact information. Said I wanted to look her up to say hello. Well, I said hello, and I asked her if she would like to come work for me. That was a little over twelve years ago. She'd worked for my father's household staff while I was out making my fortune. God, how long did she work my father? Thirteen years? And twelve for me?" He covered his face with both hands. "And fucking Gina just...gunned her down. For no reason."

"I'm so sorry, Valentine."

"Me, too." His expression twisted into hatred. "I'd like to bring Gina back just so I can kill her again."

"Valentine, you can't think like that." I shifted closer to him. "I want that part of our lives to be over. The guns, the killings...I just want it to be over."

He shook his head. "While Vitaly is out there, that's impossible." Roth stood up, shoved his phone in the back pocket of his pants, and paused at the top of the stairs. "You should rest."

"Don't leave, Valentine. Don't—don't leave me alone."

"I was just going to grab you something to eat...."

I reached for him, tugged on his sleeve until he sat back down on the bed. "We have a staff, don't we? Have it sent up." I waved my hand in dismissal. "I'm not hungry anyway. I just...I can't be alone right now." I tried to close my eyes, to rest again, but images of Tobias, and Gina, and Lisa, bloody and ravaged and brutalized, kept popping into my head. I remembered the scene in the library and Gina pulling the trigger. I could almost feel the bullet hitting my knee again. The thirst and the hunger. Tobias's breath on me, his weight, his leering grin as he prepared to rape me.

My vision blurred, my eyes hot and stinging.

"God, Kyrie, I'm so sorry. I'm sorry." His voice cracked. "I failed you. I fucking—I failed you." He shook beneath me, struggling for control.

"It wasn't your fault, Valentine." I twisted so I could look up at him.

He wouldn't look at me. "Yes. It was." He shrugged. "I underestimated Gina. I got complacent. I thought she'd forgotten. Moved on. Ten years. She left me alone for *ten* years. And then, out of the blue…she just…she ruined everything. Me. You. Us. The life I'd worked so hard to build."

"You think I'm ruined?" I asked in a high, small, tremulous voice. "You think you are?"

"You were almost raped. You were *shot*. Beaten. You saw…you—"

"We *both* went through really horrible shit, Valentine. Not just me, not just you."

"I didn't protect you." He stood up, paced away and back. "And now you're on Vitaly's radar. So even if you wanted to…I don't know…start over somewhere else. With—with someone else, you couldn't. He'd find you. He'd kill you."

"Roth, what—what are you saying?" I lunged forward, struggling to my feet, hopping, grabbing onto Roth for balance, turning him to face me. "Start over? Someone else? What are you talking about?"

He held onto my arms, keeping me upright. "I failed you, Kyrie. I promised you'd be safe. I *left* you. I left your side. I should have stayed." He shook his head. "How can you trust me now?

"You can't take all the blame yourself, Valentine." I fought the panic inside me. "I *knew*…I felt something—I knew something was wrong when I went looking for you. If I'd just waited for you—but I didn't know where you were—"

"Because I *left* you." He tilted his head back, blinking hard. "Then they were shooting at me. I tried to get back to you, but Harris, he knew…if I'd made a run for the door, they'd have shot me. They could have. At any moment, they could have killed me. But she wanted me alive. She wanted me out of the way. If you hadn't gone looking for me, she probably would have blown the door off its hinges or something. She would have gotten you. But if I'd stayed with you—if I'd done like I promised, you wouldn't have—"

"Roth." I grabbed his face and made him look down at me. He shook his head, but I held on. "*Valentine*. Listen to me. Baby, listen. Please. I don't *want* to start over somewhere else. I couldn't, even if none of this had happened. I couldn't leave you. I couldn't go back to…a normal life, to life without *you*. I just…I can't. I won't."

"Why?" He seemed honestly puzzled.

"Because I *love* you, you big idiot." I hobbled closer to him, pressed myself against him, and looked up into his distraught blue eyes. "Valentine…I love you. Do you hear me? I fell in love with you the first time I heard your voice. I was so scared then. I didn't know what you wanted with me. You plucked me out my life and you dropped me into yours—"

"And now look where you are. What you went through, because I dragged you into my world."

"Shut the fuck up, Valentine. I'm trying to make you understand." I hopped again, losing my balance. "Jesus, this knee sucks."

I clung to his neck and hung on until I regained my balance. He gazed at me, one finger dragging over the stubble of my scalp. Shit. I'd forgotten that I was bald. Ugh. I ran my hand over my head, wincing.

"You're beautiful, Kyrie."

"Even with no hair?"

He nodded. "Even with no hair."

"You're distracting me." I shook my head, running a palm over my scalp. "Listen, the point here is that I love you. No one could have predicted what would happen. I mean, yeah, I wish you'd told me about Gina. She wasn't just an ex-girlfriend, you know? She brings the whole 'crazy ex' thing to a whole new level, right?" I tried to make it a joke, but Roth didn't laugh. "Too soon, huh?"

He gave me a disgusted look. "How can you make jokes, Kyrie?"

I laughed, but it was part sob. "How the fuck else am I supposed to deal with all this, Roth? I'm a fucking nobody. I didn't grow up rich. I'd never shot a gun until all this. My dad was murdered—" Roth flinched at this, but I didn't stop. "I didn't *see* it happen, though, you know? One day he was there, the next he was gone. I was an average girl living an average life. And you—you fucking changed *everything* for me, Valentine. You can't undo that. You can't take that back. And I—I don't know how I'm supposed to deal. I *killed* two people, Valentine. I shot them with a gun. I put *holes* in their fucking bodies. I blew their fucking heads open. And the worst part is, I don't feel guilty about it, and I should. I ended their lives. I *killed them*…but they were evil, weren't they? They

were both horrible, nasty, awful, evil people…they
were killers, and they deserved to die, and I don't feel
guilty. But…I can't stop seeing it happen over and
over and over…."

I tried to sort through the millions upon millions of thoughts whirling in my head.

"None of this feels real," I said. "It feels like a
dream. Like I'm watching a Jason Bourne movie or
something, and I just got caught up in it somehow.
But it *is* real, and I don't know how to deal with it.
And…I *need* you. You're the only thing I have. You
have to be strong for me. You can't give up. You can't
let feeling guilty take over everything, and yet that's
exactly what you're doing. Yeah, you shouldn't have
left me alone in the shower, and I wish you hadn't.
I wish you'd come in the shower with me, and I
wish we'd just kept having sex. But you didn't. You
did what you thought needed doing, and I get that.
Okay? I *get* it. I don't blame you for what happened.
None of it. But now…now I *need* you. More than
ever. I need you to tell me it's going to be okay. I need
you to pretend like this is another vacation around
the world. I need you to kiss me like you can't get
enough of me. I *need* that…." I ducked my head,
blinked through the emotions, breathed through the
ache in my chest. "As long as I know you love me,
and that you *want* me, and that you don't—that you

don't…*regret*…us, I'll be okay. *We'll* be okay some-how. One day at a time. We'll handle whatever Vitaly can throw at us. I'll stay on this boat with you forever. Whatever it takes. But I just…I *need* you, Valentine. You got me into this. Now you have to take care of me." I realized I was crying. I hadn't even been aware of it, but now I tasted the salt on my lips, felt the wetness on my cheeks. "You have to—you have to take care of me, Valentine."

An odd thing: I wasn't sobbing. I was just cry-ing. The strange thing was how vastly different the two things were. I hadn't just cried in…I didn't even know how long. I'd sobbed, bawled from agony both physical and emotional. I'd wept so hard it felt like everything inside me was cracking open and seeping out through my tear ducts.

This was just crying. Soft, quiet tears slipping down my cheek, dripping off my chin. They were quiet, understated. And yet, somehow they went deeper, struck harder, cut more sharply. Sobbing was a bludgeoning blow, crushing you and crushing you, blunt force trauma to your soul. This kind of crying, this was a razor blade to soft flesh. So sharp you didn't even feel it slicing down to the bone in a single motion.

Valentine's arms wrapped around me with the swiftness of a striking serpent. I was crushed to

him, feeling his ragged breathing and his hammering heart, feeling something damp touch my scalp
where his cheek was pressed to my head. "Kyrie…
god. You've been so strong through all this. You
never faltered. You never hesitated. No matter
how fucked up things got, no matter how far into
my own shit I was wallowing, you were there." His
lips dragged over my ear, across the stubble where
my hair had been, kissing my temple. "You're *not*
nobody. You're Kyrie St. Claire. You're the woman
I love. You've come through so much in your life,
and you've come through it stronger than you have
a right to. Everything that's happened, you haven't
wavered from my side. You've been through hell,
and you're still strong."

Something in me tremored, faltered. My voice
was barely a whisper. "I don't feel very strong."

"You don't have to be. Not anymore." He swept
his palm over my scalp. "You can relax now, love.
You can let go. Close your eyes and let go."

# 19

## THE STORM BREAKS

*VALENTINE*

THE LAST TIME I TOOK A NAP, I WAS FOUR YEARS OLD, AND I did so grudgingly, angrily. Naps have always felt like a waste of time. There were always a hundred, thousand other things I could be doing instead of sleeping. And really, do you ever actually feel better after a nap? No. You just feel sleepier. Groggy, disoriented. And then it's always that much harder to fall asleep at night.

But that nap…with Kyrie?

It was the best…thing…ever.

I held her, inhaled her scent, her presence. For the first time in a long, long time, I didn't feel worried, pressured, anxious, or desperate.

There had always been something driving me, pushing me. At first it was the need to prove to myself that I could make it, that I could survive on my own out in the world as a seventeen-year-old kid. Then it was the need to prove myself to Gina, and then Vitaly. And always, in the back of my mind, was the need to prove myself to my father. He wasn't someone I thought about terribly often. I hadn't spoken to him since that day twenty years ago, and I wasn't sure I ever would. I couldn't forgive him, but I was thankful, in some odd way, because it made me the man I was today. Everything I did, every dollar I'd ever earned, every building I'd bought or built or sold, every business I bought and dismantled and resold, every corporate charter I ever signed my name to, I did so with him in mind, to prove to him that I could do it. That I could make my way and do just as well as he did, if not better.

But there was still Vitaly Karahalios to deal with. I wasn't worried about him just yet. It would take him time to formulate a plan and put the various pawns into action, and then that shit wouldn't go away. But for now, I knew we would be okay.

For now, we had the boat, more money than we could ever spend, and we had several good men keeping watch. That was enough.

And I had Kyrie. I didn't deserve her. I didn't. Yet she still loved me. Why? I didn't know. And I wasn't about to question it.

I wasn't really awake, but I wasn't really asleep. I was in that twilight place between the two, aware that I wasn't asleep but not ready to move. I was warm. Content. Kyrie was a pleasantly soft weight on me, her hand curled on my chest, her cheek on my shoulder, her breath a sweet susurrus. I let my hand rest on her back, feeling the expansion and contraction of each breath.

I felt her take a deep, waking breath, stretch, and then yawn. Her hand opened, and her palm flattened against my chest. My shirt had rucked up while I'd slept, and her hand found my flesh, diving under the cotton to slip and slide across my stomach.

I opened my eyes then, and I saw that she was looking at me, her vivid blue eyes soft with tenderness and love and a million other emotions I couldn't parse or name, all of them somehow directed at me.

The question was in my eyes, I knew: *You love me?*

The answer was in hers: *Always.*

Her hand explored my stomach, my ribs, and my chest, pushing my shirt up as she went. My own hand was busy as well, seeking the bottom of her shirt, seeking her skin and the warmth of her flesh, the softness. I found it, and slid my palm across her lower back, feeling the muscles tense and soften as she breathed, and then I found her spine, the ridges and knobs, and carved upward, lifting her shirt as I went.

Mine was the first shirt to be removed. It slipped off the side of the bed to the floor. Moments later, hers joined it.

God, was there anything in life better than the feeling of skin against skin? Of feeling her naked breasts press against your chest, her stomach to your side, her hand on your shoulder and your jaw and in your hair? I didn't think there could be.

Perhaps sunrise over the Manhattan skyline, or a glass of expensive Scotch, or the roll of the ocean beneath your hull could be close seconds.

But all of those other things? They'd be empty and meaningless without Kyrie.

Her lips touched my cheek, and her eyelashes fluttered against my temple. I twisted my face, and captured her lips with mine. We kissed slowly, and deeply.

I take that back. The best thing, the absolute *best*, was the way she sighed at the first kiss, when our lips first met and she let herself fall under. The way her lips moved and slid against mine, the way the kiss took on a life of its own and our mouths moved as if each of us was fighting for dominance in the kiss, as if we were each trying to prove with the kiss that we were more desperate than the other.

Did I slide her underwear down? Or did she kick them off? I don't remember. But somehow they were off, and her fingers were working the button of my jeans, and we were both pushing them down and I was kicking them off. Her leg slid over mine, her knee touching mine, and then her thigh covered my own—and no, wait, *that* was the best thing in the world, when she was lying on her side next to me, her face in the nook, that special place between arm and shoulder and chest where she fit just so perfectly, and then we'd start to kiss and the clothes would come off, and that, *that,* the way she slid her leg over mine.

I loved that so much.

It made my heart pound in my chest, because I knew all I had to do was take her by the hips and she'd be on top of me, and I could be inside her within seconds. But I didn't, usually. I savored. I usually let the moment play out, let her thigh rest on mine, teasing both of us. Usually.

Not this time. No, this time, I gave in to my impulse. I cradled her hips in my hands and tugged her over me, settled the "V" of her core over my stomach. She was kissing me. It wasn't us kissing, wasn't me kissing her—no, this was all her, I was just following along, tasting her tongue as it slid against mine and trying to keep up with the wildness of her mouth.

Kyrie's hands feathered through my beard beside our joined mouths, her forehead pressed to mine, our noses nuzzled together side by side, and I had her hips in my hands, because how was I supposed to let go of such perfection when I had it in hand?

I couldn't.

I could only cup her hips in my hands and lift her, savor the crush of her generously portioned tits on my chest

and let her kiss me, and

slide into her.

There was no other possible course of action. It was as necessary in that moment as breathing. As involuntary as the beat of my heart to pulse my life's blood through my veins, because Kyrie *was* my lifeblood.

When Valentine pushed into me,

filling me,

stretching me,

I gasped.

His mouth was locked on mine, his tongue slippery and hot and strong between my lips, his body a mountain beneath me, his hands around my hips, and his eyes, god, his eyes were a pale perfect blue, the sky at noon, soft and deep and endless. Somehow the kiss had broken, but our lips were still touching, trembling, our eyes both open, both of us refusing to look away from this.

I felt him enter me, and I gasped.

I knew this would not be rough and wild, not the demanding and furious fucking of a man and woman who couldn't get enough of each other. Nor would it be the slow and emotional lovemaking of two lost souls who had found each other and knew the life-altering importance of the love binding them to each other. It wouldn't be the lazy early morning sex of a couple who knew each other so intimately no words or buildup or foreplay was necessary.

I knew this would be something of all of that.

And it would stem from him taking control. That was how I'd fallen in love with him. I'd been blindfolded, dependent on him to show me each step I took, dependent on the sound of his voice. I'd known nothing else, had nothing to go on but his voice, and the gentle touch of his powerful hands. I'd fallen for him without ever seeing his face. Without seeing the brawny beauty of his sculpted body, without knowing the pale glory of his sky-blue eyes.

When I finally got to see all that, I'd only fallen that much harder.

He'd captured me, taken possession of my soul and demanded ownership of my body by demanding that I trust him before I'd ever even laid eyes on him. He'd demanded that I give him total control over me.

I had been so, so foolish to do so. I'd been reckless.

I'd been a naive, hopeful, desperate girl.

A lucky girl, because he'd known exactly what to do with me.

He was the kind of man who could read the subtlest of clues in my body language and on my face, and knew what to give me, what to take away, and how to make me need every touch he gave me.

His language was control.

I was not by nature a submissive or meek woman. So me giving him control, submitting to him, that was me speaking his language back to him.

We'd learned a balance in the time since he'd first welcomed me into his foyer, a scared, blindfolded girl meeting a guarded and dominant man.

But sometimes he just needed me to give in to him.

Lucky for me, doing so always led to universe-shattering ecstasy.

Like now.

He slid into me, pierced me, and glided deep. He held my hips in place, refusing to let me move. I couldn't give back, couldn't provide counter-thrust.

All I could do was take him.

*VALENTINE*

Holy shit. She was so tight, squeezing around me so hard it almost hurt. My fingers dug into the flesh of her hips and held her in place as I drove into her until our bodies were flush, so deep inside her I couldn't go any farther. Her forehead touched mine and her lips trembled against mine, and I could feel her not breathing, feel her heart beat harder to make up for the sudden lack of oxygen.

And then I drew back, holding her hips in place still, and she made a small noise in the back of her throat at the loss of me within her. Her mouth opened wide as I pushed back into her, a slow, hard glide. Her fingers, pinned between our bodies, curled into the muscle of my chest, and her entire body shook with the need to move with me. But I wasn't moving. I was buried deep, holding still, savoring the tight, hot warmth of her.

And then I moved again, pulled out, held, and thrust in. She gasped into my mouth, and her hands

snaked out from between our chests to clutch at my
face, and her hips rolled against my grip, fighting
me. But I held her still, held her in place. Another
hard, grinding thrust, and I filled her, her breath
of relief and need and pleasure drowning me with
its desperation and its sweetness. So I gave it to her
again, pulling back slowly, so slowly, so she could
feel every millimeter of me sliding between her taut
folds, and she could only moan this time, and bury
her face against my neck, crushing her body closer to
mine, shaking all over.

We did this slowly, thrust by thrust, each one
intentional, not one motion wasted, not one sensation lost.

I felt the tightening of her walls around me, felt
the shiver in her delicate flesh, tasted the abandon
on her lips, and knew that she was about to come
undone. She was groaning into my chest, her forehead in the hollow at the base of my throat, her fingers clawed into my shoulders, her legs resting on
either side of mine, all of her weight on me, perfect,
trusting, so strong yet so fragile. And she became yet
more delicate and precious to me as she fought to
move with the hurricane force of her climax, but I
wouldn't let her, would not allow her one single inch
of motion. I would only let her take me as I gave
her rhythm, using her desperation to fuel my own,

because I was teetering on the verge of losing myself within her.

My lips devoured her skin, everywhere I could find it. Shoulder, neck, behind her ear, her arm, her cheek. I sought her lips, but she wouldn't give them to me. I found the corner of her mouth and kissed there, fit my tongue there, but she drew down, shrank lower, pressing her mouth to my sternum and driving me deeper inside her.

And then I felt her come, and I was unmade.

Every inch of my body was pressed against Valentine's, even my feet resting on his ankles, my calves on his shins, balanced, held in place by the relentless grip of his hands on my hips—not my ass, not my thighs, but my hips, pulling me down and holding me in place. He moved slowly, each thrust a full range of motion, all the way out, nearly falling free of my body, and then he pushed all the way into me, forcing me to stillness so I could do nothing but feel every inch of the slide of him, the thick heat of him, the rock-hard fullness of him stretching me to a sweet, slow burn.

When he started a rhythm, gliding in slow but hard, withdrawing like the relentless inevitable out-rushing of the tides, I wanted to scream and wanted to move with him, but I couldn't. I could only shake above him and gasp.

Could only take him, and take him, and take him.

All of him.

I could only welcome his body inside mine, penetrating me, piercing me.

Could do nothing but

Love

Every

Inch.

And then I came.

It was an earthquake. A typhoon. A volcano. My fingertips buzzed and hummed and dug into his skin, my toes curled and scraped against his shins, my thighs quaked, my stomach tensed...my soul shook.

## *VALENTINE*

When she came, I released her hips. I grabbed the swell of her ass and moved her, thrust into her, pulled her down against me and lifted her away. She whimpered in utter relief, wrapped her arms around my neck, pressed her face to my throat, and ground her hips against mine, moving on me with such uninhibited bliss that I could only groan with her

even though my own climax was still several minutes away. I sighed when she sighed, moved when
she moved, let her be free, let her move.

And my Kyrie, she surprised me.

Instead of grinding every last drop of orgasm
out of herself on top of me, she rolled us over so I
was above her. Wrapping her legs high around my
waist, she rocked against me. Her mouth fell open
as I was pulled deeper inside her, and her eyes widened as I pushed in, then stilled. Held back, forced
myself away from the edge of orgasm. I stared down
at her, taking in the carved perfection of her face. I
marveled at her beauty. With her hair gone, the love-
liness of her facial features was accentuated, high-
lighted. The angles of her cheekbones, the fullness
of her red lips, the delicacy of her jawline and chin,
the wide sapphirine glitter of her eyes, and now the
curved smoothness of her scalp and the fragile pulse
of her temple and the column of her throat....

"You...are so...beautiful." The words were
pulled from me, involuntary, raw truth brought to
my lips by her goddess perfection.

Her eyes moistened, and she blinked and lifted
her hips against mine, and I was lost to her. She
moved. Beneath me, her good leg folded and pinned
between us, stretching herself open for me.

I palmed the inner thigh of her outstretched leg and held on, curled my other hand around her bent leg, and matched her rhythm. But then I couldn't even do that, I could only push my hips against her and let her move for both of us, let her draw the release from me, let her take control then.

Our eyes were locked, a laser-hot cord binding our gazes, and she moved, thrust, thrust. Her hips flexed with relentless speed now, her taut stomach tensing, her tits bouncing, and I saw only her blue gaze. Saw only the incredible soul of the woman beneath me shining through her eyes, a beautiful, flawed, immensely powerful soul shining bare and vulnerable, shining just for me.

The physical release was nothing in comparison to the emotional climax we shared in that moment, and god...the physical release I experienced then was like no other, wrenching and twisting every muscle and tendon within me. She drew it all out of me, bucked against me, writhing furiously to milk it all out of me, dragging it from me.

Finally, when I was spent, she stilled.

She wrapped her arms around me, lowered her leg to the mattress, and clung to my neck, cradled my face to her breast.

*I love you,* my being cried out, shuddering.

*I love you more,* her hands tangling in my hair responded.

We had no need of voices to say the truth in that moment, for we were linked mind and body and soul, attuned, attached,

One.

Merged.

Enmeshed.

A tree growing from one root, split into two trunks, entwined and woven one around the other, reaching together heavenward.

I woke to evening light like liquid gold spread across the world. I was alone in the bed of our yacht, but there was evidence of Roth, the pillow beside mine, warm still, the sheets rumpled and recently lain in. I sat up, blinking, and there he was, standing at the window, one hand on the glass, the other tucked with idle grace into the pocket of his pants. He was dressed to kill. A black tuxedo, custom tailored to his powerful physique, the suit coat buttoned once, tails draping past his hips. He turned at the sound of my waking, and my heart stilled.

He was glorious. His hair was slicked back, long enough now to be held behind his ears and brush the pristine white of his collar. His beard was still thick, but he'd trimmed it to neat perfection. And his eyes? The color of the sky an hour past dawn. I've watched sunrises and sunsets and stared at the noon blue, and I've realized now that Roth's eyes are a very specific shade of blue, the palest shade that can still be called blue. When he saw me, a smile spread across his lips, starting deep within his soul and shining out with the brilliance of the sun, fraught with love and exquisite tenderness.

"God, you're gorgeous," I said. "Why so fancy?" I asked, rubbing my eye with the heel of my palm.

He strolled leisurely toward me, his grin turning mysterious, a thumb scratching at his beard. "A surprise." He held up a finger. "I wanted to be here when you woke, but I've got something for you. Hold on, love."

I wiggled my legs, testing the motion of my knee. It was stiff, but not painful. My head whirled with curiosity. What could he be planning? Why would he be wearing a tuxedo? I knew with Roth that there was no way to conjecture. He was back up the stairs within seconds of his descent, carrying a sheaf of plastic-wrapped fabric over one arm, carrying a wide black crushed-velvet box in his other hand.

He set the box on the edge of the bed and pulled the plastic off the gown, then held it up so I could admire it. "It was one I had made for you back in New York. I had it delivered to us."

It was black silk with a halter, open in the back with see-through cutouts at my hips, the hem long enough that it would brush my toes. "It's beautiful, Valentine."

He shook his head. "It's just a dress. You're beautiful. You will be beautiful in it."

"Where are we going?" I looked out the windows and saw nothing but ocean, the setting sun a massive crimson ball resting on the horizon to our left.

He just grinned. "I'll never tell. Why don't you shower and get ready, okay? I'll be in the lounge if you need help."

I wanted to ask a thousand questions, but I didn't. Instead, I decided to trust him and go with it. "I might need help getting down the stairs," I admitted as I stood up and felt my knee wobble. He took my hand and wrapped his other arm around my waist, letting me move on my own, holding tightly to me so I wouldn't fall. "I hope there won't be a lot of walking, because you'll end up carrying me."

His only response was to descend several steps below me, wrap his huge hands around my waist, and lift me, spinning with me and setting me on the landing of the stairs. His lips touched my shoulder, my neck, and then he was behind me, his hands sliding around my ribs and across my stomach, pulling me back against his chest. "Shower, Kyrie. Before I decide I can't wait any longer."

I twisted out of his grip and backed away into the bathroom, grinning. "If you think I'm going to discourage you on that score, then you've got the wrong girl." I ran my hands up my torso, lifting my tits and letting them fall with a heavy bounce, teasing him.

He growled at me, grabbing the frame of the door and leaning toward me. "Kyrie…." My name was a feral rumble on his lips. "Get…in…the shower."

Stealing a glance away from Valentine, I twisted the knob to get the spray going. I waited until the water was hot, steam rolling between us. I palmed the wall for balance and stepped in, hissing as the scalding water pattered on my skin. I adjusted the temperature so I could move under the spray, and then let the stream douse my head, keeping my eyes on Valentine. "Sure you don't want to come in with me?"

He hung his head between his shoulders, gripping the frame of the door as if physically and literally holding himself back. "More than you know."

I lathered myself up, most of my weight on my good leg, leaning against the wall of the shower as my soapy hands scrubbed across my skin. Roth leaned forward farther as if straining toward me. I made a show of it, lathering slowly across my breasts and between my thighs. Roth growled as I met his eyes, slipping two fingers inside myself, more to tease and torture him than for anything else. I heard the frame of the door crackle under his grip. He held out, though, until I was rinsed off and stepping out. I grabbed a huge, thick black towel from a rack just outside the shower stall and unfolded it, covering my face with it. Momentarily blinded, I didn't see him move, only felt myself lifted, the towel between us. I batted at the fabric as Roth carried me upstairs, taking them two at a time. I found his eyes as we reached the bed, just in time to feel myself thrown to the mattress.

He didn't say a word, only rumbled in his throat as he swept the towel across my body, drying the water from my skin, and then tossed it aside. I stared at him and tried to scoot backward on the bed, but he fell to his knees, caught my thighs in his hands, and pushed my legs apart.

"Roth? What are you—?" His thumbs spread me apart and his tongue found me, and my words were stolen. "Oh. *Ohhhh*...."

Two fingers slipped inside me, and his tongue circled my sensitive flesh, and I was rising up off the bed, writhing and moaning in an instant, his lips sucking at me, his tongue moving in tantalizing circles. He didn't draw it out, didn't tease me. No, he devoured me as if he was ravenous, growling low in his throat as I rocked my hips against him, grinding my core against his face.

I came with a scream, and he continued devouring me, riding out my climax until I was limp and begging him to stop, to let me catch my breath.

He leaned back on his heels as I gasped for breath.

"Jesus, Valentine…." I wiped my hand across my forehead.

He stood slowly, passing his wrist across his lips. "You just had to tease me, didn't you?" He rumbled, adjusting himself with one hand. "Now I'm going to be hard all through dinner, and it's your fault."

"Sorry?"

He grabbed my heel and pulled me to the edge of the bed. "No, you're not." He stood over me, so tall I had to crane my neck to look straight up at him, and then his lips were on mine, and I tasted my essence on him.

I wiped at his mouth and beard with my palm. "You taste like me now."

"Good," he murmured, and then backed away. "You're distracting me, Kyrie."

He plucked a scrap of black lace off the bed, a slinky, tiny pair of lingerie panties. Taking one of my feet in his hands, Valentine slipped my leg through one side and eased my other foot through, and then lifted me to my feet so he could draw them up the rest of the way. I kept my eyes on his as I adjusted them slightly, and then he was helping my arm through the strap of a matching bra. I couldn't help but laugh when he tried to hook the bra on behind my back, and couldn't quite manage it.

"Never put one on before," he mumbled. "Harder than taking it off, it seems."

"That's not how I put them on anyway," I said. "I hook it first, get myself adjusted in the cups, and then put the straps on." I showed him what I meant, and he watched, rapt, as I tucked my boobs into the soft, cool silk and lace of the bra.

By the time I was finished with that, he was unzipping the back of the dress and holding it out for me. I stepped into it and pulled it up, and then he was spinning me in place, pulling the zipper up. He took several steps backward, away from me, passing a hand across his mouth as if overcome.

"You…Kyrie, you're so beautiful. You take my breath away. You know that?"

I scraped my hand across my stubbled scalp self-consciously. "Roth, I don't feel—"

He was there in front of me, one hand on my waist, the other cupping my cheek, then moving over my head. "I like it, rather."

I laughed, disbelieving. "Okay, sure," I said, my voice dripping sarcasm.

He shook his head. "I'm serious, Kyrie." His lips touched my forehead, then my temple, and then he tucked me against his chest and kissed the top of my head. "It accentuates how perfect your face is. It makes your eyes so huge, and so, *so* blue."

I laughed. "You just say that because you love me."

He shrugged. "True. I do love you. More than I could ever say, or ever hope to make you understand." His fingers touched my chin, lifting my face so I was looking up into his intense, vulnerable gaze. "But Kyrie, you *are* beautiful. More than beautiful. You are lovely. Perfect. Gorgeous. I don't think I can find all the words to describe how breathtaking you are."

"You really think so? Even like this?" I couldn't help but run my hand where my hair used to be.

"You think I could possibly find you any less incredible merely because of your hair?" He frowned at me, cupped my cheeks with both huge hands. "You haven't seen yourself in the mirror, have you?"

He pulled me toward the stairs and descended backward behind me, holding my hands in his. I made it down the steps on my own this time, and he brought me past the bathroom to a pair of double doors, which opened into a massive walk-in closet. He guided me to the center of the room and pivoted me in place so I faced a full-length mirror.

I hadn't seen myself in a mirror yet, I realized.

Maybe it was because I had Valentine behind me, or maybe it was because I had his words ringing in my ears. Or maybe it was because I really *was* beautiful. All I knew was that, looking at myself in the mirror, that I felt beautiful. He was right. My eyes were huge, vividly blue, standing out in my face even more now than when I had a full head of hair. My head was a smooth round curve, my cheekbones high and sharp, my jawline strong but still feminine and delicate.

I looked strong. Striking.

"See?" His voice rumbled at my ear. "You could never be anything less than perfect."

He reached into his suit coat pocket and pulled out the jewelry box, holding it in front of me with one hand, reaching around my body with the other arm. When he lifted the lid, my breath left me. It was the same set of emerald earrings and necklace I'd worn to the Met, so many months ago. A lifetime ago, it felt like. He set the box in my hands and lifted the necklace free, draped it across my neck, and fastened it.

"I don't think I can manage the earrings," he said, grinning in embarrassment.

I slipped one hook in, and then the other.

He pressed his cheek next to mine. "Do you see yourself, Kyrie? Do you see how lovely you are?"

I held in my breath, fighting to speak evenly. "All I see is your love, Valentine."

He kissed my cheek. "That works, too." He took my hand and pulled me away from the mirror. "Come on. There's more."

There was an elevator, thankfully. It was glass-faced in front and back, the cables whirring on either side. The sun had sunk below the horizon, bathing the rolling waves in fading orange and purple and crimson, darkness lowering quickly. The elevator slid to a gentle stop, the polished metal doors opened, and Roth was leading me across the deck of the boat. The cabins rose up behind us, a sleek expanse of tinted black glass and white walls between each level. The deck was a long spearhead, the prow some eighty feet ahead of us.

In the very bow of the boat was a single round table, draped with black cloth, several thick white candles clustered in the center, lit, flickering flames dancing. A stand with a silver bucket stood to one side, containing a chilling bottle of champagne. Valentine tangled our fingers together and led me across the deck, turning back to look at me every few steps, his eyes glittering with happiness and excitement and love. My heart thudded in my chest even as I was melting for him. He stood behind one of the chairs, pulled it out, and slid it in as I sat down.

Once he was seated, a door opened somewhere, and an attractive young man approached, dressed in black with a server's black apron tied around his waist. He plucked the bottle of champagne from the bucket and deftly opened it without a word, pouring a measure into my glass and then Roth's. He bowed at the waist, and retreated, even as another, nearly identical man appeared, carrying a tray piled high with covered plates. He arranged them on the table, pulled off the covers, and identified the dishes in thickly accented English. I wasn't paying attention to anything he said, though; I was too busy staring at Roth and at the ship and at the incredible beauty of the sea. We were anchored within sight of shore, although I had no idea where we were. The deck rolled gently with the waves. The sun had fully set, and darkness was thick around us already, stars pricking the sky one by one.

I heard someone strum a guitar, and twisted around to see Alexei standing on a balcony overlooking the deck, a guitar in his hands. He smiled at us, dark eyes glinting in the rising moonlight, and strummed again, then began singing. His words were in Russian, the melody slow and mournful, his voice strong and rich, a powerful baritone.

"This is incredible, Valentine," I said.

"What is?"

I took a sip of the champagne, and then answered, gesturing broadly around us. "Everything. The yacht. You. This date."

He took my hand. "You deserve romance, Kyrie."

I had no response for that.

We chatted idly as we ate, sipping champagne and discussing where we might go next, reminiscing about places we'd already been. On the balcony above us, Alexei was leaning against the railing, playing his guitar with masterful effortlessness, singing still, the lyrics unintelligible to me, but still full of romance and meaning. When we were finished eating, one of the young men appeared and cleared everything from the table except the candles and the champagne flutes.

Roth twisted the stem of his flute between his fingers, his other hand in the pocket of his pants. He seemed lost in thought.

"What are you thinking about?" I asked.

His gaze flicked away from the candle flames up to my eyes. "You."

"Me?"

He nodded. "After all that's happened, I just find it amazing that you can sit there and look at me the way you are right now."

I tilted my head in question. "How am I looking at you, Valentine?"

"As if I'm all there is."

I plucked the glass from him and set it aside, slid my fingers through his across the table. "Because you *are* all there is for me." I swept my hand around. "The ship? It's amazing. Incredible. As amazing as your tower, as amazing as the chateau and the vineyard and that place in the islands. They're all amazing. But, Valentine? None of that matters. All I need is you."

He sat forward, his eyes earnest and intense. "I've been thinking about this moment since I first saw you in my foyer, blindfolded, scared, and beautiful." He left his chair, not letting go of my hand, and rounded the table, kneeling in front of me. Not on one knee, but on both. He took my hands in his, rubbed my knuckles with his thumbs. "I knew then that I would do this. I just never imagined what it would take to get here. And I still don't know what I'm going to say, despite having scripted this in my head a thousand times."

My heart was in my throat, pulsing rapidly. My hands shook in his. Alexei had vanished, leaving his guitar propped against the railing of the balcony.

Roth let go of my hand and reached his right hand into his pocket. "You belong to me, Kyrie St. Claire. That is true now, and it will always be true." He opened the small black box, revealing a simple but breathtaking ring, a round two-carat diamond set in a concentric circle formed by the setting of the ring. He lifted the ring out and looked up at me. "Be mine. Forever, be mine."

I worked words past the lump in my throat, held my left hand out to him. "Valentine—I've always…." My breath left me as he slid the ring onto my finger, and I had to try again. "I've always been yours. And I always will be."

The guitar sounded and Alexei was singing again. Roth stood up with me, pulling me to the middle of the deck, dancing with me as the high, full moon shone on the rippling sea.

# 20

## VITALY

Slim, polished, expensive Italian leather loafers crunched slowly across the smashed glass. A pant leg, slate gray, pressed and pleated, fluttered in the wind. A matching slate-gray blazer, tailored to fit the man's broad frame, was held across an arm. He wore a dress shirt, blindingly white, the sleeves rolled up to just beneath his thick, tanned forearms. No tie, the shirt unbuttoned to the third button, letting a few tufts of black chest hair peek out. His shoulders were broad, his chest thick and powerful, his arms stretching the sleeves of the button-down. He wasn't a tall man, standing a couple of inches under six feet, but his presence was dominating.

A dozen men milled around him, checking for pulses, collecting weapons, keeping a lookout.

Pretending to be busy. Not one of them dared to look at the man in the gray suit. He exuded threat. Fury bled from every pore. His deep-set black eyes were narrowed, constantly shifting and assessing, his square, hard jaw grinding and pulsing.

Ignoring the opening of the shattered window, he unlocked and stepped through the twelve-foot-high front door. His eyes flicked and roved, counting fallen bodies, counting bullet holes. Naming the fallen men. Through the foyer, across the open-plan living room and to the stairs leading down.

His lackeys followed him warily, their eyes meeting each others', questioning. He was in a rage the likes of which none of them had ever seen before. Even the oldest of them, a grizzled man with salt-and-pepper hair, had never seen their boss like this before.

"No one speaks unless he addresses you directly," he said in Greek. "It is best to just stay away from him if you can." His dark eyes moved in his weathered face, going from man to man. "Someone will die today."

Everyone nodded. Everyone knew it.

They descended the stairs, cursing as they found body after body, fallen comrades. None of them could be said to be friends, not in this business, but when you worked side by side with a man every day, when you drank with him and shared whores with him, you felt at least a glimmer of emotion at the sight of his corpse.

Down and down they went, spreading out from room to room until they were sure the house was clear. This was just a precaution, of course. The house was dead. But still, they moved with guns drawn, until they came to the lowest level, where the rock was cold and damp, where ghosts lived and you were convinced you could hear a scream echoing in the distance.

A cluster of men stood around a single door, pressed shoulder-to-shoulder, silent, uneasy.

The oldest man, whom they knew only as Cut—the English word—pushed through the knot of thugs, knocking them aside with the barrel of his AK-47. "Move aside. Move aside." He took one glance through the doorway into the room beyond and then paled, his eyes going wide. He cleared his throat, sucked in a deep, nervous breath, and then started herding the men away from the door. "Up. Go. Go away. Clear out. Start carrying the rest of the bodies out."

When they were all gone, Cut stepped into the room and stood beside his boss.

Silence lay thick between the two men. Eventually, a deep, smooth baritone voice broke the quiet, speaking in Greek. "How did this happen, Cut?"

Cut shook his head. "I have no answers, boss. But I will find out."

"HOW DID THIS HAPPEN?" His voice was effortlessly powerful, echoing in the small room. His eyes were locked on the bullet-riddled, bloodied body of his daughter. "Who would *dare?*"

His eyes flicked briefly to Tobias's body but returned immediately to Gina. He withdrew his hand from the hip pocket of his slacks, passed his trembling fingers through his thick, wavy black hair.

"Who did this, Cut?"

"I do not know." Cut shook his head. "But whoever it was, they are dead men."

"Death is too good. Too quick." He spoke through clenched teeth, shaking with rage. "Their families. Their friends. Everyone they know and love. I will pull the world down around their ears, Cut. This is not just war, my friend. Oh, no. They have opened the gates of hell." His voice was quiet now, clipped and precise, as thin and sharp as the edge of a razor.

He handed his suit coat to Cut, and then crouched beside the body of his daughter and picked her up, heedless of the mess. He carried her up to the ground floor. Cut radioed ahead for someone to have a wrapping sheet ready.

He laid Gina on the ground and lowered the white cotton over her face, then turned away, his shoulders shaking. He unbuttoned his soiled dress shirt and tossed it aside, standing now in a tank top and his slacks. He looked back at the house, the stack of bodies, the shattered glass.

Turning to one of the men, he spoke in a voice so calm it belied the fury sparking in his eyes. "Have you checked the footage?"

"Footage, sir?" The man straightened, wiped at his forehead with a wrist, looking puzzled.

A slow blink, as if in disbelief. "The security camera footage." He said this with mocking precision, as if the man was dense, or deaf.

"No sir, I mean—not yet. I did not know I was supposed to—"

He held out his hand, and Cut placed a silver-plated pistol in it, diamonds spelling out a name across the barrel.

*BANG!*

The body dropped, eyes wide and staring. A glance at Cut had the older man jogging across the grounds to the room containing the security tapes.

Cut accessed the previous day's footage, rewinding through the hours of nothingness until bodies began unfolding themselves and jerking in reverse. The door opened, and the room was filled with a cold, deadly presence.

"Well?" His voice was low, expectant.

Cut didn't answer, but continued rewinding.

"*Stop!*" The command snapped through the silence, and Cut paused the footage.

The playback screen showed a tall man dressed all in black, with blond hair, a thick blond beard, and pale blue eyes. The man on the screen was staring directly at the camera, as if he knew it was there, although the camera was only a tiny thing hidden in the corner of the ceiling, not much more than a pinprick in the plaster.

"Roth?" The name was spoken with disbelief. "Here? *He* is responsible for this?"

"It looks that way." Cut knew Roth, too. Remembered the problems the man had caused in the ranks with his defection.

"Show me the room." He didn't have to be more specific.

Cut tapped a few keys, and the playback switched from the main room to views of each level, descending successively downward to the lowest level. In reverse, he saw a bald, battered, bleeding, limping girl wearing Tobias's clothing emerging from the room, falling on the stairs, found and carried away by Roth. Before that, Gina, alive, walking into the room, accompanied by Tobias.

"Must have been one of Gina's...experiments," Cut suggested.

"No. This was...something else."

There was no camera in the room itself, but the footage, rewound further, showed Tobias dragging a bloody, naked girl away, and then Gina and Tobias dragging a young girl into the room, and then hours of nothing, and then Tobias with a different woman, a beautiful blonde unconscious in his arms, one knee bloody. This was clearly the woman on the stair from earlier, before she had her head shaved. Tobias was followed by Gina, who moved past him and opened the door for him.

Cut paused the footage then, and leaned back in the chair. "Looks to me like Gina took some girl for her little games, only the girl belonged to Roth. This was the fallout."

"There is more to it, I think. There were two girls, for one thing."

"The second one was just a fear tactic," Cut said. "Showing the first one what would happen to her."

A nod. "And then somehow she overpowered Tobias, killed him, and then killed Gina." A long pause. "The problem we had at the house on Oia, did you ask Gina about that?"

Cut nodded. "She said it was nothing to worry about, so I did not bother looking at the footage. She handled it, whatever it was."

"Something tells me she was lying to you." He passed a hand over his face. "I let her run a little too wild, I think. If Roth was here, there was more going on than just this one girl being tortured. Roth wouldn't cross me like this unless he had no choice, especially for some random woman. This is not his style. This was not just one of Gina's games."

"We go to Oia, then?" Cut suggested.

He shook his head. "No. I bury my daughter first. Have someone bring me the tapes. Find out what really happened on Oia."

He stood alone in front of a crypt. The cemetery was ancient, some of the crypts dating back several centuries, a few even older. Many of the names on the crypts, if you could read Greek, said Karahalios.

Cut stepped across the grass, careful not to walk over any buried headstones buried in the grass. He stopped beside his boss. "I am sorry for your loss. I helped raise that girl."

"I know you did." He turned away from the marble with the freshly engraved name and dates of birth and death. "What have you found?"

Cut let out a breath. "I did some digging. I looked at the tapes from Oia and followed the trail backward. My most educated guess is that Gina never really forgot Roth. She was always waiting for the right moment, I think. After he left, she acted like she had gotten over him. None of us ever really spoke of him again, least of all Gina. But then, a few weeks ago, there was a big mess in France. A car chase. Alec was killed. Shot in the head at close range. No one really knows exactly what happened, but my feeling is Alec was sent to clean up, you know? Only it didn't go so well. And then another mess in Athens. Four of our guys were killed there. Whoever did them was a professional. Clean, quick, and accurate."

"Who?"

"Who what, boss?"

"The men in Athens. Who were they?"

"Marcus, Niko, Gino, and Anthony."

He nodded. "Continue."

Cut hesitated as if he didn't want to share the next part. "Oia...that was bad, boss. Gina nabbed Roth. In France, I think. She had him snatched, and then sent Alec to take care of Roth's girl, only the girl got away, and someone helped her get away. Someone *very* good. Yevgeny, Kiril, and Tomas were all killed in Marseilles. They stashed the girl with Henri, and Gina sent some men after her. Henri got them. She sent more men after Henri later. Burned his bar. Tried to kill him." Cut hesitated. "That did not go well, either. Tino, Vasily, Micha, Stefano. All dead at Henri's hand. Henri was at the fortress, too."

"Foolish girl. I warned everyone to stay away from Henri. He was to be left alone."

Cut nodded. "I know. She did not listen, obviously." He blew out a breath and then waved a hand, continuing. "Gina…was into some pretty nasty shit. You know that. Well, she had Roth chained to a bed in the Oia house for three days. The girl, the one Gina had in the cellar, with the shaved head? She and another guy stormed Oia, blew the gates off, rescued Roth, and got away. Big mess. Gina covered it up, though. Kept you from finding out till she had the gate and the wall fixed, took care of the bodies, made sure no one would rat her out to you. She obviously wanted this kept quiet, right? She knew you would put a stop to it."

"I told her, I fucking *told* her to let him go." An irritated sweep of a hand through his hair accentuated his words. "Forget him, I said. Roth did not worry me. I knew he was planning to vanish, and I let him. He was a good kid, just not cut out for this life. He did not have the stomach. He was no rat, though. Never said shit to anyone, and he knew a *lot* about my operations. Fucking Gina tried to have him killed, and I took her privileges away from her over that. Let him go, I said. Forget him, I said. Ten years, he kept his secrets and mine, and then she goes and kidnaps him?" He paced away from the crypt, running his hand through his hair in frustration. "She couldn't leave well enough alone, could she? *Fuck.*"

Cut let the silence stand for a few minutes. "Like I said, I did some digging. The girl is Kyrie St. Claire. An American, from Detroit. The other guy, the one who helped her take Roth out of Oia…his name is Nicholas Harris. Former Army Ranger. Highly decorated. Works for Roth."

He nodded. "Good work." They strode across the cemetery and got into a waiting car, a black Maybach. "Any idea where they are now?"

Cut shook his head. "Not exactly. There was a super yacht sold in Marseilles, the kind of thing only a few men in the world can afford. It was bought with cash, false names on the paperwork. It sailed out of Marseilles almost a week ago. They could be anywhere at this point. Somewhere in the Mediterranean, or out through the Bosporus and into the Atlantic. I have eyes out at the major ports, but it'll take time to find them."

"Make me a list of everyone connected to this. Everyone who has touched the lives of Roth and this St. Claire girl. *Everyone.*"

"What is the plan?"

A shrug. "I am not sure yet. I cannot let this stand. I *will not.* They killed thirty-three of my men. Destroyed one of my homes. Killed my daughter." He pinched the bridge of his nose between a thumb and forefinger. "I should have reined her in, Cut. But I did not, could not, and now she has caused me this mess, and got herself killed in the process."

"What about the deal with the Russians?"

"Finish it. We cannot back out now. But put a hold on things after that. I need time to figure out what I will do. Recruit new men. Good ones. No sloppy shit, you got it? They pay for their pussy. They keep their hands clean. No more messes." He rubbed his face with both hands. "I did not want this. Roth was a good kid. I had a soft spot for him, you know? I kept tabs on him over the years. He did good for himself. Now? Now, because of my daughter's mess, I have to do something I was hoping not to have to do."

"I can take care of it for you, boss. You know I can keep it quiet."

"No, Cut. I appreciate the thought, but no. I have to do this myself. Just get me the list of names."

Cut nodded, and fell silent.

"This will not be pretty." He said it low, more to himself than out loud.

Cut sighed. "Vengeance is never pretty, boss."

"It's not just vengeance, Cut. I have to punish him." He idly traced a circle on his knee with his finger. "You do *not* cross Vitaly Karahalios."

# 21

## A PROMISE

*VALENTINE*

I STOOD AT THE WINDOW OF OUR BEDROOM, LOOKING out at the moonlit sea, Cape Town in the distance. Behind me, Kyrie slept. She was on her stomach, the blanket draped across her ass, her back bare. Her hair had grown in over the last few weeks, covering the healing scars on her scalp.

Things were okay. We were both healing, inside and out.

A soft knock echoed at the base of the stairs. I grabbed my shorts off the floor, stepped into them, and met Alexei in the lounge. "What is it?" I asked.

"Sorry to bother you at this late hour, but this is something I think you would wish to see right away."

Alexei handed me a folded sheet of paper. "It comes from your man Robert, from New York."

I unfolded the paper.

It was an explanation from Robert: *This came in the mail yesterday, delivered via DHL to the midtown office. It was addressed to you personally. To Valentine Roth. There was no return address, no signature, no explanation, nothing. Just the document attached. I've had it assessed by a trusted forensics expert, but I don't think we'll get anything from it. What's going on? ~RM*

My blood froze in my veins.

The document was a handwritten list of names:

*Nicholas Harris*

*Robert Middleton*

*Henri Desjardins*

*Layla Campari*

*Kyrie St. Claire*

*Calvin St. Claire*

*Katharine St. Claire*

*Albert Roth*

*Olivia Roth*

*Valentine Roth*

~~*Eliza Gutierrez*~~

My heart thudded in my chest. I folded the paper into quarters. "Thank you, Alexei."

He nodded, turned to go, and then stopped, glancing at me over his shoulder. "I am only a man who is good with guns. I do not know much of people, or fixing problems. I do not know much about you. But I *do* know a threat when I see one."

"That's exactly what this is, Alexei."

"What will you do?"

I didn't answer for a long time. "Take precautions. Get eyes on everyone on this list. Protect them."

"I think we will need Harris for this," Alexei suggested.

I nodded. "I think so, too." When Alexei was gone, I called Harris. "Sorry to do this to you, my friend, but I need you back."

I heard a smile in his voice. "Roth. What did you think I was gonna to do? Sit on some beach somewhere and drink mai tais? I'm in Chicago at the moment, about to interview a potential recruit."

"Recruit?"

"For Alpha One Security. It's my new gig. It's not connected to you in any way. It's all under my name, paid for out of my pocket."

I cleared my throat, confused. "New gig?"

"Yeah. By the way, boss, I quit." He laughed. "But don't worry. Alpha One Security has only one client: you."

"Alpha One Security, huh?" I thought it over. "Okay. Well, name your price. And hurry up with the recruiting. There have been some...developments." I read him the list of names.

His voice was quiet when he spoke again. "I still can't believe Eliza is gone." He blew out a breath. "He named your parents? Kyrie's mom? Even Layla? Shit. This isn't good."

"No."

"Listen, my recruit is here. I've gotta let you go. I'm on this, Roth. I'll get my guys on every single one of the people on the list."

"Thanks, Harris."

His voice was muffled as if he'd put his hand over the mouthpiece of his phone, and then he came back on. "Before I let you go...how's Kyrie?"

I sighed and stopped at the bottom of the stairs leading up the bedroom "Good. Doing better. She can move around pretty well now. She's adjusting."

"And you?"

"He's out there, Harris. He's coming for all of us," I said. "How do you think I'm doing?"

"Stay offshore. Stay low. We'll handle this." He hung up, and I put my phone into sleep mode.

The paper in hand, I ascended the stairs as quietly as I could, hoping not to wake Kyrie. She was sitting up in bed when I cleared the top step, the sheet tucked beneath her arms.

"What's going on, Valentine? I heard you talking to Harris."

"Sorry," I said. "I didn't mean to wake you."

Her eyes lit on the paper. "What is that?" She leaned forward and held out her hand.

I hesitated, then gave it to her, my heart in my throat. "A…message. It's from Vitaly."

Her eyes raced across the page, and then she looked up at me briefly before reading the list of names a second time. "This…this is *everyone*. My mom, your parents. My brother. Even Layla! What does this mean, Valentine?" By the tone in her voice, I knew she understood what it meant.

I sat down on the bed beside her and pulled her onto my lap. "It's not really a threat so much as… him making sure we know he hasn't forgotten. He wants us to be scared. To panic."

"Well, it's working." Her voice was small.

I caressed her back in slow circles. "I promised you I wouldn't let anyone hurt you again. Well, that goes for everyone on this list, too. They don't have anything to do with this. I won't let him hurt you, or anyone else."

"What are you going to do?"

I buried my face in the soft brush of her fine blonde hair. "Protect them. Harris is going to work from the States. He's forming a security company. He's going to have armed and highly trained men watching over everyone, night and day. No one will get near them. I swear to you, Vitaly will not get anywhere near them. I won't allow it."

"What about Layla? She doesn't have anyone." She sniffled. "God, Valentine. I've been so focused on everything that's happened to us…I haven't spoken to her in weeks! She doesn't even know what's going on, what happened. If she sees some strange guy following her around, she'll freak."

"I'll have—"

She snatched my phone out of my hand. "I have to call her. How do you dial out on this thing?"

I gently pried the phone from her hands. "Kyrie. Listen to me. I'll take care of her, too. I promise."

"How? By siccing some ex-Marine on her? That's only going to worry her more, Valentine. She doesn't even know she's in danger! She's…more than just a friend to me. You have to do something."

I called Harris. He answered on the second ring. "Harris? Listen, about Layla. Get her here, will you? We'll stay in the Cape Town area for a few more days. I want her on this boat in seventy-two hours."

Harris didn't miss a beat. "Got it." A pause. "Will she be expecting me?"

"I'll have Kyrie alert her, yes."

"Sounds good. See you in a few days, then." Typical of Harris, he didn't end the call; he just hung up.

I scrolled through my phone book until I reached Layla's number, dialed it, and handed it to Kyrie. "Don't try to explain everything to her right now, okay? Just convince her to come see us."

Kyrie held the phone to her ear, resting against my chest.

I could hear the tinny ringing, once, twice, three times, and then a sleepy voice on the fourth ring. "He—hello?"

"Layla…hi. It's Kyrie."

"Bitch, don't you know it's four in the morning?"

I heard the smile in Kyrie's voice. "Sorry, hooker. It's only ten here."

"Where's 'here'?"

She glanced at me in question. I grinned and leaned closer to the phone. "We're just off the coast of Cape Town, South Africa, Layla. This is Roth, by the way."

Kyrie lifted the phone and put it on speaker. Layla's voice came through loudly. "Well, no shit.

It's the man himself. You taking care of my girl, Mr. Roth?"

Kyrie answered for me. "You know he is." Her voice wavered a little, though, and Layla caught it.

"Key? You know I can hear all the shit you aren't telling me, right? You can't keep anything from me, not even through the phone line." I heard a rustling, and then the gurgling of a coffee maker in the background. "What's going on?"

Kyrie sucked in a deep breath and let it out slowly. "It's…there's just too much to fill you in over the phone." She glanced up at me, and I nodded at her, smiling my encouragement. "What do you have going on?"

"Right now? Or in general?"

"In general."

I heard the stuttering of the coffee maker finishing and the chug of liquid filling a mug. "Classes. Work. Same as ever."

"Why don't you come and visit us?"

"Where? South Africa?" She laughed. "I ain't going to South motherfucking Africa."

"Not South Africa itself, per se, more…near there. On our yacht." She bit her thumbnail. "Come visit us. For…a while."

Layla clearly sussed out the fact that Kyrie was leaving something out. "Key? What the fuck is going on?"

Kyrie sighed. "Babe…you wouldn't believe me if I told you. I just…I need you to do this for me. Okay? Please? You know I wouldn't ask if it wasn't important to me."

"What about classes? I can't just drop out—I'll lose credit and a whole shitload of money. I've got rent due, and also, how the hell do you expect me to get to South Africa or wherever the fuck you two are?"

I spoke up. "Layla, you have my word that any and every expense you could possibly think of will be covered. My man Harris is on the way from Chicago to pick you up right now. He'll help you pack, and he will personally fly to you us." I made a snap decision. "Your tuition will be paid. You won't need to worry about rent, or anything else. Not ever. All right?"

Suspicion tinged her voice. "Why would you do that? You don't even know me."

"You're important to Kyrie. Thus, you are important to me."

A long pause. "Fine. But something tells me some heavy shit went down." She sighed. "Do I get to ride in a private jet, like Kyrie did that one time?"

I laughed. "Nothing but the finest for you, Miss Campari, I assure you."

She chuckled. "Miss Campari. That's a new one. Never been called that before." She yawned. "Listen, I need to drink my coffee. Let me talk to Kyrie real quick."

"I'll see you in a few days, Miss Campari," I said.

"'Bye, Mr. Roth."

Kyrie turned the phone off speaker mode and held it to her ear. "Layla, yeah, it's just me now. Look, just go along with whatever Harris tells you, all right? You can trust him, I promise….yeah, yeah, I'm okay, really. Look, hooker, I'll tell you everything when you get here, I swear. Okay…yeah. Love you, too, bitch-face." She hung up the phone and tossed it onto the bed. Her eyes found mine. "Thank you, Valentine."

I smiled down at her, shoved the phone off to the side, and leaned forward, laying her down on her back. "You are my everything, Kyrie. I swear to you, I swear on my soul, I will not let anything happen to you again, especially not because of my past. I won't allow my mistakes to hurt anyone else. He won't harm a hair on your head."

"I know." Her smile was trusting as she pushed my shorts off and tossed them aside. "I trust you, Valentine. I know you'll protect me."

I knocked her knees open with one of mine, and fitted our bodies together. "Everything will be okay. I'll make sure of it. I'll do whatever it takes to protect what's mine." I moved, and she gasped. "You belong to me."

## THE END

# PLAYLIST

As with ALPHA, the playlist for this book is kind of absurdly long. And again, I'm not going to apologize. Music helps me focus, gives me rhythm, provides atmosphere and mood. I hope you take the time to check out some of these artists, because they're all amazing. I know some of them are a little...obscure, and some of them have appeared on other playlists, but each and every song is chosen for the mood and setting they provided for specific scenes. Enjoy!

"Harper Lewis" by Russian Circles
"June Ipper" by Irepress
"Ephemeral" by Pelican
"Unresolved Kharma" by Don Cabellero
"Say You'll Haunt Me" by Stone Sour
"Moving Mountains" by Two Steps From Hell
"Last of the Wilds" by Nightwish

"The Eternal City" Michele McLaughlin

"The Tempest" by Jennifer Thomas

"The Omega Suite" by Maroon

"David's Jig" by Natalie MacMaster

"Phenomena" by The Section Quartet

"Solid Ground" by Break of Reality

"March to the Sea" by Pelican

"Cleaning Apartment" by Clint Mansell and Kronos Quartet (Requiem For a Dream soundtrack)

"Plunkster" by The Bible Code Sundays

"Misirlou" by 2Cellos

"Fragile" by 2Cellos

"Lux Aeterna" by Clint Mansell and Kronos Quartet (Requiem for a Dream soundtrack)

"Broken Pieces" by Apocalyptica ft. Lacey Mosley

"The Alleged Paradigm" by Epica

"Sahti-Waari" by Turisas

"Vivaldi's Winter" by Dark Moor

"Nae Tongues" by Isa and the Filthy Tongues

"Seven" by Karma to Burn

"Don't Concentrate on the Finger or You'll Miss the Heavenly Glory" by We Be the Echo

"March Into the Sea" by Pelican

"Evolution" by Tone

"Perseverance" by Michele McLaughlin

"Foc (live)" by Rodrigo y Gabriela

"Just Jammin'" by Grammatik

"El Cielo" by Radio Citizen

"Que Sera" by Wax Tailor

"Sandrang (Acoustic) by Niyaz

"Toe to Toe" by Zeb

"Dope Crunk" by Beats Antique

"Melee" by Russian Circles

"Rattlesnake" by Caravan of Thieves

"Farewell" by Apocalyptica

"Requiem for a Tower" by Escala

"Martyr of the Free Word" by Epica

"Eternal" by Evanescence

"Lord of the Rings: Return of the King, Film Score" by Howard Shore

"Wheel of Time (Orchestral Version)" by Blind Guardian

"The Three Little Jigs" by Enter the Haggis

"One" by Rodrigo y Gabriela (from the Live in Japan album)

"Acoustic Ninja" by Trace Bundy

"Coma" by Buckethead & Friends, featuring Azam Ali and Serj Tankian

"Running from the Light" by Buckethead & Friends, featuring Gigi and Maura Davis

"Faraway (Extended) by Apocalyptica

CONTINUE READING FOR A
SNEAK PREVIEW OF

# TRASHED

By
Jasinda Wilder

"...AND IF YOU'LL LOOK TO OUR RIGHT YOU'LL SEE the old fort. It's the highlight of the island, really, situated on the bluff the way it is. Built in 1780 by the British, it was intended to replace the older wooden structure of Fort Michilimackinac, which was built by the French around 1715." The driver of the horse-drawn carriage pauses to cluck at the two huge horses, encouraging them up the hill, then continues. "The British commander thought Michilimackinac was too difficult to defend, so he began construction here on the island, using the natural limestone, at first. The fort was used to control the Straits during the Revolutionary War, and, despite the terms of the treaty, the British didn't relinquish control of the fort until 1796."

The driver tugs on one of the reins, and the carriage swings around a corner and we're climbing an even steeper hill running past the fort itself. It's a hot day, and even the shade of the carriage roof isn't enough to cool us off. My co-star, Rose Garret, lounges on the bench beside me, a half-empty bottle of water in one hand, her phone in the other. She's as bored as I am. The benches ahead of us contain the director, Gareth Thomas, as well as the two executive producers and some of the supporting cast.

We're all hot and bored, and ready to go back to the hotel, but the carriage ride is supposed to last over an hour and half, and goes all the way around the island. I've heard the tour is supposed to be a lot of fun, but so far—less than ten minutes in—I'm bored, hungry, and irritable, and restless. It's nearing dinner time, and I can be a dick when I'm hungry

I tap my fingers on my knees, my gaze roving from one side of the street to the other, tuning out the constant drone of the tour guide and driver. No one is paying attention; we'd all rather be back at the Grand Hotel. I know I would. That place is the shit. A little fancier than I usually like things, but there aren't many hotels like it, even among the four-star places I've stayed in for on-location shoots.

We're on Mackinac Island for the weekend, doing a huge fundraiser gala dinner for charity. It's a publicity event, the kind of Hollywood obligation I hate attending, but don't have any way out of. I'm *really* not looking forward to the dinner. It's a swanky black tie affair, the kind of thing you need a date and a coat with tails to attend, where you have to use the right fork and your inside voice. It's going to be stiff and formal and awkward, and I hate wearing suits, tuxedos even more so. Worst of all, the only appropriate date I could get to go with me is my ex-girlfriend, Emma Hayes. I'd rather stab myself in the fucking face than see that bitch again after what she did to me, but I don't have much choice. You can't bring just anyone to these things. The pop will be there, cameras flashing. All the more reason to not be seen with Em, because then the tabs will be thinking I took the cheating skank back.

I'm lost in thought, trying to figure out how the hell I'm going to get through an entire gala with Em and stay civil. I'm not paying attention to anything, ignoring the sweat trickling down past my nose, ignoring Rose as she yammers into her cell. Ignoring everything.

And then I see her.

All I see is her hair. Fuck, her hair. Must be damn near waist-length, a river of black locks. She's facing away and has her head tipped backward, her hair loose and cascading down her back in a glimmering, glinting black waterfall. Her hair is so raven's-wing black it's almost blue, catching the sun as she shakes it out, pulls a hair tie from off her wrist, and then pulls it back into a ponytail, which then gets twisted up into a loose bun at the nape of her neck. My sister Lizzy would call it a chignon. I don't know how I know that, but that's the word that pops into my head when I see it.

And god, her neck. When she tilts her head back, her neck is a delicate curve, baring her throat to the sun. It's the kind of throat a man could spend hours kissing.

She flops her bun with one hand, wipes her palm across the back of her neck and rolls her shoulders. She pivots and her face is turned toward me.

I'm mesmerized. Caught. Trapped. I can't blink, can't look away.

Her skin is tan, not ethnic-dark, just naturally tan and made darker by hours in the sun, and her eyes, they're huge, wide and dark brown like pools of chocolate. I'm less than ten feet away from her as the carriage passes her by, and she looks right at me, pausing with one hand on the back of her neck, her eyes finding mine and widening as she realizes who I am. I'm not even aware of moving, but I'm hopping off the carriage, jogging to bleed off the momentum of the moving carriage. Rose just rolls her eyes at me and Gareth is leaning out the side of the carriage shouting, "ADAM! What the hell are you doing, Adam?"

The girl, she grabs something she had propped against her legs, and then turns swiftly away from me, starts walking as if afraid, or embarrassed. Maybe both. Chicks get intimidated around me sometimes, I've been told.

I catch up and slow to a walk beside her. "Hey," I say, as I pull up along side her.

She ducks her head and keeps walking, doesn't look at me. "Hi." Her voice is pitched low, as if she's not sure she should even be talking to me. Which is stupid, since I approached her.

I take a long step to get in front of her turn to walk backward, duck my head to try and get those big brown eyes to look at me. "I'm Adam."

"No shit."

Not the response I was expecting. I laugh. "All right then, I guess you know my name, then." I wait, walking backward in front of her. "Gonna tell me yours?"

She shakes her head and brushes past me, swerves to one side, and uses a little broom to sweep an empty, crumpled water bottle into a handheld dustpan, and then moves on, not looking back at me. For the first time, I realize what she's wearing: a one-piece jumpsuit, light gray with green trim running down the sleeves and down the sides of the legs. She's wearing scuffed black combat boots, and the front of the jumpsuit is unzipped to just above her navel, revealing a white wife beater-style tank top.

Shit, is that a hot look.

And that's when I realize how *tall* this chick is. I'm six-three, and she's not much shorter than me. Three and half inches, four at the most. And she's fucking *stacked*. I mean, even with the fairly shapeless jumpsuit disguising her frame, it's clear the girl has curves for days.

"What are you doing?" I ask. Not my most intelligent question ever, I'll admit.

She pauses in the act of sweeping a stray napkin into the dustpan, gives me a look that says *what are you, stupid?* And then, deliberately, each motion screaming sarcasm, she finishes sweeping up the napkin.

"Working."

"You work on the island, then?" I'm not usually this slow, but I'm scrambling for some way to get this girl to interact with me.

She rolls her eyes at me. "Well, this *is* an island, I'm pretty sure, and...yep! I'm working. So it would seem that, yes, I do in fact work on the island." She keeps walking until she reaches a rolling trashcan and dumps her dustpan into it, then pushes the trashcan with one hand, holding the broom and dustpan in the other hand.

I stand and watch her walk away, realizing how stupid I sounded. Shaking my head at myself, I glance across the street. There's a fudge shop, and I can make out the shape of a refrigerator. An idea strikes me, and I head across the street and into the fudge shop. Or, shoppe. I buy a pound of fudge in three different flavors and two bottles of water, trying desperately to act casual, keep my head down, and hope no one notices me.

The clerk girl behind the counter, however, gasps when I set a fifty dollar bill on the counter. "Holy shit! You're—you...you're..." she's stammering, clearly distraught.

I smile at her, my brightest, fakest photo-op smile. "Adam," I say, holding out my hand.

She takes my hand in hers, a goofy, shit-eating, delirious grin spreading across her features. She's pretty enough, for a seventeen-year old schoolgirl. "Adam Trenton." She has my hand now and won't let go, until I literally tug my fingers free from hers. "Holy shit. Holy shit. You're Adam Trenton."

I nod. "Yep. That's me." I slide my bill closer to her. "Gonna let me pay for my fudge, sweetheart?"

She stares blankly, and then starts. "Yeah. Yeah! Sorry, sorry, Adam. Mr. Trenton, I mean. Um. Yeah. Change."

There's a crowd behind me now, a few mutters, cell phone cameras clicking. Had to stop for fucking fudge, didn't I? Dumbass. I get my change, offer the girl another million-dollar smile, and turn away.

"Would you—I'm sorry, I'm not supposed to do this, but—I've never met anyone—I mean, um..." she stammers.

I turn back, take the napkin she's holding toward me, and sign my name with the Sharpie I always carry in my pocket.

"Here ya go, hon." I hand the napkin and marker to her. "I really do have to go now, though. Nice to meet you."

I try to slip past the crowd, but someone else is calling my name, and someone else is shouting "Marek! Marek!" which is the name of the character that made me famous, the hero from a popular graphic novel series. I stifle my sigh of irritation, shuffle my bag and the bottles of water so they're all clutched in one hand. I sign two backpacks, three hats, six notebooks, three receipts, and pose for ten pictures before I can slip out and away from the fudge shop. Shoppe? What the the hell is a "shoppe" anyway?

By now the girl is gone. I scan the streets, keep moving, ignoring the long stares I get every now again from the crowds on the sidewalks. I'm nearly run down by a pair of massive black horses pulling a long carriage and have to dance backward out of the way, and then re-cross the street, heading back the way I came. I hear casters rolling across cobblestone far ahead of me, and set off in a space-eating jog.

I catch her as she's rounding a corner, heading into a courtyard. "Hey! Hold on!"

She stops, turns, and rolls her eyes when she sees it's me. "Still working, dude."

Although, judging by the surroundings, she's about to be done. There are other people in similar jumpsuits coming and going, and there's a sign reading "Sanitation Personnel Only" on one wall.

"You're clocking out now, though, right?"

She wipes a strand of hair out of her eyes. "Yeah. Why?"

I hold up the bag of fudge and the water bottles. "Have dinner with me?"

She actually laughs at this, and her smile lights up her face, makes her eyes shine like there's sunlight behind the brown orbs. "Fudge? For dinner?"

I shrug. "Sure. Why not?"

She gives me skeptical look. "What do you want?"

"Just your name. And for you to have some fudge with me." I crack my water bottle and take a long swig.

It doesn't escape my notice that, even though she's trying to act unaffected, her eyes follow my throat when I swallow, flick down to my chest and arms when she thinks I'm not looking.

She hesitates. "Why?"

I shrug. "I'm bored, and you're gorgeous."

She frowns. "Nice line, asshole."

I laugh. "It's not a line! That tour was hot and boring as hell and I'm hungry. And you really are beautiful."

Her cheeks color, but she gives nothing else away. "Uh huh. Sweaty, stinking, and in a jumpsuit. It's a sexy look, I'm sure." She turns away from me. "Not sure what you're after, Adam, but I'm probably not the kind of girl you think I am." With that parting shot, she pushes through a set of double doors, shoving her trashcan ahead of her.

Shot down. Jesus. That hasn't happened in a while.

I grin; I've always enjoyed a challenge.


What the hell is Adam goddamn Trenton doing on Mackinac Island? And more importantly, why is he talking to *me?* That was Rose Garret on the carriage with him, I'm positive. *Rose Garret.* Starred in *Gone With the Wind* with Dawson Kellor. She's got three Oscars and two Emmys, and she's of the hottest actresses in Hollywood as well as being one of the most desirable women in the world.

I shake my head, pushing the mystery out of my mind. A freak occurrence, obviously. Probably figured I'd fawn all over him, maybe beg him to let me blow him behind the shop.

Right.

But his eyes won't leave my mind as I dump my bag of garbage into the dumpster and put away my can, broom, and dustpan. Those eyes, such a strange shade of green, so pale they were almost pastel in color. And so, so vivid, so piercing. He looked at me like he was actually seeing *me,* like he could read my secrets in my eyes.

I clock out, wave goodbye to Phil, the supervisor, and then unzip my jumpsuit the rest of the way, tying the arms around my waist. It's a hot, humid, sticky kind of day. I stink. I'm dripping sweat, and all I want is to get back to my little room and take a shower. Cold first to cool off, and then hot to get clean. Maybe meet Jimmy and Ruth for some drinks later.

I'm out of the shop and through the courtyard at a quick walk, lifting the neck of my wife-beater to wipe the sweat off my face. With the shirt in front of my face, I'm momentarily blinded as I walk, and so I don't see him. I feel him, though. Or rather, I feel the icy plastic of a water bottle against the back of my neck.

Instinct takes over; I'm not the type of chick you want to startle, not with the kind of neighborhoods I grew up in. I pivot and shove, and my hands meet a solid, heavy, hot mass of man, sending him stumbling backward.

"Fuck, man, I was just trying to cool you off." He's laughing though, not angry.

I'm a tall girl. Strong. And I've had to defend myself more than once, so I know I can push pretty damn hard. But this guy? He barely moved. Like, two steps, if that. A shove that hard, most men would have gone flying.

And yet, despite my reaction, he's laughing and shuffling toward me as if approaching a dangerous dog, the water bottle extended. "Here. Take it. I won't hurt you, I swear," he says, using a low, soothing voice. "Take it. It's all right. Take it."

I shake my head and huff out a laugh, wanting to be irritated, but he's too fucking gorgeous, and also funny. And gorgeous. He's massive. Only a few inches taller than me, making him maybe six-three or four, but his body is…all muscle, and big, and muscle. Which makes sense, since Adam Trenton is the biggest action star since The Rock—big in terms of muscle and stature as well as fame and popularity.

I take the water bottle, twist the top off, and take a long swig. So cold, so good. I can feel him watching me as I drink, and I pause to glare at him. "What?"

He just shrugs and shakes his head. "Nothing."

I finish the water in two more long swallows. "Thanks," I say lifting the bottle in gesture.

"No problem." Awkward silence. "So. Dinner?" He pulls out the box of Ryba's. "I've got dark chocolate, chocolate peanut butter, and chocolate with nuts of some kind."

"Walnuts," I tell him.

"Walnuts?" He seems puzzled. Is he not good at following conversations?

I point at the fudge. "The nuts in the fudge. It's walnuts."

"Oh. Right. Yeah, I knew that." He peers at me as if assessing something about me. "You look like a dark chocolate girl."

God, if only he knew. I steal another glance at him as he cuts the dark chocolate fudge into huge slices. He has dark skin, as if he's got heritage from the South Pacific or somewhere like that, naturally dark and tanned even darker by the sun. His eyes, though, the pale, pale green of them throws me off. I'm not sure what his heritage is, but I'll take his brand of dark chocolate any day.

Not that anything of the sort is happening. Not with him and certainly not with me. He's A-list Hollywood. He probably has Natalie Portman's phone number in his cell or something. And I'm nobody. Less than nobody. A garbage collector.

A distraction for him, if that.

My thoughts have soured the moment.

But then he hands me a hunk of fudge, and obviously I can't turn that down.

"You still haven't told me your name." His voice is close.

Too close. I look up, and he's leaning against a lamppost, mere inches from me. His voice is like the purr of a lion. He has a piece of fudge stuck to his lip, right at the corner, and he doesn't notice. He takes three more bites, and still doesn't notice, and then wipes his hands and his mouth, and somehow misses the bit of chocolate. I want to reach out with my thumb and wipe it way, maybe even lick it off my thumb.

What the hell am I thinking?

But my hand clearly doesn't have any common sense or restraint, because I'm touching his mouth, his actual real mouth and I'm wiping the dark spot away. He's frozen, tensed, and both of us are watching my hand and wondering what I'm doing.

It only gets crazier.

I feel something huge and rough wrap around my wrist, look down, and realize that he has my hand pinioned in his, and even though I don't exactly have dainty little hands, his are paws, actual paws. The spread of his hand from pinky to thumb could easily engulf both of my hands together, and his palms are callused, his fingers gentle on my wrist but implacably powerful.

"I'm sorry, I—I'm not sure why I did that," I admit, realizing he has to be pissed that I would touch him like that. "You just had something—"

I'm not sure I'm going with that, so I stop talking abruptly.

He doesn't respond, his leaf-hued eyes boring into mine, bright and intense and inscrutable. I can't fathom what he's thinking. Can't even begin to wonder.

And then, absurdly, he brings my hand toward his face. My hand is splayed out, fingers spread apart. He twists my hand so my thumb is pointing toward his mouth.

No.

No way he's going to—

Yep. He is.

My heart actually literally and totally stops beating, just freezes solid in my chest, and my lungs seize, and his mouth is hot and wet and warm around my thumb, his tongue sliding over the pad of my thumb, licking the chocolate away. His eyes never leave mine, and now I have to breathe, have to suck in a gasping breath, and his eyes flick down to my tits, which, admittedly, are fairly prominent at the moment, even in my sports bra and tank top. But his gaze doesn't linger, just notices and appreciates and returns to my eyes, and my thumb is *still* in his mouth, sucking, pulling out, his lips wrapping around my knuckle and then my thumb is free.

And he still has my wrist in his hand, not letting go, just holding, gently but unbreakably.

I swallow hard, blink, and then jerk my hand free. Step away from him before I combust or do something utterly idiotic, like agree to whatever he's about to ask me.

"Have real dinner with me."

"No."

"Yes."

I stare at him. "Um. Not sure you're getting how this yes and no thing works."

He just grins at me. No, it's not a grin. It's…a *smolder*.

I remember sitting in the living room of my last foster home in Southfield, visiting with my favorite foster-sister. She insisted that I watch *Tangled* with her, so I did, and the main character, Flynn Ryder, has this moment where he goes, "I didn't want to have to do this, but you leave me no choice. Here comes…the smolder."

This is that kind of smile.

But, unlike Flynn, this one works for him. Like, *really* works. The way his lips just slightly curl at the corners, the way his eyes narrow to intense, piercing slits, the press of his lips against each other, those lips, just begging to be kissed…it works. God, does it work. I can't look away. I'm trying, but I can't.

He's just so fucking *hot*.

And it works, because I want to say yes. I want to have real dinner with him. I want to pretend like this ripped, famous, gorgeous hunk of a man could actually like me, and want to spend time with *me*.

He starts walking, pulling me with him, and again, he's gentle but totally, irresistibly powerful. I'm pulled into motion behind him, and somehow my hand is in his, clasped palm to palm. Our fingers aren't tangled together in that intimate way of holding hands, he's just holding my hand and pulling me behind him, and I can't help but follow, watching his long, tree-trunk thick legs move in his khaki shorts, his sculpted calves rippling. Even his calves are muscular. It's totally ridiculous. I didn't think guys this built actually existed in real life.

Yet here he is, pulling me, walking ahead of me, larger than life and holding *my* hand.

What the actual fuck is going on? What's happening?

"Where are we going?" I manage to get intelligible English words out, arranged into a grammatically-correct sentence.

"Dinner." He's leading me, and I'm wondering if he knows where we're going, since he's got us headed in the wrong direction.

"But I said no."

He glances back at me. "Yeah, so?"

"Which means I don't want to have dinner with you," I say, sounding reasonably firm.

That's a damned dirty lie, but he doesn't need to know that, and I'm not going to admit it to him. Or to myself. Because going to dinner with Adam Trenton is a bad idea.

He's going to expect something from me that I won't be willing to give.

He stops, and then somehow he has *both* of my hands in his, and his eyes are sliding down to mine and searching me and reading the lie in my heart. "Do too."

I may be many things, but I'm not a liar. "I'm in my work uniform. And I've been outside all day, sweating."

He leans toward me. "Sweaty is sexy." He says this in that leonine purr of his, and manages to make it sound promising and dirty all at once.

It's hard to swallow or even breathe, because he's so close to me you couldn't fit a piece of paper between my chest and his, and his presence is over-whelming, dominating, blocking out the island and the *clip-clop* of a horse-and-carriage trotting past us and the caw of a seagull overhead.

"Nice line, asshole." That was good. That sounded like I'm unaffected.

He ignores that. "It's just dinner. I'm only here for the weekend, okay? What can it hurt?"

"Just dinner?"

He nods. "Just dinner. Promise."

"Okay. But let me rinse off and change first."

He grins, and lets me lead the way to the co-op dorms.

Did I just agree to dinner with Adam Trenton?

This is a bad idea.

I know it is, but for reasons I can't fathom, I'm ignoring my gut.

# ABOUT THE AUTHOR

*New York Times* and *USA Today* bestselling author Jasinda Wilder is a Michigan native with a penchant for titillating tales about sexy men and strong women. When she's not writing, she's probably shopping, baking, or reading. She loves to travel, and some of her favorite vacations spots are Las Vegas, New York City, and Toledo, Ohio. You can often find Jasinda drinking sweet red wine with frozen berries.

To find out more about Jasinda and her other titles, visit her website: www.JasindaWilder.com.